softened tenderly. . .

and they kissed again, this time with gentle, fragile balance. In that second, time froze and the clarity and meaning of the moment struck her. What they were about to do would change their lives forever.

Laura wanted it that way; she wanted the passion and the sensation of being truly, completely alive. She knew she would remember forever the whisper of his clothes against hers, the warmth of his skin emanating through the cloth, the gentleness of his touch, and the splendid sight of him, so tall and handsome, so drawn to her. She wanted to cherish it, draw it out and make it last. So much of the good in her life had passed in an instant. But not this.

This was one moment she was going to savor and hold on to for the rest of her life.

ABOUT THE AUTHOR

Cathy Gillen Thacker is a full-time novelist who once taught piano to children. Born and raised in Ohio, she attended Miami University. After moving cross-country several times, she settled in Texas with her husband and three children. *An Unexpected Family* is Cathy's twenty-sixth novel.

Books by Cathy Gillen Thacker

Don't miss any of our special offers. Write to us at the following address for information on our newest releases.

Harlequin Reader Service
P.O. Box 1397, Buffalo, NY 14240
Canadian address: P.O. Box 603,
Fort Erie, Ont. L2A 5X3

CATHY GILLEN THACKER

AN UNEXPECTED FAMILY

Harlequin Books

TORONTO • NEW YORK • LONDON
AMSTERDAM • PARIS • SYDNEY • HAMBURG
STOCKHOLM • ATHENS • TOKYO • MILAN

Published September 1991

ISBN 0-373-16407-6

AN UNEXPECTED FAMILY

Prologue

"Is it going to hurt, Mom?" ten-year-old Melinda Matthews asked.

Laura Matthews swallowed the raw knot of emotion in her throat. What was she supposed to say to that? The whole last week had been a nightmare. The whole last month. It had started with that cold of Melinda's that just wouldn't go away and escalated a little more with the large purple bruises that had begun appearing on her legs and arms for no reason. And it had increased even more when her pediatrician had found the lumps under Melinda's arm and simultaneously discovered that her white blood count was sky-high.

That had been hours ago. Now, at Children's Hospital, an oncologist had recommended yet another battery of tests and exams. Laura took her daughter's trembling hand in hers, clasping it warmly between her palms. "It probably will hurt just a little," she said honestly, "but I'll be here with you the whole time. I promise."

"Mrs. Matthews," a resident behind her whispered, "I don't think you understand how painful a bone marrow test can be. I strongly suggest you wait out in the reception area. We'll handle your daughter."

Laura turned to face him fiercely. "I'm staying with my daughter." Though her voice was calm and even, her eyes flashed a powerful warning.

Reading it, the resident backed off. "All right," he said gruffly, "just as long as you can stay out of our way."

The next few minutes weren't easy. Laura cried right along with Melinda, and when the painful procedure and round of X rays had been finished, she held her in her arms, cradling her much as she had when she was a baby.

Hours later, exhausted, Melinda was asleep in a semiprivate room upstairs, Laura still right beside her.

"Mrs. Matthews?" the pediatric oncologist, a pleasant woman in her mid-forties, said from the doorway. "May I see you for a moment?"

Laura gently released her sleeping daughter's hand and walked unsteadily out into the hallway. Dr. Baker led her into a deserted coffee room. "I've got Melinda's records." She sat down, spread them out over her lap and clicked her ballpoint pen into writing position. "I just want to go over them to make sure there's been no mistake."

"Okay," Laura said slowly, not liking the puzzled look on Dr. Baker's face, or the slightly aggravated note underlying her smooth melodious voice.

"Melinda is your only daughter?" Dr. Baker asked crisply, without looking up.

"Yes," Laura said, feeling more baffled than ever by the near animosity she suddenly felt emanating from the doctor. Dr. Baker hadn't been this way earlier in the day. What had she done to annoy her?

"And your husband—he's deceased?"

"Yes, he died in a car accident several years ago."

Dr. Baker looked up. "Melinda was his biological child?"

"Yes," Laura said, feeling more bewildered than ever.

"And yours?" Dr. Baker queried.

Laura leaned forward in her seat and said firmly, "Yes. I don't understand. What's going on?"

"I'm sorry, Mrs. Matthews, but I'm going to have to be blunt. Melinda is very ill. She's going to need blood transfusions and chemotherapy, perhaps even a bone marrow transplant." Her face softened sympathetically. "I really need for you to tell me the truth about this so we can proceed as quickly and efficiently as possible."

"I *am* telling you the truth!" Laura railed back.

Dr. Baker sighed, her patience exhausted. "Mrs. Matthews, please. We already know you and your deceased husband both had AB blood. Melinda's blood type is O."

Laura shrugged. "So?" None of this was making any sense to her.

Dr. Baker studied Laura. "So any child of you and your husband's would have had A, B, or AB type blood. It's scientifically impossible for you and your husband to have sired a child who has type O blood."

The fear she'd felt all day became unmanageable. Laura was so panicked she could barely breathe. "What are you saying?" she finally choked out.

"That either you're not telling me the truth—" Dr. Baker frowned.

"I am." Laura protested. She'd never been intimate with anyone other than Rob.

Dr. Baker's look turned even grimmer. "—or Melinda isn't your biological child."

Laura stared at her, the knowledge cutting her like a knife. This couldn't be true, none of it. It was bad enough that Melinda was ill, but for them to imply... no, she knew Melinda was her child, her flesh and blood. The doctors had made a mistake. Somewhere they'd screwed up the records or the tests. That had to be it. Had to be...

Chapter One

"Eric, you're going to be late for school," Laura Matthews called.

"I'm hustling," her sixteen-year-old son shouted as he bounded downstairs. Laura thrust his letter jacket at him. He wouldn't remember to take it unless reminded, no matter how cold it got outside. And today the temperature was in the low forties. "Got your car keys and lunch money?" she demanded, following him toward the front door.

Eric nodded affirmatively. He scooped up the stack of books he'd left heaped haphazardly on the front hall table and crammed them willy-nilly into his Central High athletic bag. "The varsity game starts tonight at seven-thirty, Mom."

"I'll be there with bells on," she promised, ruffling his naturally curly dark brown hair.

"Yeah, well try not to yell too loud," he teased, ducking the goodbye kiss she aimed at his cheek. "It's embarrassing when you tell the ref to get glasses."

"Sometimes they need them!" Laura retorted.

"Hey Gramps!" Eric said, when he opened the front door. "What are you doing here?"

Laura's father smiled. "I came over to talk to your Mom." He glanced at his watch. "Aren't you going to be late?"

Eric sped past. "Nope!" he yelled cheerfully over his shoulder.

"And even if he is he'll probably manage to charm the attendance clerk out of a tardy slip," Laura said, watching briefly as Eric stuffed his six-three frame into his battered red Mustang. The car roared to life seconds later. His seat belt on, Eric backed carefully out of the driveway. Laura waved and shut the door behind her dad.

"So, what's up?" he asked, already taking off his coat and heading into the kitchen to watch her work. Although he'd retired from the Navy three years prior, he still wore his graying haircut military short. His aging body was trim and fit. Her dad tucked his perfectly ironed flannel shirt into the waistband of his chinos. "You said last night you had something to tell me and asked me to come over—without your mother. You sounded very upset."

"I have been upset," Laura admitted, picking up the pie dough she'd been rolling out. She sighed, not knowing where to start. She'd kept this a secret for so long.

"I'm listening," her dad said gently, after pouring himself a cup of coffee.

She knew if anyone would understand, he would. He could also be trusted to keep a confidence. Trying hard to keep her lower lip from trembling, she said, "You remember three years ago when Melinda first got sick?"

Although momentarily taken aback by the subject, her dad nodded grimly.

"Well, something happened then that I've never talked about," she continued shakily. He watched her in disciplined silence. "Dad, the doctors ran some blood tests and they found out that Melinda couldn't possibly be my biological child."

For long moments, her father was too stunned to speak. Finally he shook his head as if that would clear it. "Honey, are you sure?"

Laura nodded. Tears stung her eyes but she held them back. Realizing she was making a mess of the pie dough she was rolling out, she put it aside, dusted off her hands, and sat down. "Yes."

"Why didn't you say anything then?" her dad asked incredulously.

Laura shrugged, battling an almost overwhelming feeling of helplessness. "I couldn't." She sought his glance, begging for his understanding. "With her sick, it took all my energy to take care of her needs and to see to Eric." In fact, that was all she'd done during those heart-wrenching days. Her home bakery business had been put on hold. Because she'd had no income, she'd gone through the insurance money she'd received upon her husband's death, and she'd incurred sizable other debts as well. Debts she was still paying.

Her father exhaled slowly. He reached over and took her hand. "I know how hard it was to shoulder all that alone."

It *had* been hard, Laura thought. Yet somehow she had managed for two years, meeting both children's needs. And then, after Melinda had died, she'd had her grief to deal with, and Eric's. Now, a year later, their lives were finally getting back to normal. They had accepted Melinda's illness and subsequent death, as they had come to accept the loss of Laura's husband years before.

Restless, edgy, Laura got up to roam the kitchen. With Eric, Laura could still put on a front when she needed to, to protect him, but with her father, there was no need. In his years as a Navy officer, he'd seen and heard everything. And because of that, unlike her mother, he was a very tolerant man. "Dad, I've tried to put this out of my mind," Laura continued. "And for a while I really thought I had." But the nearing anniversary of Melinda's death had brought it all up again—all the emotions, fears, and nagging doubts she'd tried so hard to bury. She knew now they weren't ever going to go away, that she wouldn't have any peace until she had some answers.

Unfortunately there were no easy answers. The news that someone else had also taken the wrong child home from the hospital, and loved and raised her as their natural child for thirteen years would be devastating. And very disruptive.

If Laura's natural child had been sent home with neglectful parents, Laura knew she'd have no choice but to sue for custody. Unfortunately, even gaining custody of her child might not be a solution. The child could resent her. The child might not get along with Eric. Laura might find that after all this time they had nothing in common. Nor would they ever have.

It was also possible that Laura's child had been loved and treasured. If that were the case, Laura knew she couldn't and wouldn't disrupt her natural child's life. She wouldn't have wanted someone to disrupt Melinda's.

Whatever happened, Laura would be causing pain. And that knowledge filled her with remorse and guilt.

"What are you going to do?" her father asked gently.

"I need to contact the hospital." Feeling more restless than ever, she dragged a hand through her short brown hair. "I've got to find out what happened."

Her father drained the last of his coffee in a single, throat-burning draught. "You realize you'd be opening up a Pandora's box, Laura."

"I know." *God help me, I know.*

"And you have Eric to think about, too. What if this is true? What if the hospital did send you home with the wrong child? What then, Laura? I know you must be curious, maybe even heartbroken, but what are you going to do if you're actually able to find this other child?"

She knew that the sensible approach was to forget she'd ever learned what she had, to accept the fact that it was too late and move on. But she couldn't.

"What then?" her father persisted. "How are you going to feel about her when you find her? About yourself? How are *her* parents going to feel?"

Laura shrugged helplessly and this time she couldn't stop the flow of tears, or the guilt and anxiety that surged within her. "I don't know, Dad," she said thickly. She remembered how happy she had been the day her only daughter was born. She'd never suspected that anything could go wrong with that happiness. But it had and now she had to deal with that, too. She twisted a dish towel in her hands. "I just know I have to find out the truth."

He got up slowly to help himself to more coffee. As she had expected, he accepted her decision. He had always treated her like a grown-up, with a capable head on her shoulders. Whereas her mother still thought she couldn't do anything right. "Have you told any of this to your mother?" he asked quietly.

"No," Laura said quickly, panic edging her voice once again. "And I wish you wouldn't, either." She knew they'd only fight about it, the way they did everything else.

"All right, I won't say anything," he promised reluctantly.

"To Eric, either," Laura cautioned protectively.

"Of course not." Her dad paused. As his initial stunned reaction faded, he looked both resigned and as if his heart went out to her. "When are you going to do this?"

"The sooner the better. This morning if possible, while Eric's in school."

"Do you want me to go with you?"

Laura nodded, knowing she needed his support to get through this. She was determined, but she wasn't superhuman. "Please."

"Then let's do it," her dad said.

They got the chief of staff to see them shortly before noon. Once in his office, Laura wasted no time in presenting him with the records she had carefully gathered. Melinda's birth certificate, her hospital identification bracelet, the records of all their blood types, and records from Melinda's illness.

The chief of staff studied the records for a long time. He looked up, disbelief etched in the kind lines of his face. "You're suggesting we gave you the wrong baby?" Clearly he thought she was some sort of nut case.

"Yes," Laura said calmly, having braced herself for exactly this kind of reaction. Her dad reached over and patted her arm reassuringly. She continued in the same matter-of-fact tone, "I'm suggesting some kind of accidental swap occurred." Her voice picked up slightly as she twisted her hands together in her lap. "The hospital was a madhouse that day. There'd been a major wreck on the interstate. I remember they drafted every available person to the ER. There were only two of us in labor at that time, myself and another woman about my age. I don't remember her name but I do remember she also had a baby girl. We delivered within minutes of one another. Then there was a crisis of some sort. I don't know what happened after that."

The chief of staff cut her off. "Mrs. Matthews, I understand your loss and I sympathize, but this hospital does not make mistakes of that magnitude. We couldn't have mixed up the two infants, no matter how shorthanded we were."

Laura challenged openly, "Then how do you explain Melinda's blood type?"

"I can't." He returned quickly, "Unless—"

"Make no mistake about it," Laura stated emphatically, "My husband was the father of that baby. This is a hospital error we are talking about, not an error of my ways."

The chief of staff's expression darkened. He looked at the protective expression on Laura's father's face and wisely kept his own counsel. After lengthy silence, he sighed and said, "Suppose, just suppose, mind you, that this is true. That it really did happen. What good would it do to bring it up now. Thirteen years have passed. You can't wish those years away."

"I know that," Laura said impatiently.

"Then what do you want?"

"Peace of mind," she said, sounding a great deal more composed than she felt at this moment. She did wish that this had never happened. She felt her stomach twist into painful knots. "And an understanding of how this could've happened." One could've heard a pin drop in the room. The chief's disapproval was palpable. Laura took a deep, bolstering breath and continued, "And most importantly, I want to know what happened to my baby. I need to know she is safe, well, and happy." Laura hoped she wasn't abused or neglected, that she hadn't been orphaned and put in a foster home.

"And then what?" the chief of staff replied with pragmatic authority. He leaned forward, elbows on his desk. "Are you telling me that if I help you, your dealings with this child would stop once you see that she's all right?"

An uneasy silence fell. Laura couldn't make promises like that, and they all knew it. She didn't know what she would do or feel when she found her child. But something deep inside told her she had to go on. And do so soon, before even more precious time had elapsed. She had to make sure that her natural child was safe and loved.

She faced the doctor resolutely. "I'm telling you I'm determined to do this, with or without your help. I need answers and I'm going to get them." She paused slightly, before bringing out her wild card. "I'd rather not bring the courts into this but if you force me to do so, I will."

The doctor studied her face. She could tell he didn't want adverse publicity any more than she did. And if she went to the courts, it would get into the papers and, perhaps, to the television stations. They talked for another hour and argued some more. Laura's father backed her up one hundred percent. Finally the chief of staff gave in. "Wait here," he said, his expression reluctant. "And I'll see what I can find out."

Laura sagged with relief as he left. When the door closed behind him, she turned to her father, worried and heartsick at the way circumstances had forced her to behave. "I think what we did just amounted to blackmail."

Her father nodded grimly, looking just as wrung-out as she felt. "I know, but what choice did we have, if we want to get to the truth?"

None, Laura knew.

After an interminable wait, the chief of staff returned. He handed her a slip of paper with a name, address, and birth date on it. "If you say I gave this to you, I'll deny it, but this child was born within minutes of your daughter and she has AB blood."

The same blood type as Eric's, Laura thought. A blood type compatible with hers and Rob's. She stared at the name on the paper. Janey Lynn Anderson, born to Zach and Maria Anderson. Many thoughts crowded Laura's mind. What would Janey look like? Would she look like Eric, Rob, or herself? Or a mixture of all three? Would Janey be healthy in a way Melinda had not been? What kind of personality would she have? Would Laura feel an immediate connection with the thirteen-year-old girl? Or would there be nothing there, no spark of recognition, no simpatico, nothing? Would having lived with another family since birth override any genetic traits so that Janey would only act like the Anderson clan? And if that were the case, how would Laura feel about that?

Her legs felt rubbery. Laura rose and, after thanking the doctor for helping her, however illicitly, prepared to go.

He stopped her with these parting words, "Think hard, before you act, Mrs. Matthews. Think very hard." His glance narrowed warningly. "There are some things that are better left alone."

"Zach, there's a lady here to see you."

Zach looked up from the blueprints that were spread across his desk and at his crew boss, Harry Cole, who stood in the doorway. "If it's the owner again—" Zach warned with a sigh. Normally he enjoyed working with the people who bought his custom homes, but Mrs. Gagglione was not the model client. During the course of building she and her husband's two-million-dollar home, Mrs. Gagglione had had the layout of the kitchen changed seven times. The first three times Zach had humored her and had his architect redesign the wiring and plumbing to fit her whim. The last four times he had calmly explained to Mrs. Gagglione that it was no longer possible to change the basic layout of the kitchen. She could fiddle with the wallpaper, countertop colors, and cabinet styles all she wanted, but not the placement of plumbing fixtures or the location of the stove or dishwasher. Each time she'd said she understood, and each time, she'd returned with yet another "plan."

Zach's crew boss grinned. "It isn't Mrs. Gagglione."

"A prospective client?" Zach asked, already tucking in his denim shirttail.

"I'm not sure. She doesn't look like a member of the Million Dollar Club but it's hard to tell. Should I send her in?"

Zach really didn't have time to spare, yet he couldn't turn away prospective business, either. Why didn't people call first? he wondered. He preferred to meet prospective clients in his plush offices in downtown Fort Worth than on the site of a current project.

"Yeah, sure. Tell her to come on in." He took off his hard hat and ran a hand through his light brown hair, smoothing it in place. Seconds later, the door to his trailer opened. An extraordinarily good-looking woman in her mid-thirties walked in. Tall and slim, she had the most arresting pair of dark brown eyes he'd ever seen. She was dressed attractively, like a suburban housewife on the way to a PTA meeting. And yet there was an aura of informality about her, a hint that she could make anyone feel comfortable with her. Zach didn't come across such warmth very often. The people he built homes for were rich, busy, and very high-strung. Not this woman. She looked remarkably well adjusted, if a tad on the nervous side. Just looking at her, Zach felt a glow of pleasure. Perhaps today wouldn't be so bad after all. Certainly this was a pleasant intrusion.

"Hi," she said, extending an unmanicured hand for a brief, confident handshake that somehow prompted him to look straight into her pretty face. Their gazes met and held. He regarded her, mesmerized. She wants something, he thought with a surge of unexpected empathy, and she's not sure how to ask. Wanting to put her at ease, he said hospitably, "How may I help you?"

"I'm Laura Matthews." She introduced herself in a husky, melodious tone.

"Zach Anderson." He gestured to a seat, noting the absence of a wedding ring, and her faint but continuing vacillation. Was she shy, maybe? He said softly, "What can I do for you, Ms. Matthews?"

She twined her hands together in her lap. "I have a personal matter I need to discuss with you. It's about your daughter, Janey Lynn Anderson."

The mention of Janey suspended his initial good cheer and held Zach motionless. Worry crept in, and he hoped nothing was wrong. Not that Janey had ever been one to get in trouble. A father couldn't ask for a better daughter than Janey, even at the difficult age of thirteen, when she teetered back and forth between childhood and her exciting teenage years. Zach focused on Laura curiously. "Are you from her school?"

"No." Laura Matthews bit her lip and hazarded a strange, uncertain glance that was also surprisingly intimate. She sighed with what seemed like heartfelt regret. "I only wish it were that easy."

Frankly puzzled, he looked at her, once again taking full inventory of her neat, pine-green corduroy skirt and matching sweater, the sensible black leather flats, and huge carryall bag she'd placed on her lap. Attractive and smart, she didn't seem like the type to play games. "I don't understand."

She lifted her head another notch. The movement caused her thick, fluffy, dark brown hair to swirl in an expertly cut wedge around her face. "I know. I wish there were an easy way to say this, but there isn't. I had a daughter thirteen years ago, Mr. Anderson, in the same hospital where your wife delivered Janey."

Zach blinked, still having no idea where this was leading. He focused on Laura's wide brown eyes. They were the kind of eyes a man could get lost in. "You knew my wife?"

"N-not exactly." She swallowed, then took a deep breath, as if bracing herself for some nearing catastrophe. "I'm here because I think there was some kind of a mix-up the day our daughters were born. I know this is going to sound crazy, but I think our daughters might accidentally have been switched shortly after they were born or while they were in the hospital nursery."

Zach stared at her, sure this had to be some kind of a gag, played on him by the practical jokers in his construction crew. But she didn't look as if she was joking. She looked scared to death. Uneasiness sifted through him, followed swiftly by anger. He stood, hands on his hips. "What kind of joke is this?" he demanded.

She stood, too. Although she tried to hide it, he could see she was trembling badly.

"It's not a joke."

He stared at her, a muscle starting to twitch in his jaw. He'd never had patience with people who profited from others' pain. Laura Matthews might be beautiful and she might look like an everyday angel, but that wouldn't stop him from throwing her out of his office. No one, absolutely no one, threatened his family. "All right," he said flatly, closing in on her until they stood nearly toe-to-toe. "If it's not a joke, then what kind of a scam is it?" Just exactly what did she hope to gain from this lunacy? Money, maybe?

She looked briefly hurt by his accusation, but recovered just as quickly. "It's not a scam." Holding herself stiffly, she reached into her carryall and withdrew a sheaf of papers. "Here." She thrust them at him.

Zach remained where he was, not the least bit willing to play her game, whatever it was.

Ignoring his refusal to take the papers, she continued softly but seriously, "You can look for yourself. The blood type of my daughter is not compatible with my blood type or my husband's." She paused and bit her lip, momentarily unwilling to hurt him. Her voice dropped another empathetic notch, and her eyes grew luminous with compassion. "I have a feeling your daughter's blood type isn't compatible with yours, either."

Zach stared at her. This was like a bad dream. And yet it was real. All too real. This lady or lunatic, he wasn't sure which yet, really believed what she was saying. Could it be true? he wondered, stunned. God knew *she* seemed to believe what she was saying. Reluctantly he took the papers. They appeared to be official.

"I know this is a shock," she said, gentler now. "I felt just as confused."

That was impossible. He looked up sharply, annoyed by her deliberately soothing tone. He didn't trust himself to continue this discussion without losing his temper. Surely this had to be a hoax, he reassured himself firmly. He advised tersely, "Look, lady, I don't know what your game is or who put you up to it, and I'm not sure I care to know, but I think you'd better leave. Now."

Her oval face whitened to the hue of parchment. She stared at him with a mixture of shock and despair. "Please," she whispered, "at least hear me out."

Feeling there might be some truth to this made him want to run. But for Janey's sake he knew he had to stay. He didn't want this woman anywhere near his daughter and if he didn't discourage her now there was a chance she'd show up at his home. "No," he said firmly, "I think I've heard quite enough."

A tense silence fell between them. She stared at him a second longer, then dipped her head in mute acquiescence, as if deep down she had expected this reaction from him all along. Rummaging through her carryall once again, she produced a small pink business card. "My name and number are on this card," she said wearily. "When you've had a chance to think this through, please call me."

He shook his head in wonderment. Either she was the best, most convincing con artist he had ever seen, or she was as vulnerable and loony as the day was long. Either way, it was best to steer clear of her.

Careful not to brush up against her, he moved toward the screen door of the trailer. He hadn't had much experience dealing with crazy people, but he sensed it would be better not to upset her. At least not until he had figured out what to do. Maybe get her some professional help? He held the door open with an outstretched arm, trying not to let the pity he felt for her show. "I'll look at the information," he promised, knowing it was the only way he could get rid of her. But only to find the flaws in it, he amended silently.

"I'd appreciate it." She looked at him, seeing the doubt in his eyes, the wariness. Disappointment turned the corners of her mouth down. "You don't believe me, do you?" she said quietly, looking very distressed.

Should he? He swore inwardly. What a question! His jaw tensing with the turmoil he felt, he repeated, "Like I said,

Mrs. Matthews, I'll look at the papers." And then he would call the police. Or the mental health authorities. Or both.

ZACH ANDERSON hadn't believed her, Laura thought, later that afternoon. She was upstairs in her room, sitting propped up against the headboard of her bed, with an afghan draped over her knees. Her own set of papers were spread out over her lap. It was all there: Janey's and Melinda's birth records, including tiny hand and footprints, and the hospital photos of each little girl.

As newborns, the two little girls had looked very much alike, with their pink faces and sparse hair. Even their weight had been almost identical. It was easy to see how the two babies might have been mixed up when the staff was shorthanded. It was not so easy for Laura to decide what to do next. Zach had refused to listen. Would he ever change his mind? she wondered dejectedly.

Downstairs, the front door slammed. Laura glanced at the clock on her bedside table and was stunned to see it was nearly six. Swiftly she gathered up the papers and stuffed them beneath the afghan. Eric mustn't see, she thought.

"Hey, Mom." Eric said seconds later, doing a double take when he passed by the master suite en route to his own room. Frowning worriedly, he asked, "Are you okay?" He knew it wasn't like her to nap.

"Yes, I'm fine," Laura reassured, although to be perfectly honest the stack of crumpled tissues next to her seemed to belie her declaration.

Book bag still in hand, Eric strode toward her for a closer look. Not one to mince words when he was concerned, he asked warily, "Have you been crying?"

Yes, Laura thought, she had been for what seemed like hours after she had returned from her visit with Zach. She'd made such a mess out of everything. In retrospect, she didn't know what she should have expected. Certainly Zach Anderson couldn't have welcomed the news any more than she did when she was first told. She was probably lucky he hadn't called the police and tried to have her arrested.

Aware Eric was still viewing her with a look of concern, she searched her mind for a plausible excuse. "I watched an old movie on TV this afternoon, one of those four-hankie kinds," she lied. "It kind of got to me." The crying jag had been cathartic really, leaving her physically exhausted and emotionally drained of all the turmoil she had been carrying around, hidden inside her, the last few days.

"Oh," Eric said, relieved. He knew what a sentimental fool she could be and didn't question her further.

"So what's up?"

"Oh, yeah." Jerked back to the present, Eric said, "I wanted to tell you that I need to eat dinner early tonight. I've got to go back to school for a student council meeting at seven. Is that okay? I mean, I could fix myself a sandwich or something—" he offered helpfully.

"No, I want you to have a decent meal," Laura said. "I'll make something in a minute. Go on down and take a look in the freezer. Pick something out. I'll be right down to fix it."

"Okay," Eric said cheerfully. "Thanks." He paused. "You're sure you're all right?"

Laura nodded. "Hormones," she said by way of further explanation, knowing no sixteen-year-old boy would question that. And to her relief, he didn't.

As soon as he was gone, Laura gathered the papers. She opened the first drawer of her bureau, which served as kind of a catchall for her personal papers, mementos, and jewelry, and slid the papers beneath her jewelry box. Satisfied they were safe, she turned away.

Zach seemed like a nice man, very protective and caring. No doubt Janey was fine, she told herself firmly. Even if she didn't have her daughter, she still had Eric. Wonderful, funny Eric. Her chin up, she went downstairs to see about rustling him up a meal.

Chapter Two

"This is going to sound strange but I need you to check on something for me," Zach told his family physician later that day. Briefly he explained about Laura Matthews's visit to the construction site.

Dr. Morris listened intently. He was as concerned as Zach had expected him to be, immediately understanding his dilemma. "You want me to verify yours and Janey's blood types?"

"You have all our blood types on file, don't you?"

Dr. Morris nodded. "Yes. It'll just take me a few minutes."

"I'll wait," Zach said. Dr. Morris left the room. Settling back in his chair, Zach's thoughts returned to Laura Matthews. She hadn't looked crazy, but she obviously was. She had to be, to come to him with a story like that out of the blue.

Not that he believed it for a second, of course. Still, it would help if he could prove that Janey was indeed his biological child.

Dr. Morris returned, looking grim. Trepidation stiffened the back of Zach's neck and made the blood pound in his temples. "What is it?" he asked gruffly.

Dr. Morris frowned, and for a second couldn't quite meet his eyes. "It's not good, Zach." He pointed at the thick manilla folder he held in his hands. "Our records show your wife, Maria, had type O blood. You've also got type O. Janey has type B blood." After a moment of silence, he offered, "I'm sorry. If our records are correct, and at this point I have no reason to think they're not, there's no way Janey could be your child."

There's no way Janey could be your child. There's no way Janey could be your child. The words kept ringing over and over in Zach's head as he drove home. He pulled into the driveway and cut the engine of his Wagoneer. Janey was his. He knew it in his heart. He would've known if she were not his child. He would've felt it. His wife would've felt it.

But they hadn't. And the fact remained, Janey's blood type was incompatible with his. *Incompatible.* He swore silently to himself, his heart aching. What a mess. If only Maria were here to help him handle it, to decide what to do. But she wasn't. He wondered despondently if he were up to handling it. He knew one thing, he wished Laura Matthews had never entered his life.

No sooner was he to the door than Janey had swung it open. In Guess jeans and an oversize New Kids On The Block T-shirt, she was the epitome of the eighth-grade student. Her naturally curly, dark brown, shoulder-length hair, with eyebrow-length bangs, was the same color, the same thick unruly consistency, as Laura Matthews's.

The thought was jarring. Zach pushed it away. That doesn't mean anything, he thought fiercely. Lots of people had hair like Laura's.

"Hi, Daddy!" As genial as usual, Janey stood on her tiptoes to give him a quick kiss before bombarding him with the usual round of after-school questions. "Can I go to the mall after school tomorrow if Chrissy's mom takes us?"

"Tomorrow?" Zach croaked, still feeling as if he was in a daze. He swore inwardly again. As confused as he was, he was lucky he hadn't had a wreck driving home.

"Yeah. After school." She tilted her head sideways and peered at him through dark brown eyes. Eyes that were the same shape and hue as Maria's. "Daddy, are you all right?"

Zach shook off his confused thoughts. He could ruminate later. Right now, Janey must not know anything was wrong. It would kill her to learn about this.

"I'm okay, just tired. Long day." He forced a smile he couldn't begin to feel. "Mrs. Gagglione was back at her home site again, demanding more changes in the kitchen."

Janey grinned and lifted the lid on the Crockpot. "Bear up, Dad. Her house'll be done before you know it."

Zach groaned. That he was beginning to doubt.

"That's what you always tell me!" Janey defended her exuberant advice energetically.

Normalcy, Zach thought, that was the key to surviving this thing. "What's for dinner?"

Janey wrinkled her nose at the concoction the part-time housekeeper had left for them and quickly replaced the steam-misted lid. "Beef stew again."

Zach put his lunch pail on the counter. "I like beef stew."

"I know. I'm the one who hates all vegetables."

"Vegetables are good for you."

"Maybe. That doesn't mean I have to like them."

"Try harder because they're good for your complexion." He tweaked her nose.

"My complexion is fine," Janey said, checking her reflection in the mirrored side of the toaster.

Zach grinned. Maria's complexion had always been flawless, too. But then so was Laura Matthews's. *Stop it,* he thought.

Across the spacious kitchen, Janey was already peering into the refrigerator. "Great. Mrs. Yaeger left tossed salad and French bread, too." Janey turned to her dad. "Want me to heat up the oven and put the bread in?"

Zach nodded. Still feeling as if he was on automatic pilot, he went to the sink to wash up. After shaking the excess water from his hands, he dried them on a towel. "How was your day at school?"

Janey pirouetted around on her stocking-clad feet. Like all the girls at her school, she had on two pairs of cotton slouch socks, layered one over the other. Today's colors were teal blue and fire-engine red, colors that matched the wording on her T-shirt. "Okay. I had a little trouble on my Earth Science test. But then that's nothing new." Janey got out the salad bowl and dressing.

Zach knew from her tone there was much she wasn't saying. "How much trouble?"

"I don't know." Janey shrugged, avoiding his pinning gaze. "Low A, maybe a B plus. I'll find out by the end of the week."

Janey was a straight A student except when she let her incessant socializing get the better of her. And from time to time this past year he'd had to remind her to hit the books more and talk on the phone less. But tonight his heart wasn't in lecturing her.

Eager to get off the subject of the test she may or may not have aced, Janey continued hurriedly, "Did I tell you we were assigned to make a rock collection? We have to find twelve different kinds of rocks and identify them. The whole project is due at the end of this six weeks grading period."

Zach nodded, not really listening. Instead he was looking at Janey's pretty face and the lively light in her clear brown eyes. What would his life be like without her? he wondered. For as long as he could remember, coming home to her had been the highlight of his day. His whole life had centered around her since the day she'd been born.

And now Laura Matthews and Dr. Morris were trying to tell him a mistake might have been made? That Janey wasn't really his daughter? She was his, in every way that counted, blood tests be damned. No one was going to take her away from him. No one. And the sooner Laura Matthews and everyone else understood that, the better.

AT 9:00A.M. the house was silent except for the soothing sounds of Michael Bolton emanating from the portable stereo in Laura's kitchen. Eric had gone off to school for the day, still beaming about last night's win over Central High's arch rival. Laura had enjoyed the game, too, as much as she was able to anyway. After her meeting with Zach Anderson, it had been hard to really concentrate on anything except Melinda and Janey.

Zach Anderson had thought she was crazy. And maybe she was, bringing this up after so much time had elapsed. If only there was another way, she thought. If only this crazy business had never happened. She had tried shouldering the knowledge alone, and learned it was just too much for one person to bear. Maybe when Zach realized that he would be willing to talk to her again, she thought.

In the meantime, she had Eric. She glanced affectionately at the photographs she kept of him on the decorative shelves on either side of the wide kitchen window.

The doorbell rang. Wiping her hands on her white chef's apron, Laura turned off the stereo and went to answer it.

Zach Anderson was standing there, in a tweed sport coat and slacks. Although he was dressed more formally than he had been at the site, he still had a very rugged aura. A man's man, he was obviously a very hands-on type of guy, not someone who would ever be content to sit behind a desk. He was also physically very daunting. His shoulders and arms bore the corded strength of a man who never shied away from hard, physical work. And he was tall, maybe six-four or so to her five-eight.

He looked very unhappy to be there, but there was no raging disbelief on his face. Worry and fear perhaps, but no expectation of being conned. Her heart pounded erratically. She wondered what he had found out in the past forty-eight hours.

There was no doubt in her mind. She had known the first time she had seen him that he was Melinda's natural father.

The resemblance was almost heartbreaking, it was so plain. He had the same genial smile, fair, freckled skin, thick eyelashes, and clear blue eyes. He had the same nose. And the same strong personality.

She was attracted to him; she felt almost bonded to him. Whether that was because he reminded her of Melinda, or because of their situation, or just man-woman chemistry, she didn't know. And she wasn't sure she wanted to know. She only knew that he had the capacity to hurt her as no one else ever had.

"May I come in?" he asked quietly. Evidently he had calmed down a lot since they had last talked.

Still, even a fool could have seen how much he was hurting, how betrayed he felt underneath the composed demeanor. Understanding what that felt like, it was all she could do not to reach out and touch him. But guessing how a gesture like that would be received, she remained motionless. He was right. They needed to talk. But that was all. She nodded her permission. "Sure. Come on in." Wasn't this what she had been hoping for, some sign of compliance on his part? Why then did she feel so self-conscious and edgy?

Holding himself aloof, he moved past her. She understood that. This had been tough on her, too, making her want to withdraw into herself, too. Shutting the door behind him, she gathered her wits and said as hospitably as possible, "We'll have to go back to the kitchen and talk while I work, though. I hope you don't mind."

He looked at her with a questioning lift of his brow. She explained, "I've got to deliver twelve fudge brownie pies to one of my customers by noon today."

Zach's clear blue eyes narrowed. "You do this for a living, then?" he asked with gentle curiosity. She thought she saw a measure of respect in his eyes. Maybe because they were both self-employed, the master of their own professional destinies.

Laura nodded her affirmation, remembering she had given him a card advertising her home-baked goods, which was how he'd known where to find her today. "Can I get you a cup of coffee?" she asked. She resumed her station at the long wooden trestle table that doubled as her professional work station. Under his watchful gaze, she began fluting the edges of a pie crust. It didn't matter, she told herself stalwartly, what he thought of her. But deep inside, she wanted him to like her, nonetheless.

This tension between them aside, he seemed like such a nice man. Had they met any other way, under any other circumstances, they would have been fast friends, Laura thought. But they hadn't. She was sure he privately wished she had never come into his life.

Zach shook his head. "No, thanks." He stood restlessly on the other side of the table, looking as if he was as upset as she was. "I thought about what you said," he began frankly, in a tension-edged tone, thrusting both his hands into his trouser pockets. His glance lifted and met hers unassailably. "And even if it is true about there being a switch—which, you understand, I'm far from convinced it is—there's no reason for either of us to do anything about it now."

Laura studied him wordlessly, aware her heart was pounding, as much from his proximity to her as from her growing apprehension. This man was running scared, just the way she had when she first heard the news. Her heartbeat slowed a notch as she felt herself miraculously regaining some control of the untenable situation. If Zach had come this far in just two days, maybe they could work something out after all. "Janey's blood tests weren't right, either, were they?" she guessed quietly.

Zach said nothing, either way.

But then, he didn't have to, Laura thought. "I figured as much." She sighed heavily, knowing how devastated he must feel, and also that there was nothing she could do or say that would really ease his pain. He would have to suffer through it the same way she had. One day, one moment at a time. And right now, he looked as if he had all he could handle.

Because concentrating on her work seemed much safer than meeting his penetrating gaze, Laura bent to trim a spare strip of crust here and there. Mindful of her noon deadline and the necessity of meeting it, she kept working on the pies, pouring chocolate batter into the prepared crust, aware that he watched her closely all the while.

"You're handling this well," he noted after a moment, wariness lighting his clear blue eyes.

His eyes were so much like Melinda's that it almost hurt her to look at them. Here was Melinda's natural father. A man of integrity and strength and a deep capacity for love. A man who would have loved Melinda deeply. Only now he'd never have the chance. She had to live with the guilt that she had denied Zach that opportunity of love.

"On the surface I am handling it," Laura admitted, briefly allowing her own emotion to show as their eyes met and held once again. "But inside, Zach, it's tearing me apart." And it was tearing him apart, too, even if he wouldn't yet admit it.

Turning back to her work, she scraped a bowl clean with a rubber spatula. Taking a deep breath, she continued to explain, "I've had three years to live with it—"

"Three years," he interrupted incredulously, staring at her in wonderment. "And you didn't do anything about it?"

She understood his skepticism. Her heart pounding again, she looked up into his handsome face, this time seeing only Zach, the man, the father and not the spitting image of her Melinda. "I couldn't," she said quietly, understanding his hurt and his desperation and his fear more than he could ever know. She swallowed hard, trying to get rid of the tightness in her throat that occurred whenever she talked about the trauma of the past. "At the time I found out about all this, my daughter was very ill."

Zach's expression changed to one of concern and compassion. Ironically that made it all the harder for Laura to go on.

"When she died last year, I was in no shape to do anything about it, nor if I'm perfectly honest, did I want to. It was enough just dealing with my grief and helping my son Eric deal with his."

He stared at her watchfully, the compassion he felt for her loss etched on his handsome face. "But now that you've recovered?" he asked curtly. "You want your daughter back, and if not her, then you want to claim someone else's?"

He was being deliberately cruel, as his fear rose. Yet she could forgive him that. She had reacted the exact same way when she had first found out about this.

He shook his head disparagingly. "It's as if now that she's gone you have nothing to lose."

And everything to gain, Laura thought, finishing what he had tactfully left unsaid. "I guess you're right," she said, knowing how she must look to him, and knowing that he understood her dilemma.

Silence fell between them, thick and unbridgeable. Zach looked as nonplussed as she felt. Needing to do something to keep her hands from shaking, Laura put another ration of unsweetened chocolate and butter into the microwave and began melting them.

Zach dragged a hand through his thatch of light brown hair, pushing the soft clean strands away from his forehead. "Look," he said, "I'm sorry about what you've gone through, the loss you've experienced. I really am. But this isn't going to bring your daughter back, Laura."

"I know that," Laura said, tears glistening in her eyes. A sob caught in her throat, choking her. "My God, don't you think I know that?" she cried.

He did, but he didn't care. Determined, he moved closer. "I want you to drop this," he said.

If only it were that simple, Laura thought with an anguished sigh. But ever since she had seen that photo of Janey as a newborn, she had yearned to get to know her, to see what she looked like now. And she knew it wasn't an ache that was likely to go away, no matter how much she wished for that to happen. "What if I can't?" she asked, troubled.

He turned away from her for a long moment, glancing at the trees in the backyard. His mind made up, he did an about-face. "You have a son, you said." He inclined his head at the photos of Eric next to the windowsill.

"Yes," Laura said, affection filling her as she thought of Eric.

"Then be happy you still have him," Zach advised.

She could see he sincerely wanted to help her, while still protecting his own. She was grateful for his kindness, but she couldn't accept his advice—and have any lingering peace of mind. Until this moment, she hadn't known what she wanted. She'd told herself it was just the knowledge that her daughter was safe. But she'd been fooling herself. She wanted more. Only how could she ask? "I don't want to hurt your daughter," Laura began carefully.

"Then keep your knowledge—or whatever you think you know—to yourself," Zach countered softly. "Because if even a suspicion of this were ever to get out, it would destroy my daughter. Do you hear me, Laura? It would destroy her."

"WHAT DID YOU EXPECT, honey, that Zach Anderson would welcome news like this?" Laura's father said, later the same morning as he helped her box up the pies one by one.

Feeling more dejected than ever, Laura sighed. "No. I don't know what I expected, Dad. I would've thought he'd at least be curious about Melinda." The same way she was curious about Janey. "But he didn't even ask to see a picture of her."

Her father was silent, thinking, she suspected, about both sides of the picture. His years as a Navy officer had given him a sense of fairness that was very deeply ingrained and unemotional. "He's protecting his own, the same way you protected Melinda all those years," her father said finally.

"I guess so."

"Laura, honey, you know I try not to meddle in your affairs, but after thinking about it long and hard I agree with Zach Anderson on this. As much as it's going to hurt us all, I think you should think of Janey and drop it."

Although she rarely ever cried, Laura felt herself tear up for the second time that day, out of frustration as much as pain. "Dad, I've tried," she explained. "But he has my natural child." *My flesh and blood.*

"You don't know that for sure," her father argued, taping each white cardboard pie box shut.

Don't I? Laura thought. "You didn't see the look on his face this morning, Dad. He's done some checking, too. I'd stake my life on it."

Abruptly her father stopped what he was doing and circled the table to her side. He put his hands on her shoulders, as he had many times when she was a child. "Laura, even if it did happen as you think, thirteen years have passed. Janey is his child in every way that counts, just like Melinda was your child. You have to face the facts. Whatever happened, happened. It's a shame you ever had to find out about it. I'm sorry you did, truly I am, but it doesn't change anything. You can't go back. You can't do that to Zach, Janey, yourself, or Eric. You lost a daughter, but you still have a son. A son I happen to know loves you very much."

Guilt assailed her. Zach had said this news would destroy Janey, and he was probably right. It would also hurt Eric.

She'd been selfish, thinking about what would make her feel better and give her peace of mind.

Before she'd gone to the hospital, she hadn't known what kind of family Janey was with. But she had met Zach now, found out what a decent and kind man he was, what a loving, fiercely protective father. Her gut instincts told her Janey was fine, every bit as fine as Eric.

Ashamed, she buried her face in her hands and struggled to find enough courage to do what she knew in her heart was right. Not for her but for the child. Janey's security was with Zach, the same way Melinda's had been with her. Laura swallowed hard. "You're right, Dad. I'm sorry. This—I guess it's the anniversary of Melinda's death—knowing that it's coming up soon." Pain and despair roughened her voice. "I guess it's made me a little bit crazy."

Her father took her into his arms and hugged her fiercely. "It's hurt us all, honey, but you're going to feel better. You'll see. Time *does* heal all wounds."

"You're right," she said again softly, feeling overcome with disappointment. Her voice hardened derisively, "I've got to be grateful for what I have and stop dwelling on the past. It won't change anything for me or for Zach." One way or another, she was going to have to find a way to put this behind her. For Janey's sake and for Eric's.

Chapter Three

"Mom, where's your calculator?" Eric asked later the same evening.

Laura was at the stove, frying chicken for dinner. Since making her decision to leave well enough alone, she felt as if she had a burden removed from her shoulders. Sending her son a lighthearted smile, she answered his question with one of her own. "Where's yours?"

"At school, I hope." Eric shrugged. "I thought I brought it home with me but it's not in my bag and I need it to do my trig."

"Mine should be on my desk, in the living room." Adjusting the heat on the stove, she turned back to the potatoes on the drain board.

"It's not," Eric said genially. "I already checked."

"You're sure?"

"Yep." Eric shoved both hands into the pockets of his jeans and leaned one shoulder against the frame.

Laura frowned, thinking. "Hmm. Well, maybe I left it upstairs in my room when I was doing the bills."

"Where in your room?" Eric asked over his shoulder, already striding for the front hall stairs.

"On top of the bureau," Laura called. "And Eric—"

"Yeah?" He turned.

"Take the clean laundry up with you."

A teasing grin dimpled his youthful face. "What laundry?"

She knew he had to have seen it when he came in from school. He just had an aversion to chores. "Those two baskets at the foot of the stairs," she said dryly. "Put yours in your room, mine in mine, and the stack of clean towels in the linen closet upstairs."

"Okay." He took off whistling.

She heard him take the stairs two at a time. The footsteps moved to her room. Then back to the top of the stairs. "Mom!" he shouted down with characteristic impatience. "It's not up here!"

Laura put the peeled potatoes on to cook. She hated this yelling back and forth. But as the alternative was running up and down stairs, she decided she could live with it. "Are you sure?" she shouted back, giving the sizzling chicken another turn. It was beginning to brown nicely.

"Positive!" Eric shouted back, sounding a tad frustrated.

"Well, it has to be somewhere," Laura muttered. "It's not down here, Eric," Laura called. "So it must be upstairs. I must've left it up there when I did the bills."

"But I already looked!"

"Well, look again," Laura advised as the phone jangled. She picked up the kitchen receiver. The call was from one of the restaurants where she sold desserts. Business had been slower than usual, the manager reported, so they were reducing tomorrow's order significantly. Disappointed but understanding, Laura made notes on the adjustment and thanked the manager for calling.

Wondering if Eric had found the calculator, she moved to the front stairs. "Eric?"

Laura waited. It wasn't like Eric not to answer her and their house was so small she knew he could hear her. "Eric?" she called again. Her heart rate accelerating, she took to the stairs. At the end of the hall a light shone from the open doorway of the master suite. Frowning, she wondered what was keeping him. And then, without warning, she knew. The papers from the hospital. She raced into the room.

Eric was standing next to the tall bureau, his face ashen. Her missing calculator was on the bed, and the papers were in his hands. "I thought the calculator might have fallen into the drawer," Eric explained. He paused, his shock at what he'd inadvertently discovered, evident. "What are you doing with someone else's birth certificate and baby footprints, Mom?" he asked suspiciously. "What's going on?"

Frantically Laura searched her mind. "I—"

Eric waved the papers at her. "Is this why you were crying the other day?"

Her thoughts jumbled, Laura sat down on her bed. She could barely get her breath and she didn't have a clue what to say. She should have hidden the papers, she realized with the clarity of hindsight, but she'd never imagined that Eric would open her bureau drawer. If he hadn't been looking for her calculator, at her instruction, he never would have. With effort, she pulled herself together as much as she was able. "It's nothing," she lied finally in a feeble tone.

"Nothing?" Eric echoed with disbelief. He approached her with all the resolute finesse of a prosecuting attorney. "Mom, they don't give you a copy of someone else's birth records for nothing. Now what's going on? Do you know this person?"

"Not exactly—"

"What then?" he demanded tenaciously, not about to give up.

Laura swallowed, still unable to come up with something. Eric's face assumed a hurt, shut-out look similar to the one he had had sometimes when Melinda was ill. She'd known then that he sometimes felt left out, overlooked, and less important. So much of Laura's energy had gone to caring for Melinda. She had promised herself after Melinda died that that would never happen again. She'd devoted the past year to making sure Eric felt very loved. But this was something she couldn't include him in. He knew it and resented it.

"Fine. Don't tell me. I'll just find out for myself." Eric tossed the papers aside. "I'll call the hospital or maybe Gramps—"

No, Laura thought, panicked. I can't lose him, too! He couldn't hear about this from anyone else.

She jumped to her feet, knotting her hands in front of her to still their trembling. "Eric, stop! I'll—I'll tell you, okay? But after dinner."

Studying her, Eric demanded bluntly, "Why not now?"

"It's a long story. And our meal is almost ready."

"Does it have something to do with Melinda?"

"Yes."

He was silent, thinking.

"And in the meantime," Laura advised, desperately buying herself a little more time to figure out how to word what she had to say, "you can do your trig."

"All right," Eric conceded finally, "but we're going to talk right after dinner."

Not surprisingly, the meal lovingly prepared stuck like sawdust in Laura's throat. Eric shoveled the food down with the same lack of enthusiasm. Finished, he pushed his plate aside. Elbows on the table, he faced her and said simply, "Okay, Mom. We've eaten. What gives?"

Her heart in her throat, Laura began to explain in halting tones, starting at the beginning when she had first learned Melinda's blood type and following through to the present. Eric stared at her in confusion. For all his size, Laura thought miserably, he looked like a frightened little boy.

If only she hadn't gone to the hospital for confirmation. If only she hadn't gone to see Zach Anderson. No one would've ever known about this devastating switch but her and Melinda's oncologist. But it was too late to back down now. And they all had to deal with it the best they could. Even Eric.

"All this time you knew and you never said anything?" Eric said, looking at her aghast.

She could see how hurt he was, how confused. Guilt flooded her anew.

"I thought we shared everything, Mom!" He stood, pacing restlessly, his long legs eating up the space in the small cozy room. "I thought you didn't believe in keeping secrets from kids! Isn't that what you said the whole time Melinda was sick, that we could count on you to always tell us the truth?"

"And I have," Laura said thickly, her guilt increasing until it choked her. *Except for this one very hurtful thing.*

Eric stared at her as if he were seeing a stranger. "Like hell you have," he snarled, striding for the hall.

"Eric. Eric, where are you going?" Laura followed him to the back door.

"I don't know," he shouted back. "I just have to get out of here, away from all the lies. Away from you."

Seconds later, the engine of his battered red Mustang sprang to life. With tears in her eyes, Laura watched him drive away. What have I done? she asked herself, feeling as if she had suddenly lost everything. What have I done?

ACROSS TOWN, Zach was pulling on his gold Lady Tigers basketball shirt, with *Coach* written across the back. He was anxious to get to the game. There was nothing he loved more than coaching the gregarious and energetic group of girls that comprised his daughter's basketball team. He grabbed his sneakers, clipboard, and play chart, and started down the stairs.

Janey was sitting at the bottom lacing up her high tops. "Come on, Dad, we're going to be late," she urged impatiently.

There was no reason, save pregame adrenaline, for them both to be so cranked up. They had over an hour until their game started. "We've got plenty of time, Janey," Zach reminded, slowing his own pace with effort.

"Yeah," Janey concurred as she sprang to her feet with a bounce, "but I want to warm up."

Zach smiled. If anyone had told him years ago that his daughter would be a basketball nut, and that he'd coach a girls' team, he'd have said they were crazy. But from the time Janey was old enough to handle a ball, she had declared it her sport.

"Been working on your foul shots?" he asked, lacing an affectionate arm around her shoulders.

Janey shrugged and leaned into the fatherly embrace. "Some."

They started companionably out the door. Unable to resist, Zach prodded gently, "Gonna remember I'm the coach tonight and not your dad?" They'd had a few fights at the beginning of the season because she didn't want to take direction from him on the court.

"I promise I won't get too mad if you tell me what to do," Janey promised good-humoredly.

As soon as they were en route, Janey imparted casually, "You know what, Dad? I found out there's a place at the mall where you can get your ears pierced for only seven dollars. They numb them and everything, use some sort of surgical gun that just zaps the earrings right in there."

Zach slanted his daughter a glance. They had been through this conversation before. "You also have a permanent hole in your ear."

"Yes, I know, Dad," Janey retorted dryly. "That's kind of the point." She grinned. "It'd be a bummer to get your ears pierced every time you wanted to wear earrings."

Zach sighed his exasperation. "Janey, you're too young—"

"All the girls at my school wear them," she defended herself hotly.

Zach had seen some of the earrings worn by the middle-school kids. Appropriate for a twenty-year-old person, they looked ludicrous on the twelve to fourteen set. "We're not talking about them, we're talking about you."

Janey's lower lip slid out at the finality in his voice. "If you were a mother, instead of a father, you'd understand."

Her remark got him where it hurt. "If you still want your ears pierced when you're eighteen, okay," he conceded finally. "But not until then."

Janey clamped both her arms against her waist. "You're being unfair."

No, he wasn't. But he knew there was no way of persuading her of that. Briefly he wondered what Laura Matthews would think of his decision. He had a hunch the easygoing woman would vote for the earrings. But Janey was his child. And she was too young. If he gave in on this, she'd start hounding him on the eye-makeup issue again, and he wasn't about to let her become a raccoon-eyed clown, like some of her friends. He'd allowed her the use of a light lip gloss and a smidgen of blush and that was all he was going to allow until she was in high school.

Stifling his usual lecture on not trying to grow up too fast, he parked his car next to the middle-school gym. Once Janey began her warm-up drills with the team, she would forget her anger with him.

It had been enough, battling Laura Matthews the past few days. He didn't want to have to fight his daughter, too. Nor did he want to think about Laura, with her cloud of fluffy brown hair and vulnerable dark brown eyes. He knew she was hurting, too, but dammit, that wasn't his fault, either. What was done was done.

As he had expected, the game with the Lady Sharks was a tough one and took all of his powers of concentration. But the girls were terrific. They won in the last twenty seconds when one of Janey's teammates, his foreman Harry Cole's daughter Tabitha, made both her foul shots.

"Great game, wasn't it, Dad!" Janey said afterward, sitting down to pull on her sweats.

"Yes, it was," Zach agreed, glad Janey had forgotten all about the earrings for the moment. If only every battle were as easy to win.

THERE WAS NO REASON for him to feel so selfish, Zach told himself later that evening as he got up around 2:00 a.m. and wandered down to the kitchen for a glass of milk.

Still, he couldn't seem to live with his actions. If the situation had been reversed, he would have been much more aggressive than Laura in seeking out his natural child. Why he should care so much about what Laura felt, he didn't know. He only knew that it bothered him.

He didn't like the uncertainty of the possible baby swap hanging over him, either. He didn't like the heaviness in his heart or the flash of fear he felt every time he saw someone with Laura's coloring or her hair coming his way.

He didn't like the fact that Janey looked so darn much like Laura, that they had the same fluffy dark hair, expressive dark brown eyes, and oval face. He didn't like the fact that Janey moved with an athletic grace that was similar to Laura's. Or that, according to the photos she had in her kitchen, her son played basketball, just like Janey.

So far, Laura hadn't met his daughter. If she did, he didn't know what would happen. Of course, Zach reassured himself firmly as he drained the last of his milk and put his glass in the sink, all this worrying on his part might be for naught. The resemblances could be coincidental. It could all be a mistake.

But why didn't Janey's blood type match his and Maria's? Why hadn't Melinda's matched Laura and Bob Matthews's?

He had been over and over his copy of the records she had given him the other day. He had even made a visit to talk to the hospital chief of staff. What he had learned had not pleased him.

That doctor felt, privately, a mistake had been made. And also that it was much too late for them to do anything about it now. Zach agreed with that. Apparently Laura did, too, for she had stopped calling him.

But what if she changed her mind sometime in the future? Could he live with this possibility hanging over his head indefinitely and have any kind of peace or happiness? He didn't think so.

And then there was Janey. Didn't she have a right to know that she might have a natural mother who was still alive? Granted, Laura didn't have any custodial rights to Janey after all this time. Nor would he ever permit her to have any. But Janey was almost an adult.

If it were him, whose parentage was in question, he knew he would want to know. He sensed Janey would want to know, too. More importantly still, he sensed she would resent him deeply if she ever found out he had kept the information from her.

So, he had to tell her. And he had to discover the truth. The only question was when. It couldn't be on a school day. That left the weekend. Figuring she'd be able to handle the news better after a good night's sleep, he waited until after they'd done the breakfast dishes Saturday morning. Knowing he had to get it over with, he stopped her before she could run off to listen to her stereo. "Janey, I need to talk to you."

Hearing the apprehension he had tried and failed to keep out of his voice, Janey turned her dark brown eyes to his, looking suddenly so much older than her years. In a canary-yellow sweatshirt and jeans, she looked like Laura.

"I know you've been worried, Daddy," she said softly, "that you haven't been sleeping. Is it something about work? About that awful lady who keeps changing her mind about her house?

"No," Zach answered with a heavy heart. Taking her hand, he led her into the living room and sat down with her on the navy-and-red-plaid sofa. "I only wish it were that simple." In contrast to this, his nonstop problems with Mrs. Gagglione were almost laughable.

Janey shot him a confused look. "Then what is it?"

Zach took a deep breath, wishing with everything he had that this wasn't necessary. Deciding the only way to tell her was straight out, he started with Laura's visit, his second talk with her, and concluded with his own talk with the hospital verifying the truth of everything that had been said. Throughout, Janey sat there in shocked silence, her face growing whiter and whiter. "Do *you* think you got the wrong baby at the hospital?" Janey asked finally in a trembling voice, looking as upset and confused as he felt.

Wrong child? "How could I have," Zach asked thickly, feeling as if his heart was breaking, too, as he took her into his arms, "when I got you?"

Janey pulled away from his enveloping hug. "But do you, Daddy?" she asked, tears running down her face. "Is my blood the wrong type? Does it match with yours or does it match with that lady's?"

Until definitive tests were run now, there was no way to be certain. And that's what Zach wanted, to be certain. Once they were, he was sure they could deal with whatever came. It was the not knowing that was tearing him, Laura, and now Janey apart. "I don't know, honey, that's why I want you and Laura Matthews to have a blood test. So we can find out." He covered both her icy hands with his own.

"And then what?" Janey asked, looking even more frightened.

"Then nothing," Zach said in a gruff protective tone, letting her know she had nothing to fear. He tightened his hands on hers. "Nothing will change. Either way you'll still be my child."

"Then why do we have to have the test?" Janey asked.

"Because we need to know the truth to have any peace of mind," Zach said wearily. "We need to straighten things out formally with Laura, get her to acknowledge legally that despite what may or may not have happened, you will always stay with me because that's where you belong."

Janey looked at him hopefully. "You think you can do that?" she asked, lower lip trembling.

Zach nodded. He had finally figured out a way to end the confusion. All he had to do now was get Laura to agree to it.

Janey stared at him a second longer, then started to cry. "Oh, Daddy, I'm so scared," she sobbed, throwing herself into his arms.

He held her close, wishing he could have spared her this pain.

"I don't want to leave you," Janey continued brokenly.

"Janey, that'll never happen," he soothed in a voice roughened with emotion, holding her tightly. "Not ever."

"But if I—if I'm not—" Janey protested.

He took her by the shoulders and forced her to look at him and listen to what he said. "Janey, you are my child. That's all there is to it." And that was final. To think that the years of loving and nurturing could be undone was ludicrous.

"But if—" Janey continued, almost hysterically.

He shook his head, cutting her off. He had parented Janey in every way that counted, made her his natural child in thought and deed and expectation, and that was all that mattered. "I'm not ever going to let anyone take you away from me," he continued firmly. "Not ever. No matter what the tests reveal. Is that understood?"

Janey nodded and threw herself back into his arms. The sobs she'd been withholding racked her body. Tears of frustration at his own helplessness in this situation flowing down his own cheeks, Zach held her until the storm passed.

MONDAY MORNING, he called Laura and arranged for her to meet him at his downtown office. She agreed readily when he told her it was about Janey. "I've been wanting to talk to you, too," she said after greeting him an hour later.

Zach motioned for her to take one of the comfortable chairs on the other side of his desk, unable to help but note how fresh and pretty she looked—how nervous.

"What about?" he asked quietly, his heart going out to her despite his earlier resolve to stay emotionally uninvolved with her.

"My son, Eric." Her skin lost some of its golden glow as she related unhappily, "He found out inadvertently about Janey and Melinda, the possibility of there being a switch." She sighed heavily and shook her head as if just remembering the incident caused her a great deal of pain and anguish. She pressed her lips together tightly. "He was very upset."

Zach knew how that was firsthand. "So was Janey, when I told her," he admitted.

Her head lifted in surprise at the soft empathy in his voice and her posture relaxed slightly as she studied him skeptically. Clearly she hadn't expected him to tell his daughter the truth. He didn't know whether to be amused or annoyed at the way she had underestimated him.

"Does that mean...?" Her eyes round, she gulped, and let her voice trail off, looking almost afraid to voice her hope.

Zach nodded slowly, still standing solidly behind his decision. "We all deserve to know the truth," he admitted frankly.

Laura bit her lip uncertainly and got up to pace the room, her heels digging soundlessly into the carpet.

As she moved back and forth, her slender legs moved fluidly beneath the full soft skirt of her peach-colored shirtdress. Zach became aware again, albeit unwillingly, of what a pretty figure she had, not too full, not too slim, but just right, with gently curving hips and breasts and a slender waist that was emphasized by a thick woven belt. Under any other circumstances he would have wanted to date her. But these weren't ordinary circumstances, he reminded himself sternly. Right now, judging from her doubtful look, he had an idea what she was thinking. She didn't seem to know if she could weather the strain and deal with her son's grief and confusion, too. But it looked to Zach as if they had no choice. "A simple blood test is all it would take," he continued gently, attempting to put her at ease. "Then we would know for sure."

Laura pivoted to face him, demanding he tell her the truth. "What made you change your mind?"

"Nights," Zach said simply, knowing they needed to be completely honest with each other. "I couldn't sleep. Couldn't stop thinking about it. Couldn't stop thinking about you and how you must feel." He shrugged eloquently. "I figured you probably felt the same."

She nodded slowly and her body relaxed. "You're right about that," she murmured.

Zach regarded her intently. "So you'll agree to have a blood test?" he asked, grateful she was being so calm and cooperative about this.

Laura nodded, looking as if a weight had just been lifted off her shoulders, too. "Yes," she said simply.

"Good." He nodded, satisfied they were doing the only practical thing they could do. Now came the hard part, the part she would resent. The part that would protect his daughter irrevocably. "There's only one condition," he continued in the same even tone.

Laura's head lifted at the forced geniality in his voice. Reading all he sought to hide in his eyes, she looked at him distrustfully, as if she should have known there would be a catch to this generous offer of his. "And what's that?" she asked.

He had never been one to shy away from playing hardball when necessary. "The catch is," he said slowly, "that you agree in writing to legally relinquish all parental rights and never to seek custody of Janey. If and only if you do that," he finished in a calm level voice, "will I ever agree to testing."

Chapter Four

Coming here had been a mistake, Laura thought as she stared at him, barely able to believe what she'd heard. "You can't really expect me to agree to that? If she is my natural child—" Laura sputtered.

"So far, Laura, that's a big if," he pointed out calmly, looking more indomitable than ever, seated behind the gleaming solid oak desk. It was the first time she had seen him in his downtown office. In a navy suit, he looked every bit the sophisticated executive. Like a man who was used to going after what he wanted and getting his own way. Trying to stand up against him would be like trying to stop a steamroller with one's bare hands. But she knew she had to try. She was strong, too. The years after Rob's death had taught her that.

She raised her chin in a posture of courage, letting him know this negotiation wasn't over yet. "I can't just give her up, Zach," she said earnestly. "Not if she is mine," she continued, looking into his clear blue eyes and finding them as mesmerizing and compelling as ever. "Not if we know that for certain."

"Why not?"

For him it was just so easy, Laura thought, on a new wave of despair. "Because you're asking too much of me. To not be sure and walk away from what might be my natural child is one thing. To know for certain and still leave her is something else entirely." He raised a dissenting brow, but she gave him no chance to interrupt her as she continued passionately, "How would that make Janey feel, Zach, knowing she'd been abandoned and rejected? How would she ever get over the loss? Especially at such a vulnerable age. An age where a young girl goes through so many changes."

Her last words seemed to hit a mark, because for a moment Zach did look conscience stricken. But the moment passed and he pushed away from the desk. Standing so close to her she could inhale the brisk woodsy scent of his aftershave, he said, his voice low and intense. "You not only can walk away from my daughter but you will, Laura. You have no choice. No matter what happened years ago, Janey's not yours to keep." He paused a moment, letting that sink in as he scrutinized her upturned face, then continued just as firmly, "Janey is my daughter in heart and soul and mind as surely as Melinda was yours. I thought we had settled that."

She still had Eric, Laura thought, and she loved him more than ever, but having a son wasn't the same as having a daughter. She knew in her heart that nothing would ever fill the emptiness Melinda's death had left.

Zach looked at her kindly, seeming to sense her inner turmoil. Instinctively he knew she had meant him and his daughter no harm. "I've just bargained with you as much as I ever intend to," he said gently. Her eyes met his and for a moment she was drawn in by the need for understanding and acceptance she saw in his eyes, a need that mirrored her own. But that faded as he set about getting his own way. "As far as I'm concerned," he continued with subdued implacability, "you can take it or leave it, but it's my only offer."

She knew from the determined look on his face he meant what he said. She had one chance to find out if Janey was her daughter. And only one. "All right," she said impulsively, giving in to his protectorate conditions.

Turning away from him, she walked to the window that overlooked downtown Fort Worth. Maybe he was right, maybe just knowing what the truth was would bring them both a modicum of peace of mind. Certainly, she thought, the confusion and doubt and guilt she felt couldn't get any worse. "You've got a deal," she conceded softly, turning back around to face him, "but I've got a condition of my own, too. I want the test done right away." Before he had a chance to change his mind, she thought. Before the not knowing drove her any crazier. "Like today."

"Today?" he repeated in open disbelief.

Laura nodded, all too aware of how the sunlight drifting in through the window brought out the gold in his light brown hair, and of how the blue in his suit brought out the blue of his eyes. He reminded her so much of Melinda. "Yes," she said.

He fell silent, gave her a measuring glance, and exhaled a lengthy sigh. Like her, he wasn't one to rail uselessly at the heavens about something that could not be changed. "Fine," he said abruptly, already moving to the phone on his desk. "I'll call my lawyer, get him to draw up the papers."

Soon, I'll know, Laura thought as she watched him flip through his Rolodex. The knowledge filled her with a certain buoyant joy. "I'll call my family doctor and get him to recommend a lab to do the blood tests."

That quickly, it was done.

HOURS LATER, Laura was not so sure she had done the right thing. She turned her attention to Eric, and told him what she had done. Not surprisingly, he was confused and torn about the situation, too, and they were still talking about the pros and cons of her actions early the next morning when her father came over to help her build a portable five-tiered rack for her pie-baking business.

"I know it sounds mean, but I really hope Janey isn't my sister," Eric confided as he sanded the edges of the wood his grandfather had cut. "Because if she is—" his young voice caught and it was a moment before he could go on "—it would mean that Melinda wasn't really my sister, you know? And, well, I find that sorta hard to believe. We were so alike...."

Laura's father nodded as he nailed two more finishing nails into the joints. "I've always thought it was who raised the child that counted, myself. The person who cares for the child is the parent, not the person who gave them life."

"Do you think I did the wrong thing, agreeing to the test?" Laura asked.

Her father shrugged and kept hammering.

She knew his silence meant he was trying to be tactful and not hurt her feelings. But she didn't want to be protected. Plus, if the two of them were to stay close, she and her father had to talk about this, even if it hurt. "Would you have done it?" Laura persisted, needing to know.

Her father straightened slowly. "Probably not," he admitted gently as he gave her an understanding glance, loving her enough to dare to be completely honest with her. "I think this is one of those things I'd just as soon not know. But that's me, Laura. That doesn't mean you shouldn't have agreed to do it. You're a grown woman now. You have to follow your heart. Only you know what's right for you and don't let anyone tell you any differently."

She smiled. "Thanks, Dad."

At the persistent blast of a horn in the driveway, Eric dropped what he was doing and ran toward an idling car. Three boys in Central High letter jackets were inside. Laura recognized them from the basketball team. They talked to Eric. Then he jogged back to Laura's side.

"Mom, can I go now? The guys are going out to lunch and then to see a movie."

"Don't you have a game tonight?"

"Yeah, but we don't have to be over at the high school until six. Please? I'll be home by four at the latest, I swear."

"You haven't finished your work," Laura's father reminded his grandson.

Laura looked back at the newly assembled shelf. All that was left was putting on the stainless-steel racks, where pies would cool, and the rollers on the bottom. There was really nothing she couldn't do herself. "I can help you finish, Dad." To Eric, she said, "Go on then, but take your jacket with you. Do you have enough money? No? Okay, you can borrow ten from me. My purse is inside."

"Thanks, Mom. Gramps, see ya later." Eric trotted off, and a scant minute later, the boys were off with yet another blast of the deafening horn.

Her father went back to work. Though he said nothing to her, she could tell by the stiff set of his shoulders he thought she was spoiling her son unnecessarily. "Since basketball started, he rarely gets any free time," she explained.

"Well, I think you should've asked him to finish what he started here. He shouldn't have left until the job was done."

Stinging from her father's disapproval, Laura frowned. They rarely quarreled, so it hurt doubly to have him speaking to her this way now. Laura countered, "He has so little time to be a kid, Dad. He's been through so much. I want him to enjoy life while he can. He'll be burdened with adult responsibilities soon enough."

Her father nodded his understanding and said nothing more. Nevertheless, she couldn't shake the feeling that he still disapproved.

"You know something don't you, Daddy? You found out what the blood test said."

Zach looked at Janey, so eager and trusting, and felt his heart break. Why had he ever agreed to the tests? "Honey, come over here and sit down," Zach said, taking her hand and guiding her to the sofa.

She sat down beside him, her face losing some of its color, her voice none of its youthful bravado. "I'm your child, aren't I, Daddy? That's what the tests showed?"

This wasn't getting any easier. Zach swallowed the lump in his throat. "Honey, you know you will always be my child, no one else's. That's why Mrs. Matthews signed that document I showed you."

Janey's expression grew pinched. She looked younger than her thirteen years.

"It would appear," Zach said, "that there was some kind of switch made at birth."

"So I'm not your little girl, not really?" Janey asked, her chin quivering.

Anger burst through Zach, fierce, unquenchable. It was coupled with a feeling of stark unreality. This had to be a bad dream, a nightmare from which he would soon wake. Needing a hug at that moment as much as Janey did, he took her into his arms. "You are my little girl, in every way that counts," he reassured her firmly, silently damning the telltale thickness of his voice. For the umpteenth time since this whole mess had started, Janey began to sob against him as if her heart would break. "And you always will be."

"You swear?" Janey demanded desperately, looking up into his face. "You swear she can't take me away from you?"

"I swear," Zach said seriously, meaning it from the bottom of his heart. "And she signed some legal papers to that effect. No one is going to take you away from me. Not ever."

"Good," Janey sobbed, clinging to him like a lifeline to safety. "Because I don't ever want to leave."

That said, Janey began sobbing with new terror. Knowing words would be useless at that point, until she calmed down enough to be able to listen to him, Zach merely cradled her close, the same way he had when she was an infant. As he did so, he remembered flashes of other times. The day she had learned to walk, and how she had fallen flat on her face. Her first words, which had been not Dada or Mama but "Go bye-bye." The fiercely intent way she looked when she concentrated on something, and the peaceful, angelic expression she wore when she slept.

No one could take those memories away from him, no one could take her. Because of what had happened, Janey was his child, biology be damned. And more importantly, he had the legal contract that Laura had signed. The fact there was no precedent for such a contract, that his lawyer didn't know how well it would hold up in court if put to the test, didn't bother him. From what he knew of Laura, she was an honorable woman. She would keep her promise. They would be able to go on with their lives and forget this had ever happened. When he thought of Melinda, there was some sadness, of course, because she had not lived her life to the normal age. But his was a kind of detached emotion, the kind of emotion you felt for a stranger you heard about on the news. Nothing like what he felt for his real daughter, for Janey.

No, that kind of love was forged only by years and years of closeness, caring, shared experiences. It didn't matter what the blood tests said. Janey was his. Melinda belonged to Laura. And that was the way it would always be.

"I CAME as soon as I heard the news."

"Mother." Laura straightened in surprise. The paintbrush in her hand threatening to splay droplets of varnish everywhere, she hurriedly transferred it to the wooden surface on the cooling rack in front of her and resumed painting, trying hard to hide the unsteadiness of her hands.

To no avail. Her mother had always been able to see through Laura's every defense, and earlier, when she was a child, her every artifice. If Grace had been understanding, or even as fair and open-minded as Laura's father, it might have been okay. But Grace was from the old school of rigid behavior and rigid expectations. Nothing Laura had ever done was good enough to suit Grace. Laura had not been ladylike enough, studious enough, or responsible enough. With her father away at sea a good deal of the time during Laura's childhood, and no siblings to run interference and distract Grace's relentless criticisms, Laura and her mother had been locked in an almost continual battle. For as far back as Laura could remember, her mother had tried to control her, to orchestrate every detail of her life. And, for as far back as Laura could remember, Laura had resisted furiously.

During the years she had been married, she had managed to exert some independence, but there were still times like now, usually the most stressful, when her mother felt it was her duty to interfere.

"Well, what are you going to do now?" her mother demanded.

I don't have to fight with her, Laura told herself firmly. It is not too late for the two of us to be friends. "I don't know," Laura said honestly, meeting her mother's probing gaze. "I still feel numb," she admitted. And sad, and scared, she added mentally.

Her mother stepped closer. Laura could tell she had just been to the beauty shop. Her graying hair was sprayed and teased so firmly into place that not even a gale-force wind could have budged a single strand. "Laura, you can't let someone else raise your child."

Laura could feel her hackles rise. "Believe me, I don't want to—" she began, her guilt at relinquishing all claims to Janey assailing her like a ton of bricks. "But I have no choice."

"Laura, I can see you're upset," Grace said firmly, using the same stiff and grating no-nonsense tone Laura had always dreaded in her youth. "That is understandable. But once the shock wears off—and it will, I assure you—you will realize what you must do. Frankly I think more than enough time has been wasted already." Her forbidding glance narrowed. "You've got to get her back."

If only it were that simple. But people could not go around trying to rearrange everyone else's lives to suit themselves. If they did, they would be as miserable as she was when her mother started in on her. Laura argued back reasonably, "I can't think about my needs here, Mother." Or yours, she thought. "I can't take Janey from the only father she has ever known."

"Nonsense, Laura, she is your flesh and blood. Your natural child. Eric's sister—"

"I lost Janey years ago, while I was still in the hospital with her. As much as we might like to do so, we can't rewrite history." As she finished, a sadness and despair deeper than any she had ever known washed over her.

A stormy silence prevailed between them. Bossy and opinionated, her mother had ruled her with an iron hand all those years her father had been off at sea. And Laura had rebelled and rebelled. If her mother had put her in uncomfortably stiff and outdated starched crinolines before Sunday school, Laura had made sure they were smudged with dirt and ripped beyond repair before the morning was over. When her mother curled her hair in ringlets and sprayed it with as much itchy lacquer as her own, Laura had accidentally on purpose dipped those same stiff curls into the water fountain and destroyed the Pollyanna look. Sweets were forbidden in her house, because they weren't nutritional, so Laura had eschewed fruits and vegetables and sneaked junk food every chance she got. Ditto with trashy novels and popular movies and rock music and anything else the normal teen wanted to enjoy. Their battle of wills had continued right up until the time Laura had married, at eighteen. In fact, it was still continuing to this day.

Laura glanced at her watch. "Mom, I've really got to finish this. Eric's got a game this evening and I haven't even showered yet."

"This matter isn't settled yet, Laura. I've let you make plenty of mistakes in the past, but I will not stand idly by and watch you turn your back on my grandchild."

You have no choice, Laura thought wearily, not about to let her mother start interfering in Janey's life. This is my natural child we're talking about and my decision. She knew she couldn't disrupt her daughter's life, or make this ordeal any worse than it already was. And it had nothing to do with that written promise not to seek custody. It had to do with what was right and wrong for the child. Nonetheless, staring at her mother's set expression, Laura felt a nagging sense of loss and depression.

Chapter Five

"Sorry I'm late, boss," Harry said as he walked into Zach's construction site trailer, turning his hard hat over and over in his hands. "I had to go over to the school. It was about Tabitha." The brawny construction worker had been with Zach since he'd started his company, fifteen years prior. They were not just boss and employee, but friends. Tabitha was in the same school as Janey and played on Zach's basketball team.

"Nothing's wrong, I hope," Zach said.

"Actually," Harry said with weary resignation, slumping down in a seat, "there's a lot wrong. Tabitha is close to failing two of her classes. If she doesn't get with it and bring her grades up, she won't be promoted. She'll have to stay in middle school another year."

"How long has she been having problems?" Zach asked sympathetically. In the past, he knew Tabitha had always been a very good student and in fact had been inducted into the junior honor society the previous year, along with Janey.

"This is the first time she's ever had trouble academically. She's—I don't know—a different kid sometimes. Surly, disrespectful. We've tried talking to her but that doesn't do any good."

Come to think of it, she'd seemed moody to Zach, too, even though she usually was attentive and hardworking during both practice and games. "What did her teacher say?"

"Basically that she's not trying. The school counselor thinks it's just a phase."

"What do you think?"

Harry shrugged. "I don't know. We got Tabitha a tutor. Hopefully that'll help."

Despite his confident words, Harry still seemed worried. Searching for a way he could help, Zach said, "Look, if she needs to drop basketball, so she can pull her grades up, I'll understand."

"No," Harry said, vetoing that idea immediately. "That wouldn't accomplish anything. It isn't that she has too much to do and too little time. The problem is her attitude. Hopefully we'll get her back on track soon."

The door to the trailer opened and Zach's chief carpenter came in. He looked grimmer than Zach and Harry put together. "Sorry to break in, Zach," he said, "but Mrs. Gagglione is going crazy over what she says we've done to her kitchen. Better get in the house and calm her down."

"All right. I'll be there in a minute," Zach sighed.

"And uh Zach?"

"Yeah?"

"You had a phone call from Mrs. Yaeger while you were out to lunch. She said Janey came home from school today, that she's not feeling so hot."

Alarm bells sounded in Zach's head but his years as a parent had taught him not to panic. "Did she say what she thought was wrong?"

"No, only that you should call or go home and she'd stay with Janey until you got there."

"Right. Thanks."

His mind on his daughter, Zach went out to talk to Mrs. Gagglione who had decided the ceiling in the room was too low. Reining in his exasperation, Zach spent the next fifteen minutes explaining why the structure of the home could not be changed to accommodate a higher ceiling. Finished, he told Harry he was leaving for the day and he went home to check on Janey.

"She's upstairs in her bed," Mrs. Yaeger said. In the middle of fixing their dinner, she had been watching her favorite soap on television, but she turned off the set to talk to him.

Zach frowned. It wasn't like Janey to head for her bed, even when she was sick. During the day, she much preferred to lounge around on the living room sofa. "Does she have a fever?"

"No, she told the school nurse something about her time of the month and cramps," Mrs. Yaeger said, an embarrassed flush lighting her cheeks. She turned her eyes to the casserole she was preparing. "I offered her some aspirin but she said she just wanted to climb into bed. I'm sorry if you were worried but, the construction site being all men, I didn't want to leave a more specific message."

"I understand completely. And thanks for staying until I could get here." He paused, worried. The past two weeks, since they had found out the results of the blood tests, Janey hadn't been herself. She seemed depressed. Subdued. Tired all the time. Zach empathized because he felt that way, too. The knowledge they had expected to free them had only increased their doubts.

Slipping off his down vest, Zach headed for the stairs. Janey was in her room, curled up on her side. Ducking to avoid the pink-and-white canopy cover, he saw she wasn't asleep and sat down beside her.

She turned to face him. "I told Mrs. Yaeger not to call you."

"Honey, she had to. Besides, I want to know if you're not feeling well."

At his expression of sympathy, her expressive eyes, so like Laura's, flooded with tears. Embarrassed for him to see, she turned her face back into her pillow and ran her open palm over her eyes.

"Honey, if you're in that much pain, I'll call the doctor," Zach said worriedly, already starting to get up.

Janey shook her head disconsolately. "No, Daddy, it's not that, the cramps aren't that bad."

There was no hurt worse than seeing your own child suffer. His throat thick, he said, "Then what is it?"

Janey swallowed hard and kept her head averted. "I'm just sad," she said in a muffled voice, with her eyes still closed against his searching glance.

"About what?" Zach said softly.

Janey lifted her shoulders eloquently and then released them. "About everything, I guess."

"Want to talk about it?" he inquired gently.

Janey shook her head. "What good would it do?"

"Well, it won't change the facts, if that's what you mean," Zach said, aware there were very few times in his life when he had felt as utterly helpless as he did now. He patted her shoulder tenderly, offering her what comfort he could. "But it might help to make you feel less alone and depressed than you are right now," he pointed out practically.

"I'm okay, Daddy," Janey said, shooting him a look of rebuke that said very clearly she wished to be left alone. But that, Zach wasn't about to do.

"No, you're not okay, and if you won't talk to me then—" Maybe a psychologist, he thought. Taking in a slow breath, he tried again, "Honey, you have to talk to someone. You can't hold everything inside. Are you worried about Laura?"

"Curious, is more like it," Janey interjected finally.

"What do you mean?" Zach said, keeping the edge of panic out of his voice with a great deal of effort.

Janey shrugged. "I just can't stop thinking about her. About everything. Daddy, I have a brother out there. And a mother. And it's all so weird. I—I haven't told you this, but I keep dreaming about her. And—and him. I dream I'm living there with them and I miss you and then I'm back here and then I'm there again, only I never know where their house is exactly or what they look like. I only know that they're like me. A lot. Is that crazy or what?" She sniffed again.

It wasn't crazy. It was something that he should have anticipated perhaps. He had been having the same weird dreams. Only his were mostly of the nightmarish variety, about loss.

"What do you want to do?" he asked softly. He felt she had already figured it out, even if she hadn't yet verbalized her desire to herself or anyone else.

Janey pleated the fabric of her pink-and-white bedspread with her fingers. "I don't know. I guess—" she continued with difficulty, not quite meeting his eyes "—I want to meet them. Just—just one time. So I know what they look like. But then that's all," she said hurriedly.

"Do you think that would help?" he asked gently, wanting only to end her distress and protect her from hurt in whatever way he could.

After a moment, Janey nodded. "I think if I could just see them once," she said slowly, "that I'd stop having these faceless people in my dreams." She looked to him for aid. "I think I'd be able to sleep again."

"ARE YOU SURE this is a good idea? I feel funny about this," Eric said as he got out of the car.

Laura straightened her pink-and-white striped chambray skirt and pink blouse. She'd had her reservations, too, but the more she thought about it, the more she knew Zach was right. Their mutual misery wouldn't end until they confronted their fears face-to-face. And considering how hellish the past two weeks had been, that couldn't happen soon enough. She turned to her son reassuringly. "It's only one meeting, honey. And a very brief one at that. Just enough to satisfy Janey's curiosity about us."

Eric's lower lip shot out glumly. "I don't see why she has to know anything," he muttered under his breath.

Determined not to have this get-together end in a free-for-all, Laura stopped halfway up the walk to Zach's house, and admonished her son firmly. "Eric, I know this is difficult for you. It is for me, too. But I expect you to consider everyone else's feelings today and cooperate to the fullest. It's not going to take long anyway. Zach felt half an hour would be plenty for Janey."

At the mention of his natural sister, Eric's expression became even more apprehensive. She knew how he felt. This was her first meeting with her natural child. She was nervous, too. She wanted it to go well, and was afraid it wouldn't.

But Zach was right. It needed to be done. Otherwise none of them would have any peace of mind. Initially, of course, after the tests had been finished, their results known, she had been so stunned and bewildered she hadn't known what to do. Now her shock was fading. She felt, as Janey did, the need to somehow tie this all up, and then move on. She wanted to get back to a normal life. She knew Eric and Zach and Janey did, too. And this first and last meeting, all in one, was the only way to accomplish that.

Satisfied she had Eric's cooperation, Laura took a deep breath and continued up the walk. Zach opened the door before she had a chance to ring the bell. "Hi. Come on in," Zach greeted them. He glanced at her son, his expression both kind and thoughtful. "I suppose this is Eric?" he asked as he extended his hand.

For a moment, Laura thought her son would not take Zach's hand. Finally he did. Unfortunately for all their mutual comfort, his expression was as reluctant when they finished shaking hands as when they started.

Maybe I'm asking too much of him, she thought worriedly. After all, he is only sixteen. This is a lot for me to handle. But then, what choice did they have? Excluding Eric from this would not make him feel any better. She suspected it would only make him feel worse. And Janey needed to meet both of them.

Laura looked over to see an adolescent girl sitting on the sofa and for a brief second her heart seemed to stop. Transfixed, Laura stared at the athletic-looking, dark-haired preteen with the oval face and dark brown eyes. She's beautiful, Laura thought. And so much like me, with her thick, abundant, naturally curly hair.

She was wearing an aqua and light gray slacks and sweater outfit, and looked, not surprisingly, just as shy as Eric. Something in Laura softened as she realized her two children had their shyness in common.

"Laura, I'd like you to meet my daughter, Janey," Zach said.

To Laura's surprise, the raw, overwhelming emotion she had expected—the burst of instinctive motherly love—didn't come. Despite the child's healthy beauty and the physical resemblance between them, Laura felt no soulful kinship with this child whom she had given birth to. Nor, it was very clear, did Janey feel any innate kinship toward Laura. Janey looked as apprehensive as Eric did.

His expression one of compassion and understanding, Zach looked from her to the children, then said pleasantly, "Why don't we all sit down?"

Unfortunately, despite Zach's graciousness as a host, the getting to know one another was as stiff and unnatural as it was possible to be. Before even five minutes had gone by, Janey was up and out of her chair, bounding restlessly toward the door. "I'm going to go out and shoot baskets, okay, Daddy?"

The way she moved, she didn't expect to be denied. And, Laura suspected as Zach looked at Janey, his expression one of concern, she wasn't going to be. Seeing she'd had all the tension she could bear, he said softly, "Sure," tolerating an action, that under normal circumstances, would have been very rude. And probably, Laura thought, gauging Zach's expectations of his child, unacceptable.

But the situation they were in broke all the rules, and hence, obliterated all normal expectations of accepted social conduct.

Eric looked at Laura, then at Janey disappearing out the door. "I think I'll go, too," he said uncertainly. "If it's okay. Mom?"

Like Zach, she nodded her approval.

Offering her his broad back, Zach crossed over to the bay window overlooking the front yard. From outside, could be heard the rhythmic thumps of bouncing basketballs. "Funny, isn't it, that they both love basketball," he murmured in a low voice laced with surprise as he watched them play.

Laura got up to join him at the window. "Maybe there's more to biology than we know."

"Maybe," he agreed softly, his eyes still on the kids.

That being the case, Laura was amazed at the calm, practical way he had been able to handle all of this. And yet there was something very wrong, she knew. Because not once had he ever appeared to want to know anything about his natural child, the child she had reared and lost. She wondered why.

Giving in to her impulse, she asked inquisitively after a moment, "Aren't you ever even curious about Melinda? What she was like or—"

"No."

His denial was kind but quick, almost too quick to be believed. Studying him, she felt he was holding more inside than any of them. And that this would inevitably hurt him.

Softly, wanting to help, she pointed out, "But she was your natural child, just as Janey is mine."

He continued looking out the window, his hands in his pockets, his posture relaxed. Turning to her, he assessed her for a long moment. "I'm not going to dwell on what was or what might have been," he said pragmatically, imprisoning her with his gaze. "We all need to just forget about it and go forward."

Laura sighed. How simple that all sounded, how easy. Only for her, she knew it wasn't quite that easy. And she suspected it wasn't quite that easy for him, either, despite his surprisingly realistic attitude. Wanting to forget something and being able to forget something were two different things. How well she knew that. "And if we can't?" she queried softly.

Zach shrugged expressively. "We don't have a choice. Trust me on this, Laura," he advised candidly, able to see she wasn't persuaded. "The sooner we put this behind us and forget about it, the sooner we'll all be able to go on with our lives."

Laura looked at the kids. It seemed safer than looking up into Zach's handsome face. Though of differing minds, they were getting along better with every passing moment. And because of that she couldn't help but be aware of him on every level. As a father, he was kind, compassionate, devoted. As a man, he was fair and levelheaded. As a lover, she sensed he would be tender and giving, and yet demanding, too. Patient and insatiable. She pushed the unwelcome thoughts away, reminding herself that they were here today to tie up this chapter of their lives, somehow resolve their conflicts, and move on. She commented, "You said on the phone that Janey's been upset the past few weeks."

Zach nodded, his expression worried as the talk turned again to Janey. "Yes, but she was a lot better once we arranged this meeting. She seemed—" he shrugged expressively as he searched for words "—at peace with everything. I think today will help her to put this behind us."

Behind them.

Was that what she wanted, Laura wondered, her heart aching for no reason she could name, for this to be over? Feeling suddenly as restless as the two kids had been, Laura moved away from Zach so they were no longer standing shoulder to shoulder. She concentrated once more on the activity outside. She watched, pleasantly surprised to see that Janey and Eric were no longer as wary of each other as they had been at the outset. They were talking to each other occasionally, Eric remarking on an easier way to shoot lay-ups, then demonstrating, Janey clumsily attempting to imitate his more experienced aim.

How alike they looked, playing together in the sunlight. How tentatively inquisitive about each other, Laura thought with a wave of optimistic satisfaction. As if now that the first barrier had been broken down the two of them really could be friends. Perhaps even brother and sister one day. Knowing how much Eric had missed having a sibling, and that Janey had never had one, she couldn't help but wish that could happen.

"I have to be honest with you, Zach," she said, sighing softly as she turned back to him, "This hasn't been as cut-and-dried as I would have wished. Since we found out the truth, I still think about her a lot." And she hungered to know more.

He let out a long uneven breath. "Then stop," he advised, his pointed words softened by the kindness in his eyes, "because no good can come of dwelling on this."

She viewed him with barely concealed exasperation, understanding where he was coming from but unable to agree with his remedy. He really expected this trauma to be over, just because he wanted it to be. He expected them to go on as if nothing had ever happened. That promise seemed as silly as it was idealistic to her. But it was also a typically male response. In her experience, men just simply refused to think about what they couldn't easily change, as if by steadfastly ignoring a problem, it would go away. Her husband had been like that. For the most part, her father still was, although his age had mellowed him somewhat and made him more prone to take emotional risks.

Again she tried, as gently as possible, to get through to Zach and offer him what he'd already offered her, the chance to know his natural child, however cursorily. "If you'd like to know more about Melinda—" she began gently, only to be cut off by the deliberate shake of his head.

"No," he refused her wearily. "I don't see any point in going back. I want this to be over. At least as much as it can be."

And for him that meant not dwelling on his loss. After a moment she carefully supposed that she could understand that. Why pine after someone you could never know? Laura suddenly wished she had come to know Zach some other way, without all this tension between them. She had the feeling they could have been friends. Maybe more than friends.

Glancing at her watch, she saw almost an hour had elapsed. And he had mentioned something earlier, when he had called her to arrange the meeting, about having a basketball practice to coach later on. It was time for her to go, past time. "I better get Eric," she said.

He looked briefly as reluctant for her to leave as she was to go but recovered promptly and moved chivalrously toward the door, offering gently, "I'll walk you out."

Together, they moved outside. "Eric. It's time," she said as she walked down the steps, her full skirt swirling around her legs.

"Okay." Slightly out of breath, he handed the ball to Janey, and then without a word, turned and started for the car.

This is the last time I'll ever see her, Laura thought, and this time she felt the pain of that. The loss. By a twist of fate, she'd been blessed with not one but two daughters, and now she'd lost them both—one to death, one to Zach. There were times, like now, when she felt life was terribly unfair.

Janey backed up, two basketballs cradled to her chest. Unlike Eric, who still looked cool and composed, her oval face was flushed with the heat of exertion. Her dark brown hair was mussed and frizzy, falling in a tumble to her shoulder. Yet facing Laura, her dark brown eyes were wary.

"Goodbye, Janey," Laura said. "I enjoyed meeting you."

Janey remained silent.

Zach didn't press her to respond, although Laura felt in any other circumstance he would not have countenanced deliberate rudeness.

"Goodbye, Laura, Eric," Zach said.

It was over that quickly.

"TEN EXTRA PIES?" Laura repeated happily. "Four pecan, two chocolate fudge, three apple, and one blueberry. Sure, I can have them at the restaurant by five." Laura glanced at the clock on the kitchen wall.

It wasn't going to be easy, of course—the three apple pies in particular would take at least an hour and a half to assemble—but business had been slow since the holidays and she needed to increase her income in whatever way she could. Besides, maybe the extra activity would take her mind off Janey and Zach. Heaven knew she hadn't managed to think about much else while she worked since meeting the pretty teenage girl several weeks prior.

By two-thirty, she was whistling and elbow deep in dishwasher suds. The phone rang. Dripping suds, she grabbed a towel and reached for it.

"Mrs. Matthews? This is Eric's basketball coach, over at Central. I wondered how he's doing."

"Doing?" Laura repeated dumbly.

"Yeah. I know he's sick today and—"

"He is?" she interrupted quizzically.

There was a very brief silence. "You're telling me he isn't?"

Eric had skipped school? Deliberately, Laura pushed away a flash of anger. She had never been one to jump to conclusions before and she wasn't going to start now. Maybe this was all a crazy mistake.

Keeping her voice calm, she reported, "Eric left for school this morning at the normal time." She glanced out the back door at the driveway, and confirmed for herself his car was gone. "I haven't seen nor heard from him since." Oh, no, she thought as the next thought occurred. Please, don't let him have been in an accident. But if he had been, she surely would have been notified.

"Well, he hasn't shown up here at school."

"I imagine if he'd had a flat tire he would've called," Laura said slowly. She frowned, perplexed. Heat flooded her face as the silent seconds ticked by. Embarrassed not to know where her child was, but still wanting to give Eric the benefit of a doubt, she continued, "I can't imagine what could have happened. He's always so dependable."

"Well, that's something else we need to talk about." The coach paused, then went on reluctantly as if picking his way through a mine field, "Mrs. Matthews, is everything okay at home? I only ask because Eric hasn't seemed to be quite with us the past few weeks, during practice or games. In the past he's always been one of our strongest players."

"I know," Laura said. On that score, she was worried, too. In the last two games he had played well below his ability, missing almost every basket he attempted. Afterward, disappointed in his own performance, he had been moody and remote. She had attributed his low mood to his "off games," not considering it might be the other way around.

"Is there anything I can do to help? Anything you'd like me to talk to him about, man-to-man?" the coach persisted. "Any girls in the picture I don't know about? Somebody in the family sick? Anything?"

"No, sorry," Laura confessed, feeling even more mortified and confused. "I don't know any more than you do at the moment."

"Well, please let me know if there's anything I can do. And as for Eric's absence, for his sake, I hope there's a good excuse."

"I'm sure there is," Laura said with more assurance than she felt, "and I promise I'll let you know as soon as I find out what it is."

Feeling further dismayed and dejected, she hung up the phone. This had never happened before. The coach was right. Eric had been acting strangely lately. Distracted, surly, upset. And when he wasn't grumpy, he was too quiet. And he had been that way ever since they'd visited the Andersons.

Well, there was only one way to get to the bottom of this, and that was to talk to him face-to-face. While she waited for the pies to finish baking, she started calling the homes of his friends. To her dismay, no one had seen nor heard from Eric all day. Nor had he contacted her parents.

By the time she was ready to deliver the pies, she was frantic with worry. By five, she had completed her business and began looking for him in earnest.

She found his car in front of a popular video game arcade. Eric was inside, hunched over one of the brightly lit machines. As she looked him over and saw he was physically intact, she didn't know whether to burst into tears or grab him by the edges of his letter jacket and shake him. She did know she'd never been so scared or angry in her life. Marching up to him, she grabbed his arm. "I want to talk to you, young man."

He straightened laconically, for a second looking like a defiant stranger. "Okay, shoot."

"At home," she specified clearly.

His face changed. His jaw hardened and his voice was curt, "Fine. I'll follow you."

"No, Eric, you'll ride with me."

He opened his mouth as if about to protest, took a second harder look at her expression, and saw the extent of her displeasure, then bit down on whatever he'd been about to say.

Unable to control her flaring temper any longer, Laura started in on him the second they marched in the door. "You skipped school today, didn't you?"

He shrugged indifferently. "Yeah, so?"

"So?" She spoke heavily, as if verbally underlining every word. "You could get expelled for that, at the very least kicked off the team."

Eric shrugged disconsolately, his expression dark and rebellious. "Yeah, well, my playing hasn't been worth a damn lately anyway. The coach told me so at practice yesterday, so I didn't think it'd be any great loss to anyone if I wasn't there, know what I mean?"

Her face softened sympathetically, despite her resolve to be every bit as tough on him as his father would have been. When she'd been his age, she had needed understanding, not scolding. But that was all her mother had given her and the resulting distance between them had only made her behave all the more foolishly. Feeling much calmer, she asked gently, "Is that why you skipped?"

Near tears, Eric shrugged in a way that let her know it was much, much more.

Bewildered by the raw emotion she saw on his face, disappointed by the unexpectedly unconscionable way he'd behaved, angry at her own unusual obliviousness to his pain, she fought back a wave of frustrated tears. Tears that had been borne as much from hours of worry as anything else. Moving closer, she took him tenderly by the shoulders, letting him know by her touch that she cared very much what happened to him. "Eric, what is going on with you? You've got to talk to me." He had never behaved this way before, not even after the death of his father.

Silence.

"Is it a girl?"

He gave a sardonic laugh and shook his head in mute aggravation, pulling away from her as if he could no longer bear her maternal touch. "Not the way you mean, no."

"Then what is it?"

He turned back, surly and defiant again without warning. "Can't you guess?" His young face was gilded with challenge.

"No." Laura shouted. "Dammit," she said, massaging her aching temples. "Eric, stop playing games. Stop expecting me to be able to read your mind and just talk to me. Tell me what it is that's eating you alive and prompting you to act this way."

"All right, you want to hear it? You'll hear it." Eric announced, flinging off his jacket and sprawling on the couch. "I'm ticked off at you, Mom."

"Me? Why?" Barely able to get out the single word sentences, she stared at him in shock. "What'd I do?"

"It's more what you didn't do." At her bewildered glance, he said plainly, "It's Janey. I don't get how you can just walk away from her that way. I mean, what if it was me, Mom?" he said, his voice breaking. "What if I had ended up in the wrong home? Would you not have cared? Would you have just walked away? Darn it, you have a responsibility to at least get to know her, especially since she doesn't have a mother. And I have a right to get to know my sister!" Finished, he clamped both arms over his chest and glared at her.

Tears streamed down Laura's face. She felt stunned and hurt. "Eric, listen to me." She held out her hands beseechingly and sat down beside him. "I do care about Janey—"

"Yeah, well, you have a funny way of showing it," he said, his eyes filling with pain and anger.

Laura struggled with her grief, her guilt, and her loss. "But she's not mine, not anymore."

Eric's jaw jutted out. He turned his face away from her and stared at the wall. "Yeah, right."

His hurt cut her to the quick. "What do you want me to do?" she asked in a broken, trembling voice.

He turned back to her, his cheeks flushed with temper. "What do you think?"

Her heart in her throat, Laura forced the words out of numb lips, "Eric, I can't—"

He got up abruptly and strode from the room, his face a mask of impotent rage and frustration. "I don't want to hear anymore. Okay?" He was running by the time he reached the hall stairs. The door to his room slammed behind him, and then echoed in the still, lonely house.

LAURA WAS AWAKE all night. By dawn she knew what she had to do. Go see Zach. She found him at the construction site. In a rough chambray shirt and cords, he had been going over some blueprints while he drank what was probably his first cup of coffee. His hair was clean and soft, brushed back away from his face in short, damp waves, his face freshly shaven. Looking at him, she felt another pang of physical awareness, then pushed it away. No matter how attractive he was, she couldn't get involved with him.

Watching her smile at him uncertainly, his bright-eyed look of welcome faded. He straightened slowly and put down the marking pencil in his hand.

"Hi," she said.

"Hi. I didn't expect to hear from you again."

Didn't want to hear from her was what he meant, she thought, sitting down in one of the upholstered chairs in front of his desk without waiting for an invitation. "I know, but some things have changed." Briefly she told him about her conversation with Eric, keeping her voice as unemotional as possible.

Zach's face softened compassionately while she talked about Eric's unhappiness. He got up to pour her a cup of coffee. "I'm sorry you're having trouble with your son," he said carefully, handing her a cup and a small tray that contained packets of sugar and cream, and little plastic stirrers.

Slowly Laura put her cup down on the edge of his desk. She faced him deliberately, her eyes direct. "I was wrong to think we could just let this go, Zach."

It took a moment for her words to sink in and when they did, he was anything but pleased. "We agreed on one visit, to satisfy everyone's mutual curiosity, and we did that."

"I know," Laura replied, "and it was a success."

"Because we knew going in what the limits were."

"We thought we did," Laura corrected. If he were unnerved by the rather intimate setting of the trailer, he wasn't showing signs of being bothered. "Unfortunately," she continued matter-of-factly, "everything we've tried to predict in this situation has turned out to be wrong. And maybe that should tell us something, Zach. Like we need to forget long-range plans and just play it by ear. Take it one day, one moment at a time." Like she had when Melinda was sick and in other traumatic or difficult times.

He shook his head grimly. "I can't do that. I have to think where all this will lead."

"And I have to think about right now, this moment, about how my son is feeling, and how Janey may be feeling."

He lifted a powerful-looking arm and rubbed at the tension in the back of his neck. "She hasn't said anything to me about wanting any more visits with you."

Laura watched as he dropped that same arm back to the arm of his chair, and tried not to think about how it might feel wrapped around her waist. Why not face it, she thought honestly, she'd never been attracted to any man the way she was attracted to Zach. But she'd never been around anyone as inherently sexy and self-assured as he was, either. There was just something about him, something physical and sensual, that she found alluring. Still, she knew she would never let herself act on those feelings.

Forcing her mind back to the subject at hand, Laura persisted, "You're telling me Janey's completely back to normal?"

Zach was quiet. He took a sip of his coffee and looked at her reflectively over the rim of his cup. "It's hard to get back to normal after all we've been through, Laura. And that doesn't mean we have to jump into something that is only going to complicate the situation more."

"All I know," Laura said tiredly, swallowing the faint catch in her throat, "is that I don't want Janey to feel like Eric does, like I've abandoned her, like I don't care."

The words *World's Best Dad* were printed on his mug. Zach traced them with gentle circular motions. "I don't, either, Laura. I'm just not sure your solution is the right one."

"Then what should we do?" she asked.

He shrugged expressively. "I don't know."

She reached for her coffee. Aware he was watching her every move, she took a sip. "What about Janey? Don't you think she has a right to know her brother, don't you think that she might benefit from some contact with a sibling?"

Zach remained silent.

He's remembering how well the two of them played together, Laura thought. She realized with satisfaction that the way the kids had interacted had touched him. Therefore, he wasn't as immune to feelings as he would like her to think.

Laura leaned forward earnestly in her chair, balancing her mug on her knee. "Talking to Eric, I realized he was right. Suppose, for instance, that you or I had discovered somewhere along the way that we had another brother or sister. Wouldn't you want to get to know him or her? At least find out if you had anything in common? I know I would."

Zach stiffened and set his mug aside. "What you or I would or wouldn't want has nothing to do with Janey's situation." His eyes lifted to hers and he made a plea straight from the heart. "She's vulnerable, Laura."

So were they all, she thought. Zach included. Not dissuaded in the least, she replied softly, "All the more reason she needs a protective older brother in her life." She paused, appealing to his practical side. "I'm not trying to be her mother, Zach, or separate the two of you. I would never do that. But I do think that we should try to become friends. Because if we don't and Janey one day feels like Eric does now, you're really heading for trouble."

He was silent, thinking. Head lifting, he gave her a neutral look. "If I say no?"

She looked into the depths of his clear blue eyes and feeling him to be a very sympathetic, compassionate individual, predicted gently, "I don't think you will once you think about it, Zach. All I ask is that we have some joint family outings. You and Janey, Eric and me. All I want is for Janey to know that even though fate has thrown us all a curve, that I still care about what happens to her and so does Eric, and so do you. And maybe if their insecurity about all this is addressed, they'll be reassured. Surely there's enough love between us to go around," she finished. "Surely we're adult enough to work this out in a way that will satisfy everyone."

Her reasonableness was getting to him. She could see it in the faint relaxing of his jaw. Zach sighed and ran a hand through his hair, the light brown strands looking like shimmering threads of silk against his work-roughened hands. "All right," he said finally, conceding with obvious reluctance. "But if this request of yours upsets Janey in any way—"

"We'll pull back," Laura promised, satisfied she had accomplished what she had set out to do. Her heart was light with anticipation and relief. The excitement she felt was normal, considering that she was going to spend some time with her long lost daughter. It had nothing to do with the fact Zach would be there, too, she assured herself, nothing at all.

Chapter Six

"Janey, come on," Zach said, rapping on his daughter's closed bedroom door, "we're going to be late!"

"I can't help it. I haven't got anything to wear," Janey said, joining him in the hall.

He stared at her robe in mute stupefaction. "I thought you were already dressed." This wasn't like her. Usually she just put on her Mavericks sweatshirt and they were off.

Telltale spots of color appeared in her face. "I was."

"And?" he prompted gently when nothing else was forthcoming.

She shrugged. "That red sweatshirt didn't look right."

It always looked perfect, Zach thought. And so did she. But she didn't want to hear that from him, not tonight. Tonight she needed a woman's reassurance. She needed her mother. Only that was impossible. He regretted the loss of Maria with all of his heart and soul.

Maybe if she had been here, Janey wouldn't have needed any contact with the Matthewses at all. Maybe she wouldn't have wanted any, he thought with guilt and resentment.

Oblivious to his disparaging thoughts, Janey disappeared into her room again, still explaining why the red sweatshirt wouldn't do at all.

Zach hesitated, then offered a way out. "Honey, look, if you'd rather not go tonight, I understand. I don't really want to go, either."

She whirled to face him. "Dad, you promised we'd be there!" Accusation mixed with the panic on her face.

"This inability to get dressed has nothing to do with second thoughts?" he queried firmly.

Janey rolled her eyes in full-blown teenage despair. "Dad, get real. I like Eric. I like him a lot. I just need to go shopping, that's all. I'll be ready in five minutes. I swear."

Zach let out his breath slowly, noticing she'd said nothing about Laura Matthews, only her newfound brother. Somehow that was less threatening to him. "Better shake a leg, then, because I told the Matthewses we'd meet them at the entrance to Reunion Arena at six-thirty." As sticky as things were, he didn't want the determined Laura Matthews to think they'd deliberately been stood up and then go off half-cocked and do something even more damaging than request time with her biological daughter.

Fortunately, Janey was as good as her word, and a few minutes later they were out the door. "Why couldn't we have gone with them to the game?" Janey asked once they were on their way.

"I thought it'd be easier just to meet there," Zach replied. It would be less awkward. And in case the evening was a total bomb, as he half feared it would be, they wouldn't have to ride home together in the same car.

"Oh." Janey fell silent.

Zach cast her a worried glance. "You don't have to get to know the Matthews family, you know. I, for one, would understand if you didn't."

"I want to get to know Eric," Janey said, her chin taking on that determined tilt that said he couldn't budge her with a crane. "He seems neat. We look a lot alike, you know?"

So much so, Zach thought, that it tore him apart. Wordlessly, he nodded.

"It's like discovering I had a twin or something I never knew about. It's weird, but kind of nice, too."

But so far, Zach objected mentally, very little had happened.

"Don't look so worried, Dad," Janey reassured teasingly after a moment. "I'm a big girl now. I can handle this."

Zach hoped so. He never would've agreed to it at all, if Janey hadn't been having trouble sleeping, if she hadn't had so many questions, and if she hadn't reacted positively to the suggestion the two families get to know one another as friends.

Then he'd known she wanted to get to know Eric, too, but had been afraid to voice the emotion. Probably for fear of hurting him. And her request had hurt and threatened him in some way. Intellectually, of course, he knew it was wrong of him to be so petty. Laura was right. There was enough love to go around. Or at least there should be. But in his heart, he wasn't sure that was at all true, or even if this was going to work out. Well, they'd find out soon enough.

They arrived at the gate to find Laura and Eric already there. She, too, had taken an inordinate amount of care dressing for the occasion. From what he'd seen of her in her home environment, Laura was an extremely casual, very happy-go-lucky person. A messy baker, she seemed to get smudges of flour everywhere, and then not mind at all. Tonight, however, she had dressed with enough care to meet the president. Her thick, naturally curly hair had been coaxed into a disciplined wedge. She was wearing eye makeup, pretty earrings, subtle but sophisticated perfume, a dignified navy-and-red sweater that might have been new, and a trim knee-length skirt. Her leather flats showed off her long slender legs to perfection.

Janey, however, seemed not the least bit impressed. She stayed unusually close to his side. But Zach hadn't expected to be disturbed by Laura's presence, too. In a completely different way. And although he would've liked to chalk up his extraordinary awareness of her to the fact he dated so infrequently, deep down it was more than her fresh, pretty looks.

Laura was just so alive. With all the grief and trauma she'd had in her life, losing first her husband, then her daughter, she could have turned inward, adopted a sour outlook. But she hadn't. Instead she was vivacious and lively. He knew from the fond glances she routinely slanted at her son that she was a very loving woman. She seemed to have a wealth of tenderness within her, just waiting to be released.

And, as he looked at her, he found himself wondering who would be the recipient of all that pent-up passion and zest for life. He found himself fantasizing about the softness of her kiss. And he knew damn well that could never happen.

"Let's go on inside, shall we?" Zach asked abruptly, taking charge.

The next few moments were awkward, with everyone trying a little too hard to please, to appear casual. After some shifting of seats, they finally ended up with Zach on one end, Laura on the other, and Eric and Janey in the middle.

Fortunately, the game was an exciting one, and the Mavericks took an early lead. Janey and Eric talked only occasionally—about the basketball being played. At halftime, they all headed to the concession stands.

Not surprisingly, Zach thought he detected a faint note of resentment on Eric's part toward him. Eric wanted to get to know his sister, but he could have done without Zach's hovering presence during the awkward process. He guessed he couldn't blame Eric. If he were in the kid's shoes, he'd probably feel that way, too.

Maybe it would go easier on all of them, Zach thought, if he could just put him at ease. "So, Eric, what are your plans when you graduate from high school next year?" Zach asked as the line to the concession stand inched forward.

Eric sent him a surprised glance. Although he was just sixteen, he was tall, and on eye level with Zach. "I don't have any."

Yet, Zach thought. "You planning to make your college visits this summer? Or are you going to go into the service like your dad?"

Eric shrugged, bewildered by Zach's interest in a subject he apparently didn't care two bits about himself. "I don't know. I guess I'll figure that out after I graduate."

After he graduated? Zach stared at him, nonplussed. By the time he had been a high school sophomore he had known exactly where he wanted to go to school, and what he wanted to do.

"Dad, look," Janey interrupted, tugging on his sleeve. "They're selling the new style T-shirts over there. Can I go get one, please? I've got enough allowance money saved up."

It wasn't so much a question of money as it was of time. If they stood in yet another long line they'd miss the start of the second half.

"I'll go with her," Eric said. "That is if it's okay with my mom," he amended as an afterthought.

Laura nodded. "It's all right with me, if it's all right with Zach. Just don't go anywhere else."

After getting permission from Zach as well, the two left. An awkward silence fell between Zach and Laura. Casting around for something to break the continuing tension between them, Zach said, "About Eric. One of the men who works for me has a wife who specializes in career counseling, for high school students. She helps them define their goals, identify their talents and interests. If you like, I could give you her name."

"Thanks, but no," Laura said firmly.

Zach didn't bother to hide his surprise.

"I don't want that for Eric unless he wants it for himself and he's just not ready yet."

He wasn't ready, or Laura wasn't ready? Zach wondered.

Reading his disapproval accurately, she continued, "When I was a kid, my mother made me adhere to all sorts of schedules and rules. I hated it. I won't put those same demands on Eric."

Zach saw it was an emotional issue for her, and for that reason he didn't want to push it. On the other hand, what he was suggesting wasn't so out of line. For Eric's sake, someone needed to talk to Laura. "Deciding on a career path is not exactly punishment, Laura," he pointed out mildly, inching slightly closer to the concession stand.

"Maybe not for you," she countered quietly but firmly, "but for Eric it would be."

Zach reached into his back pocket and pulled out his wallet. "Don't you think you're underestimating your son? He seems like a very together kid."

"He is. But he's also been through a lot." She sighed, going on, "Most of Eric's early life, our whole family existence was dictated by the whims of the Navy. It encompassed where we lived, how we lived, how often and even when he saw his dad. Then his dad died and everything was dictated by our precarious financial situation, and the demands that were made on me as I moved us back here, found us a place to live, and got my business going. No sooner had I managed that than Melinda got sick and for the following two years after that, our lives were completely ruled by her illness. Since Melinda died, we've been content to take it day by day, to just appreciate what we have every moment. The way Melinda did during her last days with us. That's how we've coped, the both of us. I'm not going to ask him to change, not even to get ready for college or whatever it is that he chooses to do with the rest of his life." Her chin thrust out stubbornly, her pugnacious expression enhancing rather than detracting from her looks.

Zach couldn't argue with her logic. But if Eric only lived from day to day that could severely limit Eric's choices later on. Well, it wasn't any of his business. So he would have to let it drop.

They reached the concession window. Laura ordered colas and hot dogs. Zach chipped in for ice cream and chips. The two of them were thoroughly loaded down when the kids returned, each with a Mavericks T-shirt in hand.

To Zach's relief, the second half proved even livelier than the first, the lead slipping from one team to the other and back again. The winner wasn't decided until the last two seconds of the game when the Mav's sunk a three-point shot. The crowd was on its feet, roaring with glee as the final buzzer sounded.

"What a game!" Janey cried exuberantly.

Zach glanced at his daughter and caught Laura's wistful expression as she watched Janey. Guilt stung him briefly, then faded swiftly as he realized he stood to lose Janey, too, if she were to transfer her affections to Laura. "Well, we better get a move on," Zach said, a bit more abruptly than he intended. "Traffic will probably be murder."

None of the other three was as anxious to depart as he. Together, they carried their trash to the receptacle, and then walked shoulder to shoulder toward the exit and out into the bracing night air. Once out on the sidewalk, they drew to a halt. Janey looked at Eric, with all the adoration of a younger sister for her big brother. "I guess I'll see you around sometime," she said.

Eric nodded. "Maybe."

Knowing it wouldn't get any easier, Zach said a polite goodbye and then hustled Janey off in the opposite direction. "That was fun, wasn't it?" she said ebulliently, practically skipping along beside him.

Zach nodded, aware as Laura probably was that although his daughter had been friendly toward her new brother, she hadn't said much more than an emotionally aloof "I like your earrings" to Laura.

Clearly, Janey wasn't that interested in finding a mother. She wanted a sibling, but that was all.

Zach wondered if her feelings would change over time. The crazy way things had been going, he decided there was no telling.

"Mom?" Eric questioned as he pulled her car into the driveway and cut the engine. "Are you okay?"

Laura looked at him, stunned by the concern she heard in his voice. "Yes. Why?"

"You've been so quiet. You hardly said a word on the drive home."

That's because I was still living the evening with Zach and Janey, she thought. She had gone into it with zero expectations, only to find the four of them could have a really good time together. A portent of other times to come? she wondered.

Realizing her son was still waiting for an answer, one corner of her mouth lifted and she favored him with a fond smile. "I was quiet because I didn't want to distract the driver."

He gave her a closer look. "I did all right, didn't I?"

"You did great." She felt she could trust his driving in any situation. "Your reflexes are great. You were patient and courteous. A mother couldn't ask for more."

"Whew! That's a relief!" He pretended to wipe the sweat from his brow. "I thought for a moment, from the look on your face, you were unhappy with my driving again."

"No, not so, not at all," Laura said with a reassuring smile. They'd had a few fights initially, while he was first learning how to drive, mostly because he had tended to go too fast or take corners more out of his lane than in it, but those days were behind them now. He drove with skill and care.

Together, they walked into the house. "Are you hungry?" Laura asked, turning on the kitchen light.

I've got to stop thinking of Zach, of how nice he looked in his dark blue sweater and light blue shirt. His khaki slacks had been perfectly pressed, his shoes shined, his jaw closely shaved and scented with the brisk woodsy after-shave he favored. She'd been proud to be seen with him. And knew from the admiring glances he'd given her when he thought she was watching the game that he approved of the way she had looked, too.

Long used to being independent in the way she was attired, she usually didn't give a second thought to what she wore. But tonight she had worried over her selection, unable to choose between slacks or a skirt. She'd finally selected the skirt, feeling it was more feminine. She was glad she had. And she didn't want to think about what that might mean. She wasn't getting involved with Zach, other than as friends. Their lives were already far too complicated. Nevertheless, for a moment tonight as she'd sat shoulder to shoulder with Zach in the noisy arena, she'd had a flash of what it might be like to be his date. And it had been a good feeling.

"Mom—" Eric said, breaking into her runaway thoughts.

Laura jerked to attention, guilty color warming her cheeks. "What?"

"I said I'm still stuffed. I'm going to bed."

"Oh." Laura leaned forward to kiss his cheek. "Good night, hon."

He shook his head remonstratively. "You were a thousand miles away."

Laura knew that. And her thoughts weren't just happy or ridiculously romantic. Seeing Eric and Janey together had stirred up a wealth of memories. Laura realized that Janey, no matter how sweet and lovable and charming, could never take Melinda's place in her heart.

And she had to face it, that was what she had wanted, subconsciously anyway. To find a way to fill the void left by her daughter's death. For Eric, it seemed to have worked, at least a little. She had known all along he missed having a little sister adoring him and tagging along after him, but it hadn't been until the two of them had been sitting side by side in Reunion Arena, their heads bent together over a program, discussing the players, that she'd begun to appreciate just how lonely he must have been the past year.

She had never had a sister or a brother herself, so she had no idea what it was like to have a sibling there day in and day out. But Eric had known. From the time he was small, he had a sister to entertain and keep him entertained, someone to share confidences and secrets and private jokes and stories. He'd lost all that when Melinda died. Now he had a chance to get some of the familial camaraderie back. She couldn't, wouldn't begrudge him that.

Being with Janey the first time had been an experience full of curiosity and wonder. Being with her the second time, Laura had experienced the sense of loss and bereavement she'd felt at Melinda's death all over again. Only Zach's pleasant companionship had softened the blow.

For Eric, it had been different. And for that, she was glad. She just didn't know how she was going to cope in the days ahead. Would spending time with Janey hurt and disappoint her? And how would she cope if it did?

"MAYBE IT WASN'T so much your interaction with Janey that's bothering you, so much as it is the anniversary of Melinda's death that's coming up," Laura's father suggested several days later over coffee.

Laura looked up and recounted soberly, "You think that's the reason behind my depression."

"My dad died twenty years ago, honey, and I still get depressed every year at that time. Sometimes I don't even know why I'm feeling as blue as I do, and I'll go along for a week or two, wondering what's wrong, and then out of nowhere it'll hit me. I'll realize what my subconscious already knows, that it was this time of year when I lost him. I'll be very sad for a day or so. Then it'll pass and I'll be chipper again."

Laura knew that was true. She'd experienced the same phenomenon after her husband had died. She rested her chin on her hand, feeling more depressed than ever. "Oh, Dad, why is life so hard?"

He shrugged with an acceptance she couldn't begin to feel. "Because it is, honey."

She lifted her coffee to her lips and took another long, enervating draught. "That's no answer."

"I know, but it's the only one I've got." He took an oatmeal cookie from the plate she'd set out. "So, how is Eric doing through all this?"

Laura smiled, thinking of the easy camaraderie that had sprung up between Zach's daughter and her son. "Better than I am, actually. He's seen Janey several times since we all went to the Mavericks game. He dropped by her house one day and shot some hoops."

Unfortunately Eric hadn't realized it would have been best to call first. Unhappy about the unscheduled visit, Zach had telephoned to let her know what was going on. Laura'd apologized and talked to Eric, instructed him to be sure to call and ask permission first in the future. Which he had dutifully done.

"But you haven't seen Janey again?" her dad persisted, looking a little disappointed.

Laura shook her head, guilt flooding over her. "No. Zach and I have both been very busy with our jobs." But that wasn't it and she knew it. Part of it was that she felt sad because she knew no one would ever replace Melinda. And maybe that was the way it should be, Laura thought pensively.

"I see."

She heard the faint note of censure in his voice and found herself bristling at it. She reached for the carafe on the table and freshened both their coffees. Keeping her voice casual with effort, she continued realistically, "I think one Matthews is enough for Janey to handle at a time."

Her dad's gaze narrowed. He searched her face carefully for any sign of emotion. "Is that the only reason you're holding back?"

Sadly, Laura reported, "She's not Melinda, Dad."

"No, she's not," her father agreed. "But you could still be close to her," her father said softly.

Swallowing hard, she hung on to her composure with a thread. "No, Dad, I'm not sure I can be."

Her father's glance softened compassionately, leaving no evidence of the tough Navy official he had once been. "This makes what I have to ask all the harder," he said. "It's your mother, Laura. She wants to meet Janey. And Zach, too."

"No. Dad, that's the last thing I need."

"Janey is her natural granddaughter."

"She's yours, too. I noticed you're not demanding the same thing."

He gestured obliquely. "I've always been more patient than your mother. You know that. Laura, she's not going to give up on this."

After all this time, Grace was still making her miserable. "No, Dad. The answer is no. And it will remain no. So you better tell her to give up." He sent her a mildly rebuking glance, prompting her to add, "Look, even if I wanted to do this—and I assure you I most certainly don't—Zach would never agree to it and Janey would never live through it. You know as well as I how critical Mother can be. Janey's a very sensitive kid. She's been through a lot."

"Your mother is just talking about meeting her, not reforming her."

"To Mother, the two are one and the same," Laura responded dryly. "And the answer is still no, Dad," Laura said, closing the argument. "*N-O*. No."

Chapter Seven

"I know you're busy," Zach began when Laura greeted him at the door on a Monday morning two weeks later. "I promise I won't take much of your time, but I need to talk to you about Eric and Janey."

As he had hoped, she had no objection to that. "Come on in," Laura said, her tone casual and welcoming. Yet her studied politeness had an edge of tension to it. He wasn't sure if they were simply friends or on the brink of something more. He only knew he thought about her a lot. And he suspected from the way she was looking at him that she thought about him, too.

"Can I get you a cup of coffee?" she continued, leading the way back to the coziest room in her entire house, her kitchen.

In the bright sunlight there, she looked unusually pale and tired, as if she hadn't been sleeping. Zach knew how that felt. He hadn't been sleeping well, either. "That'd be nice, thanks," he said.

Looking around, he was surprised to see her kitchen was devoid of the usual baking clutter. "You're not working today?" he asked Laura.

"No." Laura's tone was crisp and purposeful, despite the fragility of her looks.

Zach wanted to tell her she didn't have to pretend to be in an upbeat mood when she wasn't, but he didn't know how to say the words without sounding too intimate.

"How do you take your coffee?"

"Black."

She handed him a cup and cut straight to the chase. "Has Eric been wearing out his welcome?"

"No, not really. It's Janey." He paused, not sure how to go about this. She already looked so fragile that it was all he could do not to reach out and hold her. Bracing himself for her reaction, he continued gently, "She wants to see one of Eric's basketball games. And she wants me to take her. I didn't know how you would feel about us both being there." It could be awkward. Janey cheering Eric on might cause people to ask questions Laura might not want to answer.

Laura's dark brown eyes lit up thoughtfully. She seemed to be considering all the angles. "How does Eric feel?" she asked finally.

Zach shrugged. "Apparently he'd like her to go. He said something about hitting a midseason slump, but he thinks he's coming out of it."

Laura nodded and smiled, proving, Zach thought, once again what a remarkably adaptable woman she was.

"Well, sure, it'd be fine. I could pick her up if you like." She sighed as the next alternative came to mind. "Or the two of you could meet me at the gym."

The thought of such an outing was very pleasing to Zach, but he knew it wouldn't be to the kids. And it was up to him to tell her so. "Uh, no," he said awkwardly, unable to help but notice how shiny and soft her hair looked in the morning sunlight. He liked the fact it wasn't all sticky with spray. "That's not what they want." Her face fell. He continued, "They both felt it was fun but a little awkward, with the two families together."

Zach stuck his hands into the pockets of his jeans. "Janey wants me to drop her and one of her girlfriends, Chrissy, off at the game and then pick them up when it's over."

A flicker of what appeared to be hurt flashed in Laura's eyes and was quickly suppressed. She moved around the kitchen restlessly. And again, Zach had the desire to hold her, to give comfort.

"And you don't have any objection to that?" Laura asked.

As a matter of fact, Zach did. And maybe it was time he voiced his suspicions, found out if they were shared. He leaned against the opposite counter and took a sip of the hot delicious coffee. "I think they're trying to deliberately cut the two of us out, in their efforts to establish a brother-sister relationship." On one level, Zach wasn't sure he minded so much. It was easier for him, not being involved, not having to fight his instinctive, involuntary attraction to Laura every time they were together.

On another level, he knew he would miss seeing Laura. And right now, getting the kids together, making them comfortable with all that had happened, was his only excuse to be with her.

At all he had revealed, her listless expression grew even more dejected, so much so that Zach felt guilty for upsetting her. "I see," she said slowly, surreptitiously wiping a tear from the corner of her eye.

Zach watched her helplessly, not knowing what to say or do, only knowing that he couldn't bear to see another human being in so much pain. "If you want to talk to them, or set down some ground rules, try to limit the time they're spending with each other—" he offered.

She shook her head and folded her arms at her waist. "No. I can't and won't deny Eric anything that brings him comfort, and being increasingly close to Janey does circumvent some of his feelings of loss." She swallowed hard.

"He's missed not having a sister. It helps him to be close to Janey."

"But what about you?" Zach was surprised to find himself asking before he could think to censure himself. "Obviously this has really upset you."

"It isn't Janey or her request," she said miserably, cutting him off. "It's Melinda." Zach was silent, waiting, sensing there was more. Finally, Laura choked out the words. "Today—it's—she died one year ago today, Zach," she whispered hoarsely, as if each word required maximum effort. "That's why I'm so upset."

The words hit Zach like a blow to the chest. No wonder she looked so drawn and pale. "I'm sorry," he said quietly, not knowing how else to ease her pain.

She studied his sympathetic expression and felt almost resentful of his calm.

He felt angry with her for resenting him and angry with himself for not knowing how to help her. "I'm sorry for you, Laura," he reiterated gently, "but she wasn't my daughter. I didn't even know her. There's just no way I can feel your loss, not now, not ever."

Abruptly the fight went out of Laura. Burying her face in her hands, she began to sob soundlessly, the shaking of her shoulders the only clue to the emotional torment she was in. Again, he wanted to go to her, hold her. But something held him back. If he couldn't feel her pain, she wouldn't want his sympathy.

"I'm sorry," he said again, lamely. "I had no idea what day this was. Or I wouldn't have come over to talk to you." And then feeling more guilty than ever, he fled.

THE DINNER HOUR came and went. Laura turned the oven off and transferred the turkey casserole to the hot plate. By seven, she was frantic. She telephoned the school, found the athletic office empty, then one by one started calling all his friends. Yes, Eric had been at practice, they all said. He'd left to go home at the usual time. No, there was nothing wrong except he'd seemed kind of out of it, down. But he hadn't told anyone why.

Laura knew because she was feeling the crushing grief and despair, too. Looking out at the darkness that had fallen, she wondered where he could be. The two of them had visited Melinda's grave very early that morning. They'd taken flowers out and said a silent prayer.

He'd seemed okay, then, as had she.

But maybe like her his grief had grown more unmanageable as the day lingered on. He wasn't with his friends or her parents. She knew there was only one other person he might turn to to ease that ache. Going back to the phone, she dialed Zach Anderson's number. He answered on the third ring.

To her relief, Zach seemed as concerned as she was. "No, he hasn't been here. Let me go ask Janey if she's seen or heard from him today." He put down the phone.

Her heart pounding, Laura waited. Please, she thought, wherever he is, wherever he's gone, let him be safe.

Zach returned seconds later, his voice crisp and business-like. "Janey said she hasn't heard from him."

Laura's whole body was trembling and so was her voice. "I—maybe he's out at the cemetery then. I—I guess I'll drive out there."

Zach's response was incredulous. "This time of night?"

She said stiffly, "I've got to find him."

"You don't sound like you're in any shape to drive."

"I'll manage," she said tightly. She didn't want to turn this into a crisis of epic proportions, that would only hurt and embarrass Eric all the more. He was obviously hurting enough as it was.

On the other end of the phone line, Zach let out his breath in an exasperated whoosh. "Let me drive you," Zach said.

Was he doing this out of the goodness of his heart, or out of guilt for his lack of feeling? Laura wondered. Did it really matter? What was important now, was finding Eric. Zach could help her. And in the process, he would see Melinda's grave. Maybe that, more than anything, would drive the full extent of their mutual loss home to him. Didn't Melinda deserve at least that much?

"All right," Laura said, knowing Zach was right. Emotionally she was in no shape to drive. Besides, if he were driving, she would be free to look for Eric's battered red Mustang. And they'd find her son all the sooner.

On the other end of the line, one hand partway over the mouthpiece, muffling the sound, Zach was talking to his daughter. "Janey, Eric's mom is looking for him, so if he shows up here while I'm gone, keep him here until I get back, okay?"

"Okay."

"Laura," Zach said, speaking to her once again, "Sit tight. I'll be right over." He hung up before she could protest.

AFTER REASSURING his daughter that everything was going to be fine, Zach drove over to Laura's in record time. He didn't know why he was so frantic, only that he was.

"You didn't have to do this, you know," Laura said in a voice stiff with pride. She got into the car beside him, the long trench coat she wore buttoned to her chin.

"I know," Zach said. It was more than chivalry on his part. It was also a mixture of curiosity and guilt. And he didn't want to run from Laura and her pain, as he had this morning. He had a responsibility to her. He might not share her feelings of grief, but he could at least be compassionate. He could at least see where his biological daughter had been laid to rest.

Over the next few minutes, Laura spoke only to give him directions. "I don't see his Mustang here," Zach murmured as he parked.

The memorial garden was well lit and well tended. Peaceful, pretty, the hillside was dotted with marble and granite monuments.

Laura got out of the car. Her collar drawn up around her face, her hands shoved into the deep pockets of her coat, she led the way. Zach followed, his mood somber and subdued.

"She always liked yellow roses," Laura said, kneeling to arrange the lovely bouquet of flowers in the vase beneath her daughter's name. "So much so that near the end, she asked me if—" Laura's voice broke and it was a half second before she could go on "—if I would see to it that the flowers at her memorial service would all be yellow roses, a blanket of them." Laura's voice hardened and she stood. "She knew from her father's funeral, how much people like to send flowers. His was military, of course." She swallowed again. "Melinda's was a different type of service."

Her composure faltered abruptly. Head down, Laura began to weep.

Zach took her into his arms and held her against him, inhaling the flowering scent of her perfume. For the first time he felt the true depth of her pain, and he hoped never to feel anything like it himself. Laura, he wondered, how did you ever get through it? How could you ever bear to let your child go, knowing you would never see her or talk to her or hold her again? But somehow she had done that and she had recovered. Today was full of sorrow for her, but she would be better tomorrow.

"Mom—how could you?" a tortured voice erupted from behind them.

Laura and Zach turned, her soft body still pressed against his, her arms wreathed around his neck. Eric was standing there, his hands shoved into the pockets of his letter jacket, his face and ears red from the cold. The look of complete disgust on his young face plainly told what he erroneously thought: that there was something licentious going on.

"On Melinda's grave?" Eric said contemptuously, getting more furious with every passing second.

Zach released Laura slowly. "Eric, it's not the way it looks," he said slowly but clearly, giving him a direct look. "I was just comforting your mother."

"Yeah, I saw the way you were comforting her!" Eric shot a fierce look at Zach, then glared at Laura as if she were the worst kind of traitor. "You disgust me," Eric continued vehemently, giving Laura a disdainful look. "You really do." Whirling, he trotted off toward his car.

More concerned than insulted, Zach started to go after Eric. Laura stopped him. "No, don't. He needs time to cool off." Mingled with her hurt was an incredible depth of compassion. "At least I know he's all right now."

Zach studied her, his heart going out to her. "Are you sure you're all right?" She seemed very fragile to him, very vulnerable.

"I'm fine," she said wearily, brushing the hair from her eyes. She straightened resolutely. "I just want to go home."

"Are you going to be able to talk to Eric when you get home?" Zach asked.

"I don't know." Laura stared out the window. "The truth is, ever since he found out about the switch, he's harbored this silent resentment toward me." She shrugged helplessly and drew her coat closer to her slender frame. "I don't think there's anything I can say or do that will ever excuse what I did, in his estimation, anyway. He blames me for being stupid enough to accept the wrong child as my own. That made me angry at first. It hurt me. But now, I don't know. Maybe I should have known I had the wrong baby. Maybe I should have guessed—And now I wish I could let go of the way I feel. I wish it were that simple," she said desolately, tears shimmering on her lashes.

"It is that simple," Zach said. "We have each other to help get through this. Eric will forgive you, in time." As he spoke the consoling words, Zach discovered he really believed them.

She shook her head disconsolately. "You say that because Janey hasn't blamed you."

He shrugged, knowing he was lucky on that score. "She's younger, Laura. It hasn't occurred to her yet."

"More forgiving."

"More sensible, maybe," Zach acknowledged matter-of-factly. He looked at Laura, fighting the urge to take her in his arms and hold her, as he would anyone in such pain, until her misery passed. "Eric will come around," he reiterated firmly.

"I hope so," Laura said. "I really hope so."

"DAD?" Janey asked anxiously, the minute he walked in the door. "Did you find Eric?"

"Yes, we did."

"And he's okay?"

Zach hesitated. If he didn't level with her, she might hear about what happened from another source. He didn't want Eric running to Janey with false stories about Laura and himself. Zach sat down beside her on the sofa. "Actually he was very upset. You see today is the anniversary of his sister's death."

Janey's face fell and she looked at a loss for words. "Oh."

"He misses her a lot, I think."

Janey rubbed at an imaginary spot on her jeans. "He never talks about her, though." She looked up at him, as if wondering what that meant.

"Maybe not to you or me, but I'm sure he and his mom talk about Melinda," Zach said. "They probably have a lot of happy memories."

"And some sad ones, too," Janey added compassionately.

Zach nodded in agreement, knowing it must have been very hard for Laura and Eric to lose Melinda. But he and Janey couldn't dwell on that. It would serve no useful purpose. Especially when he had something more important to tell her. "Honey, when we were out at the cemetery, Mrs. Matthews started to cry. I held her in my arms, you know the way people do when they're trying to comfort each other?"

Janey nodded acceptingly, and Zach continued in the same matter-of-fact tone. "Well, Eric saw us and he misinterpreted what was going on." At Janey's blank look, Zach was forced to elaborate, "He got angry. He thought we were defiling Melinda's grave by having a romance there."

"You and Mrs. Matthews!" Janey said, aghast.

"Yes. Of course there was nothing going on. When Eric calms down, I'm sure he'll realize that but I wanted you to know about it, in case he wants to talk about it."

"Okay." Janey gave her agreement readily, then said, "Daddy, did it make you sad, seeing where Eric's sister was buried?"

Zach said, "I felt sad for Mrs. Matthews. And Eric. And Melinda, too, even though I didn't know her."

Janey frowned and looked depressed. "It seems unfair, her dying so young."

"To me, too."

Janey shook her head in mute sympathy. "Poor Eric," she murmured.

But not poor Mrs. Matthews, Zach thought. Initially, the way Janey cut Laura from her life had been a source of relief to him. Now he wasn't sure it was so good.

"Well, I guess I'll go to bed," Janey said, smothering a yawn with the back of her hand. She looked as relieved as Zach that the immediate crisis was over, even if Eric now had some misconceptions. "And maybe I'll call Eric in the morning or something, just to see how he is."

"Better wait a few more days," Zach advised, taking the cautious view. In the mood Eric was in, there was just no telling how he would react.

LAURA was just getting into bed, hoping her age-old cure of an extra hour or two of sleep would make her feel better after the draining trauma of her day, when the phone rang.

"Hello."

There was a second of silence on the other end, then a low, familiar male voice. "Laura...Zach," he began kindly. "I won't keep you. I just called to see how everything is. Did Eric get home intact?"

Glad it was Zach and not anyone else, Laura nodded. She could use his calm, soothing demeanor right now. Talking to him would make her feel as safe and protected as she had when he'd been holding her in his arms. How she had needed that, she thought, yearningly. "Yes, he got home about half an hour ago," she related with a slightly harried sigh.

"And?" Zach prompted cautiously.

She only wished she had better news. Or that Zach could be there with her, to hold her and tell her everything was going to be all right once again. But he couldn't. And she had to accept that. Sighing, Laura continued, "And I told him that what he saw was no more than a hug between friends."

"Was he okay with that?"

"No, but I think when he has time to calm down, he'll—" Laura glanced up to see Eric standing in her open doorway, one arm stretched out and planted against the frame. From the stony look on his face he had obviously surmised who she was talking to. Her spirits plummeted to an even lower depth. Partly because she did feel guilty, at least on some level, about what he'd seen. It was true—she and Zach had been doing nothing wrong when Eric had spied them together—but her thoughts were not as blameless. She had been attracted to the man for a long time, since the day they had met.

"I heard the phone ring," Eric grunted in way of grudging explanation as to why he had come to her room.

Knowing, despite her own private, guilt-filled yearnings, that she had nothing to hide, Laura calmly said "It's Mr. Anderson. He wanted to check and make sure you got home safely."

Eric's mouth curled skeptically at one corner. "Sure." Without further comment, he dropped his arm and stalked away.

Watching his retreating back, Laura sighed. It was obvious Eric didn't want her to become involved with Zach. And she wasn't. Wanting Zach didn't count! If only Eric would stop behaving so irrationally.

"Laura?" Zach said, concern lacing his low tone. "Are you still there?"

Laura cast a glance heavenward and exhaled slowly. "I'm fine. As you probably heard, Eric's still in a surly mood."

On the other end, Zach sighed his frustration. She could guess what he was thinking, that her son probably needed a good scolding, but that wasn't the way she worked. Feelings were allowed in her house, no matter how prickly. It was the suppression of feelings that caused conflict, not the healthy venting or discussion of them.

"Well—" Zach seemed to be searching for something to say. "Is there anything else I can do for you? If you want me to talk to him or—"

His concern for her, his willingness to help, was endearing. "No," she said, "there's nothing you can do. I'll manage. But thanks for offering. And Zach—" Her voice softened gratefully as she continued, "thanks for being there for me tonight." She swallowed around the reflexive tightening of her throat, glad he wasn't there to see her blush. "I know I was really overwrought. I just couldn't help it. But I feel a lot better now. Drained but better."

His reply was soft, sympathetic. "I'm glad."

And suddenly, there was nothing else to say. "Well..." Laura said as the moment drew out even more awkwardly.

"I better let you go."

She gripped the receiver tighter. "Thanks again."

"Good night."

"Good night." Their conversation over, Laura hung up the phone, feeling strangely consoled and feeling strangely bereft. His call was just a polite courtesy, nothing more, the kind one would give any neighbor in trouble. There was no reason to make anything more of it. Or of the way he had held her...

Chapter Eight

"Is Eric home?"

Laura put down her account ledger and pen. "No, he's not," she said carefully, suspecting from the girlish timbre of the speaker's tone, that she was not speaking to one of her son's friends from Central High. "He's still at basketball practice."

"Oh."

Just one syllable, Laura thought, and yet so terribly dejected. Laura recognized the speaker's voice. "Janey? Is there something I can help you with?"

Janey sighed. "No, not really. I was just going to ask Eric if he could go rock hunting with me. I've got this collection due, and I—well, I kind of forgot all about it."

Laura remembered Eric having to do the same thing in eighth grade. It was a required project for the Earth Science classes every year. "Oh, my," she said, sympathizing with Janey's panic. "When's it due?"

"Day after tomorrow. My dad's going to kill me when he finds out I haven't even started it. Plus, I don't even know where to begin to look for the dumb rocks. I have to have twelve, from three different categories."

This really isn't any of my concern, Laura thought. I should just let her call her dad and deal with the consequences. On the other hand, if I were to help her, I'd get to know her a little better. And suddenly she wanted that, very much. She hadn't realized until this moment how shut out she'd been feeling the past few weeks, watching Janey get closer and closer to Eric, all the while holding her deliberately at arm's length. Impulsively Laura offered, "I could help you, Janey. If you want, that is. I know where we ended up getting Eric's rocks. And I imagine they're still there. In fact, we've still got several books upstairs on identifying rocks."

Janey sighed her relief. "Would you? I don't want to impose or anything, but I really need to get this done or I'm going to flunk for sure."

Laura smiled at the drama in the teenager's tone and reassured pleasantly, "I don't mind at all. When do you want to go?" Laura consulted her watch. "We've still got two hours before dark. I could be over there in say, twenty minutes?"

"That'd be great. Thanks, you're saving my life."

"No problem. And Janey? Wear old clothes. Where we're going it can get pretty muddy."

Janey was waiting for Laura on the front stoop. She looked both pretty and raring to go. Laura breathed a silent sigh of relief. As she had driven over, she had wondered if she was doing the right thing, especially when she had realized this impulsive idea of hers could very well backfire on her. What if they didn't get along? What if they didn't find any good rocks and Janey failed, then blamed it on her?

Laura didn't know how she would handle any of that. But so far, so good, she thought, looking at Janey's determined and thoughtful expression as she thumbed through the books on rock collecting Laura had put on the front seat.

Fifteen minutes later, the two of them were hiking down a hillside on the outskirts of town, collecting muddy specimens, big and small. "They all look alike to me," Janey moaned as she tossed yet another rock into the plastic bag Laura had brought.

"That's because all we're seeing is the mud," Laura soothed. "That'll change when we give them a good scrubbing."

Back at Janey's house, that was exactly what they did. Filling a bucket with warm water and soap, they took the rocks onto the back patio, and scrub brushes in hand, went to work.

"STILL NO WORD from Janey, huh?" Harry Cole asked as he nailed wallboard to one of the upstairs bedrooms in the Gagglione mansion.

Zach shook his head, using a trimming knife to cut another sheet. "No. And I've called every ten minutes for the past hour."

"Maybe she went over to a friend's house," Harry suggested hopefully, picking up yet another nail.

Zach shook his head negatively. Finished cutting one piece, he began trimming the next. "She always calls me and lets me know where she's going to be. It's a rule we have."

Harry began to look as worried as Zach felt. "Have you checked your answering service?"

"They haven't heard from her, either."

Harry was silent. "Look, I don't want to say anything to upset you, but the police caught Tabitha hitchhiking last Monday, after school."

"What?" Zach said, shocked.

"Yeah, she and some friends were just trying to get a thrill." Harry stopped hammering and gave Zach another worried look. "Fortunately for the girls, the police picked them up before anyone else could. I only mention it because Janey and Tabitha are in the same class at school. They don't hang around that much there but you know how contagious fads can be. From what little we got out of Tabitha, there's been a lot of peer pressure to prove they're daring, adventurous. I don't want anything similar to happen to Janey."

Neither did he. Quickly, Zach unhooked his tool belt and took off his hard hat and put them aside. "I'm going to knock off a few minutes early and head home," he said brusquely, knowing he could trust Harry to disperse the crew and lock up. "If Janey should call, tell her to meet me there."

"Sure thing," Harry said. "And Zach, I'm sorry if I worried you. I just wanted you to know what's been going on with some of the kids."

Zach nodded grimly. "I appreciate the warning."

Janey wouldn't do something that stupid. She's a smart kid, he told himself firmly as he climbed behind the wheel. Janey had been thrown a lot of curves lately. Maybe like Tabitha, she was feeling the pressure to keep up with the so-called cool kids in her class.

The drive home had never taken so long. By the time he reached his house, he was both tense and worried. Janey, where are you? he thought. Why are you worrying me this way? Why are you breaking the rules we set up to keep you safe?

Foot on the brake, he stared at the car parked in his driveway. Laura Matthews? What was she doing here? he wondered, easing in behind her and cutting his engine.

As he strode toward the house, he heard the distinctly feminine sounds of laughter emanating from the backyard. Circling the house, he came upon Laura and Janey. Mud, soap suds, and water streaking her from head to toe, Janey was turning off the garden hose. In jeans, hiking boots, and an old sweatshirt, a mud-streaked Laura was kneeling on the wet cement, busily drying off rocks with paper towels. Even in the dimming daylight, he could see that her short, dark hair was damp and curling wildly around her flushed face. Never, he thought, had he seen her look so animated or quite so beautiful. "Do you think we got enough?" Janey asked excitedly, dashing back to Laura's side the moment the hose was turned off.

Her face whitening, she noticed Zach. "Dad—uh—hi."

Laura looked up, like a kid who'd just been caught with her hand in the cookie jar. She grinned mischievously. "Uh—hi." She glanced at her watch and rose awkwardly to her knees, ineffectually brushing off the dirt, her casual movements drawing the shirt closer to her breasts. "Gosh, I didn't realize it was so late. Eric's probably home, wanting supper."

"I guess I can take it from here," Janey said, smiling adoringly at Laura. In that instant, when Zach saw the two of them standing side by side, he was struck by how much they looked alike. Mother and daughter, it was as clear as the day was long. The knowledge combined with his fear of losing Janey and stabbed him like a knife.

Immediately he wanted to lash out at someone for inflicting this kind of hurt and worry on him. But the practical side of his nature forced him not to overreact. Pulling his thoughts together, he forced himself to forget his fears for a moment and concentrate only on why and how this had happened.

Laura gently touched Janey's shoulder, looking Zach thought resentfully, more maternal and loving than any woman had a right to look. "If you have any trouble," Laura advised Janey softly, "you can call Eric or me. We'd be glad to help you identify them."

Janey lit up like a beacon. "Thanks, Laura."

When had they gotten so close? he wondered. He only knew he felt hurt, excluded. And mad. Janey might have been careless, but Laura knew better. Hadn't she gone through hell just a short time ago when Eric was missing?

"Janey, why don't you take your rock collection and go on in the house and wash up," Zach suggested.

Janey looked at him, the guilty expression on her face telling him she knew full well she'd been remiss in not letting him know where she was. Or who she was with. At least now he understood why she had been so secretive. What else had been going on that he didn't know about? Had Laura been undercutting him like this all along? Was that her intention, to tell him she had no interest in Janey and then go behind his back and court her anyway? He had thought Laura was his friend, that he could trust her. Apparently not.

Reading his expression, Janey said awkwardly, "Laura— Mrs. Matthews—was just helping me with my science project, Dad."

"I can see that." Zach forced the most civilized smile he could manage. From the very beginning of his association with Laura, he had feared a showdown like this. He had never expected it would be tonight. "Would you wash up and set the table please?" he asked.

Recognizing an order when she heard one, Janey nodded and slipped inside, shutting the patio door behind her.

He faced Laura in silence.

"I have an idea how this must look," she began slowly, approaching him as cautiously as she would a wounded bear.

Her wariness only added fuel to the fire burning in his gut. "Do you?" Zach asked. "I had no idea where Janey was tonight. None! I was worried sick, scared something might have happened to her, that she might have been kidnapped." He paused, letting his words sink in, then gave in to his soaring temper and added silkily, "I wasn't far wrong, was I?"

At his thinly veiled insult, Laura advanced on him angrily. "Now wait just a minute. Janey called me, not the other way around. Or rather she called Eric and he wasn't home."

"And you couldn't wait for the chance to step in and see her behind my back, could you?"

Laura's face grew more flushed. She touched a hand to her hair, pushing the tousled strands into place as best she could with her fingers, the reflexive action only serving to make her look even more as if she had just tumbled out of bed. "I admit I welcomed the opportunity to get to know her better, without having to compete with my son."

Her honest words struck a nerve. He knew how hurt she'd been by Janey's previous indifference to her. Obviously, judging by the companionable way the two had been washing the rocks together, this was one hurdle that had been cleared. He saw how much that had meant to Laura, and knowing how much she missed her own daughter, his heart went out to her on that score.

Calming slightly, Zach asked, "Is this the first time anything like this has happened?"

Laura nodded stiffly. "Yes. And I would've told you about it before I took her out rock hunting, had I any idea you didn't know what was going on. Although," Laura sighed with weary regret, "thinking back on it, I should've realized she wouldn't call you. She said something about not wanting you to know she had been remiss in not starting her project." Laura ran a harried hand through her hair, adding informatively, "It's due the day after tomorrow."

That explained a lot. "So you bailed her out," Zach supposed quietly, calming as the misunderstanding between them was gradually but painstakingly cleared up.

"Yes," Laura said, echoing his soft, patient tone, "when Eric wasn't home." Her dark brown eyes beseeched his understanding and forgiveness. She shifted her shoulders expressively and her voice grew choked with emotion, "It was the first time she's ever reached out to me, even a little bit."

For a second he thought she was going to start to cry and then she pulled herself together and finished frankly, "So, yes, Zach, I am guilty as charged. I took the opportunity to be with her, and I enjoyed doing it." She shook her head and said lamely, "Maybe you can't understand that. Maybe you don't have to understand it. Maybe you just need to know that's the way I feel." She reached out and touched his arm.

Her soft hand felt warm even through the layers of his clothes. Zach fell silent, unable to refute her soft earnest words.

She continued genuinely, "I should have made sure she had your permission. I just didn't think."

Nor had he, if he hadn't realized this would happen eventually. Laura was impulsive. She lived moment to moment. Whereas he was not. He liked to plan for everything. He studied her silently. Realizing no real harm had been done, he said finally, "You had a good time with her?"

Laura smiled, the happiness she felt lighting up her face. "Yes. It was fun, traipsing around the canyon, hunting for ordinary rocks as if they were the most precious treasure. It was also the first time she's ever really relaxed around me. She's a lovely girl, Zach. You've done a wonderful job raising her."

But I don't want her to relax around you, Laura, Zach realized with a start, surprised by his own selfishness. He didn't want to lose Janey, not even a tiny bit. And at this point in her life, Janey needed a mother, maybe more than a dad. But he also knew Laura wasn't the kind of woman who would ever try to drive a wedge between him and his child. If she had been, he would have seen evidence of it long before this. She had just been doing what she thought best, helping out. He couldn't fault her for that.

Laura glanced at her watch. "I really do have to go," Laura said, stepping by him.

As she skirted past, he caught the whiff of sunshine and flowers in her hair. He knew it was probably just her perfume, yet it seemed so much like the sunny personality of the woman herself. A woman Janey and he had both started to bond to. Feeling suddenly ashamed at the way he had let himself blow up, he trailed after her. She had just circumvented a schoolwork-related crisis in Janey's life and all he had done was berate her for it. "Laura, wait."

She turned, lifting her eyes to his.

"I'm sorry if I snapped at you," Zach said penitently.

She reached out and touched his hand. "It's okay. I understand."

And looking into her eyes, he saw she really did.

"DADDY, you aren't mad at Laura, I mean, Mrs. Matthews, are you?" Janey asked as they helped themselves to Mrs. Yaeger's casserole.

"Why didn't you call?"

"I was afraid you'd get mad at me for waiting till the last minute to start my science project. I just forgot about it. There's been so much going on."

That much was true, Zach thought. Under the circumstances, it was a wonder Janey had been able to keep her grades up at all. He knew it was hard for him to concentrate on his work. Deciding Janey had learned her lesson, he extracted this final promise from her. "Just let me know if you're going someplace from now on, agreed?"

"Agreed." Seconds later, she told him what was really on her mind. "Daddy, you know how we always do something nice for people who've done something nice for us, to show we appreciate what they did? Well, I think we should do something nice for Laura."

Laura, Zach thought a trifle jealously. Not Mrs. Matthews anymore.

"Like what?" he forced himself to ask in a reasonable tone.

"Like I don't know. Maybe—well, we'll think of something," Janey finished airily, the momentary sunniness in her disposition reminding him acutely of Laura.

She wants to keep up the contact, Zach realized with growing clarity, resentment, and confusion. Before today any contact with Laura Matthews was a threat to Janey, now the contact was appealing, necessary almost, for her continued happiness and contentment. If Laura could manage to do all that in only one afternoon, what would she manage in subsequent visits? he wondered. Used to being the only parent in Janey's life, he found the possibilities unsettling.

"May I be excused? I've got a lot of work to do. And if you're not too busy, maybe you could help me identify some of the rocks we collected? Laura lent me some books of Eric's that tell me all about them."

"Sure," Zach said, knowing full well if he didn't, Laura and Eric would be only too happy to do it in his stead.

"HERE ARE THE BOOKS you lent Janey," Zach said two days later. He'd stopped by on his lunch hour, en route from his office to the construction sites where he had crews working.

"Thanks." Laura wiped one flour-covered hand on the tail end of her long white chef's apron and then took the books. "Did she get everything she needed?"

Zach nodded, wondering if Laura knew she had flour smudged on her chin and the uppermost curve of her right cheekbone, or that she was unerringly beautiful even when wearing old jeans and a sweatshirt, with her dark hair all tousled.

In the background, the oven buzzer sounded. Laura sprinted off, her high-topped sneakers thudding on the carpet.

As he entered the sweetly scented kitchen, she was lifting a delicate chocolate soufflé from the oven. She turned, the hot pan cradled between two gloved hands, then saw belatedly that she had nowhere to set it down. She sent him a helpless glance. "Would you mind lifting those two pecan pies, the ones next to the refrigerator, and putting them on the five-tiered rack next to the back door? Thanks." When he'd finished, she slid the perfectly formed soufflé on a neatly folded dish towel to cool.

"Sometimes I think I need about ten hands instead of two," she remarked.

"Ever think about renting space and working out of a professional kitchen?"

Laura smiled wistfully. "I dream about it all the time, but I can't afford it, not now. Although I admit it gets a little crowded in here, especially when I get special orders."

"Special orders?" Zach asked, watching as she bent to put two more pies into the hot oven.

"From neighborhood customers. For bridge parties, luncheons, or whatever." Silence fell between them. Zach knew he should get out of there, but it wasn't so easy to leave such a nice, cozy and warm place. Laura Matthews's kitchen felt like home to him, and everywhere he looked there was a woman's touch, from the embroidered picture on the wall that said *Laura's kitchen* to the fresh flowers growing in the windowsill. He wasn't sure but he thought they were red geraniums. Whatever they were, they were as healthy as could be, and very well tended.

"I hope Janey gets a good grade on her project," Laura said. "I know how important schoolwork is to her."

And to me, Zach thought. Curious, he asked. "What about Eric? Does he get good grades?"

"Oh, yes. Rob and I both were very big on education. Me, because I never finished mine. Rob, because he did. We live by the motto if something is worth doing, it's worth doing well."

Zach smiled, pleased to find they had that in common. "I live by that, too."

A second buzzer went off. Laura moved to the other oven. Slipping on the oven mitts once again, she lifted an apple pie out of the oven, and again found she had no place to set it.

"What you need is more counter space," Zach said as he moved to clear a spot.

"Tell me about it," she moaned.

Remember how you're always telling me to do something nice for someone who's done something for us? Janey had said. Laura had looked for rocks with his daughter, scrubbed the dirt off them, and lent Janey books, which saved him a trip to the library. Like it or not, he owed her for this and he was a man who always paid his debts.

Zach looked around thoughtfully. "Maybe you should consider having a wall shelf built for your microwave, to get it off the counter, and then another for your cookbooks," Zach said. "That would give you another four feet of counter space, easily."

"I don't have a budget for remodeling," Laura said.

"The materials wouldn't be that expensive," Zach argued. Especially if he got them at wholesale prices for her, he thought.

"It's not that, it's the labor."

Zach offered, "You don't have to bother with hiring someone. I could do it for you." Then they'd be even, he thought, and Janey wouldn't have to get involved.

Laura looked shocked, then intrigued, then disappointed. "Zach, that's sweet of you, but I couldn't possibly—"

"It would only take half a day at most," Zach continued persuasively.

Her dark brown eyes widened speculatively. "You're sure?"

"Positive."

"All right," Laura said finally. "It's a deal."

Chapter Nine

An hour and a half later, Laura sat at the dining-room table, going over her accounts, trying to ignore the electric whine of a power saw just outside her back door. Business had been slow right after Christmas, as was usually the case. Now that February was here, people were beginning to eat out more again. Restaurants were upping their orders, though not with any predictable consistency. Laura never knew from one day to the next whether she was going to be asked to deliver as little as ten pies or cakes, or as had happened more than once during the weekends, as many as thirty. She liked not knowing, though. If her business had been the same day in and day out, she would have been bored stiff.

The back door slammed. Heavy footsteps sounded on her kitchen floor. Zach. If she lived to be one hundred, she would never figure that man out. One minute he looked at her as if she were the most opportunistic, least trustworthy person on earth. And the next he was offering to build her a shelf for her microwave. He'd said he wanted to pay her back for helping Janey with her rock collection for school, but she sensed it was more than that. He both wanted to get close to her and to get rid of her.

In the kitchen, Zach began to hammer in steady, precisely measured intervals. Bucking the urge to go in to see how it was going, Laura picked up a cookbook, paper, and pencil. Turning to the page she had marked, she used her calculator to begin quadrupling the recipe for Praline Pie.

She was nearly finished when Zach strode into the room, his tool belt jangling on his waist. "Want to come and see what I've done?" he asked. "Tell me what you think?"

"Sure."

Feeling suddenly self-conscious, Laura put her paperwork aside and got to her feet. He waited for her to take the lead. Acutely conscious of his presence behind her, she hurried to where he had been working.

I can't believe he did this so quickly, was her first thought. Her second was that it was a marvelous job.

"The wood needs to be stained to match your cabinets. I'll have my paint crew call and arrange a time to come over. They'll match it precisely for you."

"Thank you. It's wonderful," Laura said, meaning it. She moved forward to touch the additional four-foot square of counter space that had been freed up. "I really need this space."

"I don't see how you do it. Keep track of all the various ingredients, I mean," Zach said casually, as he slid a hammer into one of the loops on his tool belt. "I find it hard just trying to make one dish at a time at home."

She shrugged. Cooking had always come naturally to her, the way building things obviously did to him. She grinned. "Well, then we're even because I have a hard time just hammering a nail in straight."

Their gazes met, locked. He gave a reluctant smile, then realizing the attitude had become almost friendly between them, abruptly stopped smiling. There were a few specks of sawdust on the floor.

He reached for the broom she had in the corner, and began to sweep, the tool belt jangling against his hips as he moved. With effort, she tore her eyes from his lower torso. Realizing she was no longer comfortable with him there, with the two of them alone, she reached for the handle. "Here, let me. You've done enough. Really."

For a second she thought he would protest, but a glance at the clock told him it was almost suppertime. Eric would be home soon. Janey was perhaps already home. "I guess you're right," Zach responded. "I better get going."

He gathered up the rest of his things, and then went outside to retrieve his power saw. Laura carried the scraps of excess wood to his truck. Zach was just loading the last of it in when Laura's mother parked at the curb. Fortunately, Zach backed out of the driveway before her mother trod carefully up the front walk.

"Laura, what's going on? I saw that man's truck here most of the afternoon. That was Zach Anderson, wasn't it?"

"Yes, that was Zach. He built shelves for my microwave and cookbooks, that's all."

Her mother stared at her as if she'd lost her mind. "You hired him to do this?"

Laura couldn't prevent a flush of reaction to her mother's probing voice. "No. He did it in return for a favor I did for him."

Her mother's brows rose. Unable and unwilling to imagine what she must be thinking now, Laura supplied dryly, "I helped his daughter collect rocks for a science project at school."

Her mother's expression turned to one of delight. "You mean you helped your daughter."

Laura felt her irritation grow. "Mom—"

"Laura, when are you going to come to your senses and do something definite about your situation?"

Her face flaming, Laura whirled and started for the house. This wasn't a conversation for the street.

"You've lost so much time already," her mother continued doggedly, her high heels clicking heavily as she followed Laura up the walk.

"Mom, please." Once inside her kitchen, Laura went straight to the sink and began scrubbing a sticky pan she'd left soaking. Was it her imagination or did the room smell of Zach and the heady scent of his cologne?

Her mother continued to grumble as she sat with lady-like precision in one of the kitchen chairs. "In the past, you've never hesitated to go after what is rightfully yours."

Laura rinsed the pan and put it in the drainer next to the sink. She had to stay calm. She did not want to fight with her mother. Turning, Laura reached for a dish towel. She propped herself against the counter. "This is different, Mom." They weren't talking about just any old thing Laura wanted, but a child. "Janey's whole life, her emotional well-being is at stake. I can't and won't destroy that." She wouldn't do it to Zach and she wouldn't do it to Janey.

Grace's eagle gaze grew even sharper as she mulled over Laura's calmly issued statement. "What about your emotional well-being? What about Eric's?"

"Eric knows I love him."

"Does he? I think he's been upset about this."

Guilt assailed her. Eric had been upset, but then that was normal, too. She wouldn't let her mother think it wasn't. "It's going to take time, for all of us. We have a lot to adjust to."

"I see." Her mother sniffed disapprovingly. "And in the meantime, Zach Anderson has your natural daughter, who he is falsely raising as his own."

Her mother spoke as if he were a heinous criminal. Holding on to her soaring temper, Laura said, "First of all, Mom, Janey is his real daughter, in every sense. Secondly, he is a nice man. A very nice man."

"What does that have to do with anything? Why are you protecting him? You're not starting to feel sorry for him, are you? Laura, for heaven's sake! Use your head this once, instead of your heart and think about what you're doing!"

Her mother shook her head, baffled. "What good could cozying up to this man possibly do you?" Her eyes glimmered. "Oh, I get it! You're trying to get friendly with her father first, aren't you, get to know him, and then get Janey back, if not officially, then unofficially?"

Laura's face flamed hotter. This time her mother had gone too far. "That is not true!" she said, outraged.

"Well, then, maybe it should be," her mother said thoughtfully. "Think about it, Laura. You're both single. Both raising one child. It would make sense, the two of you combining your households.

"You're jumping the gun here, Mother," Laura pointed out calmly, hanging on to her composure by a thread.

"Perhaps I am," Grace continued, smoothing the strand of pearls at her neck. "And perhaps, Laura, this is something you should think about. That is, if you haven't already."

Laura fell silent, resenting her mother too much to be able to speak and maintain a civil tongue.

"However, if you can't do that, you might consider doing something else, especially now that the two of you are on friendly terms. Your father and I want to meet Janey, Laura."

"Mom, no!"

"She's our granddaughter. We have rights, too."

"Zach would never agree to it."

"What could be the harm in a simple dinner, with all of us?"

"It's impossible," Laura declared, seething.

"You could at least ask."

"No, Mother, I mean it. I won't ask Zach any such thing. It would only make him furious."

Her mother studied her shrewdly. "You really think so?"

"Yes, now can we drop it?"

Grace shrugged. "You leave me little choice.

Silence fell between the two women. Her emotional energy depleted, Laura said quietly, "I have to get back to work, Mom."

Knowing she'd pushed her welcome to the limit, her mother said a few more words and left. Laura waited until the door clicked shut, then sank onto the closest chair, unspeakably disturbed. What her mother had suggested about her and Zach was completely ludicrous.

First of all, she wasn't interested in any man, period. And if she were, it wouldn't be someone like Zach who was able to separate himself so completely from his emotions, someone who could and would deny the heartbreaking loss of his own natural daughter. She was the kind of person who needed to be in close touch with her emotions, and know that was not only understood but accepted by the man she loved. And by the same token, she wanted to know what her potential partner was thinking and feeling, and she could only do that if her partner was willing to take the time and energy to delve into his own emotions. And Zach just wasn't. Second, that conflict aside, she had enough to do, just running her business and taking care of her son.

She had been in one relationship with a man for all the wrong reasons, to heartbreaking results. She didn't want to go into another for anything less than all-out love. She was sure Zach didn't, either. He was too smart to make a mistake like that.

Then why was he here today on a trumped-up reason of returning the books? she wondered. Why had he insisted on paying her back and building those shelves for her, free of charge? And when he had finished, why had he acted as if he were so ill at ease?

"...SO I BUILT THE SHELF and now it's all taken care of," Zach told his daughter as the two of them popped popcorn before their evening television shows. Or it will be when my painters finish.

"But I wanted to do something nice for her, too," Janey protested, giving him a betrayed look as she poured lemonade into tall glasses and then set about searching for the popcorn salt.

"This was from both of us," Zach said, watching the hot-air popper.

"Yes, but I wasn't part of it," Janey said sullenly. "I wasn't there."

"Laura understands."

Janey turned mutinous. "You just don't want me to be around her. You're jealous because I'm starting to like her."

Was he that transparent? He hadn't meant to be. "Honey—"

"Dad," Janey said in a soft, reassuring tone, "you don't have to be scared of her. I'm not, not anymore anyway. She really is nice."

Zach knew that, too, and it was killing him inside. It would have been so much easier if Laura weren't so nice. Then he could have ignored her.

But now—now all he thought about when her name came up was her dark brown eyes and soft brown hair, the gentle, loving way she interacted with her son, the way she gave Janey space, the way she had cried when she'd visited her daughter's final resting place, the fragile way she had felt when he held her in his arms, and the vulnerable look on her face when he had released her. She was a very smart, sensitive woman. And, like it or not, she was Janey's natural mother.

Maybe it was time he admitted his jealousy to himself and dealt with it. He felt guilty for surreptitiously wanting to keep Laura away from Janey, even though on a legal basis he had every right to do so. And he felt threatened by Janey's newfound receptiveness to Laura. Because now Janey wanted to be close to Laura, to get to know her, and to exchange mutual kindnesses.

Perhaps it would've been different if Maria were still alive, if Janey'd already had a mother in her life. But she didn't have that and she was at an age where girls needed a caring, female influence in their lives. So what was he going to do? What *could* he do?

"We could ask them to go out to Granbury Lake, or to the Log Cabin Village near the botanical gardens. Please, Dad," Janey continued urgently as the last kernel popped out of the popper. "You said the four of us could get to know one another."

This is a battle I am not going to win, Zach thought. The more I fight, the more determined she will be. Nothing attracts a kid more than the forbidden. "All right," Zach said reluctantly at last. "I'll get in touch with her tomorrow and see what she says."

ZACH MADE GOOD on his promise to his daughter. Figuring he'd just wing it, rather than make a big deal out of it, he decided to just drop by and make it casual, rather than call first. As he had expected, Laura was home and in the midst of icing a tray of chocolate éclairs when he rapped on the kitchen door.

"Hi." After wiping her hands on her apron, she let him in. His attention moving to his handiwork, he looked past her, to the shelves he had built. "I see the painters have been here," he remarked with satisfaction, striding over for a closer look.

"Yes, they did a nice job."

Zach frowned, not as pleased as she obviously was. He stepped back, squinted, then stepped closer once again. He touched the smooth, glossy finish on the new shelves, admitting, "I was afraid of this. You always run into that problem when you try to match a new stain to cabinets that are slightly weathered. There's a slight difference in the stains."

Her expression bewildered, she moved over to stand in the light. "Zach, I can't see it."

Glancing around her kitchen, he picked up two collapsed white cake boxes, and held them by both the new painted and the existing cabinet. "Come here and look."

Her expression still perplexed, she moved closer. He lifted his arms slightly, and with a nod of his head, directed her wordlessly to slip beneath them.

Being careful not to touch him, she did. With her slim body ensconced between the warmth of his body and the cool wood, she took a closer look. "Oh." Zach knew she was seeing what he had, that the new stain was a shade darker than the old.

Sighing his disappointment, Zach stepped back. "I'll call the painters and have them come out again."

"No." Laura stopped him from going to the phone with a light touch to his arm. The light touch was oddly stimulating, and he turned to face her in silent, subdued reaction. As if realizing what she'd done, she dropped her hand. Swallowing hard, she continued, "You and your paint crew have already done a wonderful job. Honest. This is fine."

Zach shot her a measuring look and his mouth tightened in exasperation. He hated anything less than absolute perfection. "It could be better," he warned.

Laura shrugged and smiled. "It's fine, really. See, look. If I slide the books up here, see how pretty they look. Help me put the microwave in place."

Dubious but unresisting, he went for the heavy appliance. She started to help. Not sure what it would feel like to be so close to her again, not sure he wanted to know, he shrugged off her help. "That's okay, Laura. I can lift it alone. Just handle the cord for me, and slip it into the wooden slot."

Careful to keep his eyes on his task and not the sunlight reflected off Laura's hair, he lifted the microwave and slid it onto the sturdy shelf. "Is it centered?"

She was standing behind him, the end of the cord dangling in her hand. "A little to the left. Yeah, you've got it." She stepped back to survey it. "The stain on the shelves is perfect, Zach."

Zach frowned suspiciously. Dissatisfaction stamped on his face, he guided her forward, urging, "Take a closer look."

Shrugging again, she said, "Still perfect."

He gave her a strange look, then peered closely at the wood. "You're right," he said with amazement. "With those books and the microwave on the shelves, you really can't tell."

Looking abruptly aware of his nearness, Laura smiled and attempted a light remark. "Are you this picky about all the houses you build?"

His answer was serious. "When people build a custom home in the half-mil range, Laura, they expect the best."

"And you deliver," she said softly, with approval in her dark brown eyes. Love of one's work was something she could not only respect but identify with.

Feeling closer to her, for the shared value, he said wryly, "I try. I don't always succeed."

She lifted a skeptical brow and crossed both arms beneath the curves of her breasts. "I find that hard to believe."

He shrugged again, feeling suddenly, unexpectedly shy. She was...so nice. He could see why Janey was so drawn to her.

"Could I get you something?" she asked impulsively. "Coffee? An éclair?"

He looked longingly at some golden puffs with chocolate frosting. "Aren't those for your business?"

"Yes, but I always make a few extra, just in case one bakes lopsided." She poured him a cup of coffee and handed it to him. "Black, right?"

He was pleased and surprised she remembered how he liked it. "Right."

Her motions quick and economical, she slid a pastry onto a china plate and handed him a fork.

"I rate the good dishes?"

"Everyone around here does," Laura countered dryly, returning his smile. Pouring herself a cup of coffee, she looked relaxed and content. "I've got a motto I live by. Never put off until tomorrow what you can enjoy today."

He could have guessed that about her, though he wasn't sure he always agreed with that. Sometimes anticipation was as heady as the actual treat. Aware she was watching him and waiting for a reaction, he took a bite and then closed his eyes briefly, savoring the sweet, creamy golden puff pastry. "Heaven," he pronounced.

She frowned, unsure. "There's not too much vanilla in the filling?" she pressed.

He grinned and finished another bite. "Now who's being a perfectionist?"

She shrugged. "It's a new recipe."

"Ah," he said. The counters weren't brimming over with her creations as they usually were. "You don't seem very busy today," he remarked.

"I'm not," Laura admitted ruefully.

His eyes narrowed with concern. "Business lagging?" He hated to think of Laura wanting for anything.

Laura nodded affirmatively. "The usual postholiday doldrums. It'll pick up with spring and get really crazy by summer. People don't want to cook in the heat then."

"Makes sense." He glanced around again, this time as a builder. "Must be hot in here in the summer, baking all day," he said.

"My electric bills for the air-conditioning are horrendous," she agreed. Getting the coffeepot, she freshened both their cups. "But it's a business expense."

"A necessary one, I imagine. Still, a ceiling fan would help."

Her chin jutted out determinedly. "I use two oscillating fans. Works fine."

He nodded and refrained from pointing out the obvious, that the oscillating fans used up valuable counter space in her already-cluttered work area. He carried his plate to the sink. She started to follow him, to take the dish for him, then stopped, apparently not wanting to be that close to him. He understood. He was a little leery of any more physical contact with her, too. He didn't need any more reminders what a vibrant, beautiful woman she was and it was impossible to get close to her and not think about it.

Finished rinsing out his dishes, he turned and looked at her. And in that second, he knew without their even realizing it, that everything had changed. They were beginning to see each other as people, rather than rivals for Janey's affection. She liked him. And he liked her.

She slid off her stool. "I better let you go. I'm sure you have a busy day."

He took the hint and started for the door, then stopped and turned. "Before I forget, one of the reasons I came over here was that Janey wants us all to get together again."

Laura did a double take. He wasn't sure what she was feeling, but it wasn't outright joy. More like reservations. "The four of us?" she croaked.

"I know how you're feeling. When she first brought it up, I was reluctant, too."

"And now?" Laura prompted, wariness in her eyes.

He didn't want her to be afraid of him. "Sitting here with you, I'm beginning to think Janey's right. We do need to spend more time together." Laura would not try to rob him of Janey's love. She was too generous a woman to ever do something like that and if he had looked harder in the beginning and not been so territorial, maybe he would have seen that.

Seeing her reluctance, remembering how Eric felt about him, he realized what a complicated situation he was creating. Understanding and respecting her reservations, he said, "You don't have to give me an answer this minute. I can see you need time to think about it. Just like I did when Janey talked to me. So I'll call you in a few days. Okay?"

Laura nodded. "I'll have to talk to Eric. He's still . . . rather prickly."

"I know," Zach said. Boy did he know.

"I DON'T GET IT," Janey grumbled to Zach later the following week. "I mean, I know Laura was busy last weekend with Eric's tournament but why can't she do something with us on President's Day? Eric told me she'd taken the day off, because he had the day off. Did you ask her about Monday specifically?"

"Yes," Zach replied patiently.

"And?"

"And she couldn't be sure what her plans were going to be."

"Did she at least agree to ask Eric about the possibility of a foursome?" Janey persisted.

"I didn't ask her." Her attitude had been so reticent he hadn't wanted to push.

"I don't get it," Janey repeated, bewildered.

Zach did. Laura was avoiding him. Perhaps out of consideration for Eric's feelings. Perhaps for other reasons of her own. And it was beginning to be very frustrating. It wasn't as if he made a habit out of going where he wasn't wanted, but dammit, the other morning in her kitchen he'd had the distinct impression she welcomed him there, that she liked his company. She had started to open up to him. And he'd liked what he'd seen. He'd thought she felt the same keen interest in him. And then she'd shied away for no reason. He'd seen the rejection in her eyes. And he'd heard it in her voice every time he'd talked to her since. She was holding him at arm's length, deliberately.

"Maybe she just needs to hear it from me," Janey said. As Zach watched, she picked up the phone and started dialing. He wasn't surprised to see that like him, she now knew the Matthews's phone number by heart.

"Laura, hi," Janey said softly, her face lighting up with pleasure as the two of them began to talk. "It's Janey. Yeah, great. I have something to ask you...." Minutes later, Janey hung up. She faced him, glowing with satisfaction. "It's all set," she crowed triumphantly. "We're meeting them Monday morning at nine."

"How'd you do that?" Zach stared at his daughter in amazement. Why could Laura respond to Janey so readily and not to him? In the past week, he'd phoned her—what— three times? And thought about doing it three times as much.

"It's charm, Dad." Janey winked. "You ought to try it sometime."

Chapter Ten

"Another strike!" Janey moaned dramatically, burying her head in her hands as Laura watched. She turned to Zach, zealously pleading her case, "Dad, this isn't fair! They're going to kill us if they're both on the same team. We've got to switch partners."

Zach looked a little embarrassed, as well he might, Laura thought. His last turn he'd only knocked down one pin. Zach glanced at Eric. "Would you mind?"

"No problem," Eric said curtly. Turning to Janey, he smiled and laced an arm around her shoulders, "I'd be glad to be on Janey's team."

He still resents Zach, Laura thought, disturbed. For reasons she sensed weren't even clear to her son. Knowing that, she'd tried to avoid putting the two males together again, but when Janey had called, insisting the four of them get together she'd found it impossible to say no.

"Would y'all mind if just Janey and I bowled for the next game or two?" Eric asked. "We wouldn't have to keep score or anything. I just want to give her a few pointers."

"Sure," Laura said.

"Okay with me," Zach said. "He's very good with her," Zach said to Laura after a minute.

"And she clearly adores him," Laura added. Just the way Melinda had. At the thought of the daughter she'd lost, sadness imbued her mood.

"Sorry you came?" Zach asked, misunderstanding the reason for the long sigh that preceded her frown.

"No, not at all."

"You weren't anxious to go out with us in the first place, at least not when I asked you. With Janey, it's a different story."

Laura cast an affectionate glance at her natural daughter and deftly skirted the issue. "It's true. I find it difficult to say no to her."

"She knows that, too."

He waited for her to confide in him and when she didn't, he picked up the questioning again. "Have I done something to annoy you? The last time we were together I thought we were getting along pretty well."

"We were." Maybe too well, Laura admitted candidly to herself.

He shrugged, unable to conceal his hurt at the change in her attitude. "So what happened?"

Laura looked down at the hands she had folded in her lap and said defensively, "I had a chance to think about it, that's all."

"And?"

She felt herself flush self-consciously. "I don't think it's a good idea for the two of us to get too close. Our situation is muddled enough already."

"Not seeing each other won't change that, it won't erase what's happened."

"No, it won't. But I don't want the two of us to become friends the way Eric and Janey have simply because fate has thrown us together." She'd had enough have-to's in her marriage to last her a lifetime.

His clear blue eyes narrowed. "Let's get something straight. I don't see anyone I don't want to, not even for

Janey's sake. You're right, of course, the first time we went out together as a unit, to the Mavericks game, you had to twist my arm to get me to go. I didn't have the best time once I got there, mainly because I was very suspicious of you. Now, I've started to see you as I probably would have all along if our situation hadn't been so complicated. I liked what I saw, Laura. I thought you liked me, too."

She lifted her eyes to his and forced herself not to look away. He was being so honest with her. She couldn't cover up her feelings. "I do like you—as—as a person." There. Maybe that would be enough to satisfy him.

Not a chance. Encouraged by her admission, he gave her a one cornered smile. "A person or a friend?"

His eyes held hers, his brows slightly raised. As he waited for her reply, she could feel her throat tightening. She wished he would stop looking at her so knowingly. "A friend." As soon as the words were out, she knew that was an understatement. The surprising truth was she was warming to the man. And he was warming to her. She didn't know where it would lead, but so what? Maybe she should just relax and enjoy it. She could handle tomorrow's problems, tomorrow.

"Okay. So now that's settled, do you think you could find it in your heart to stop avoiding me?"

She smiled shyly, "I guess, yes."

"Mom!" Eric came back to stand before the two of them impatiently, and she could tell by the tone of his voice it wasn't the first time he had called to her. "We're ready to start the game now. That is if you guys are done talking."

There was an unconscionably rude undertone to her son's voice, one she had never heard before. Laura stared at him, stunned. Realizing he'd gone too far, Eric flushed bright red and said nothing more as he waited for her to reply.

Two months ago, Laura would have reprimanded him on the spot for his behavior, albeit in a quiet fashion. Of course, two months ago, it wouldn't have been necessary.

But now she couldn't fault him for needing to find a target for his overwrought emotions. And who else would he blame, but the two of them?

Janey's eyes twinkled merrily and she teased, "If the two of you are done talking, maybe we could play a real game? Please?"

Zach smiled, as susceptible to his daughter's sweetly voiced request as Laura. "Sure," he said, offering Laura a hand up. "Laura? Who wants to go first?"

"I'M HUNGRY," Janey announced as they turned in their bowling shoes. "Can we go for pizza with Laura and Eric? Please?"

Zach looked at Laura. They were having fun. Why not? She nodded her okay, adding, "There's a Pizza Hut right down the street. We could go there."

"Sounds good to me," Zach said, then turned to the younger members of the entourage again. "Kids?"

"Yes!" Janey said enthusiastically.

Eric gave Zach the once-over, then shoved his hands into his pockets and nodded. The tension between the two males was unmistakable.

And it only got worse as they moved on to the restaurant. After they'd placed their order, Eric slid out of the booth. "Come on, Janey. Let's go play video games while we wait."

Zach reached into his pocket for a handful of change. He counted out four quarters and handed them over to his daughter. "That's all you're going to get, so use them wisely."

Janey made a face. Eric gave Zach a contemptuous look. "Don't worry, kid," Laura and Zach both heard him soothe as he walked away with Janey, "I'll lend you some money if you run out."

"Eric," Zach said firmly. Both children turned and he continued in the same no-nonsense tone, "I said one dollar. That's all."

Janey blushed, embarrassed. "Dad—he was just kidding around!"

No, he wasn't, Laura thought, looking at Eric's face.

Eric shrugged uncaringly. "Whatever." His jaw set, he turned back and laconically continued for the video machines in the corner.

"I've always made it a firm policy never to interfere in other parents' relationships with their children, but I think you should nip this attitude of his in the bud."

If the situation hadn't been so complicated and emotional, she wouldn't have hesitated to act. "He's never acted this way before. He'll come out of it," she said with the assurance of a mother who knows her child. "We just have to give him time."

"And until then?"

"Ignore his temper and don't pick up any gauntlet he throws down."

For a moment, Zach looked as if he wanted to argue. But to her relief he thought better of it and let the subject drop. "So," he said after a moment, when the waitress had brought their drinks and left again. "How is your week shaping up?"

"It's going to be busy."

"So is mine. Maybe we could do something this weekend?"

Laura nodded. "Maybe."

"Just the two of us?"

I don't know, Laura thought. Considering how Eric still felt was she asking for trouble? Fortunately, she was saved from replying as the two children returned to the table.

ERIC STARTED IN on her the moment they arrived home. "You really like Janey's dad, don't you?" He went to the refrigerator and got out a carton of milk.

Laura tried to be honest. As gently as possible, she said, "All things considered, he's very nice."

Frowning, Eric reached for a glass. "That's not what I mean," he said, still radiating disapproval.

Laura had been afraid of that. Sighing, she sat opposite him at the kitchen table. It was clear from the disgruntled look on her son's face that he considered her budding interest in Zach a form of disloyalty to his father. "I loved your father very much, but I can't bring him back."

"I know that." Eric shifted defensively and reached for the cookie jar on the counter behind him, extracting a handful.

"What is bothering you about this?"

Eric's mouth tightened. He gave her a surly look. "That night, when I saw the two of you hugging or whatever, you told me it didn't mean anything."

"It didn't."

But something *had* started that night.

"What about now?" Eric demanded.

"We're friends."

"Is that all?"

"For the moment," Laura answered cautiously, evading what she hadn't yet had time to figure out for herself.

"But it could be more," Eric pushed. "Couldn't it?"

"Maybe," she admitted cautiously as their gazes meshed and held.

Eric was silent, taking in all she had said.

"What is it, Eric?" Laura asked again, deciding to be just as tenacious as her son. "You've never reacted this way to any man I've been friends with before."

He scowled and got up abruptly to get some more milk, then accused gruffly, "That's because you never looked at any guy the way you look at Zach."

Laura struggled to keep her voice level. "And how is that?"

He scowled, resenting the fact he had to spell it out. "The way you used to look at Dad, like he's some sort of super-hero."

This was dangerous territory. "Does anything else bother you about Zach?" So much depended on his answer.

Eric shrugged, accusing, "I don't think he likes me much."

"You haven't exactly been polite," Laura pointed out.

"Yeah, well, he bosses Janey around too much. He's too strict."

"He's her father. That's his job. You have to remember she's younger than you are."

The challenging set of her son's jaw was back. "Are you going to keep seeing him?" Eric asked finally.

"I don't know," Laura said honestly.

Wordlessly, Eric got up, rinsed his glass and then put it in the dishwasher. "I'm tired," he said gruffly, keeping his back to her as he closed the appliance door. "I'm going to bed."

Laura sighed, exasperated and worried. "Eric—"

Finally remembering to mind his manners, he said, almost shyly, "Thanks for letting us all go bowling. Janey and I had fun."

The vulnerable look on his face made him seem so much younger. Her heart went out to him and the disciplinarian in her faded. "You're welcome," Laura replied softly. There was no use letting the sun go down on their anger, she thought. There would be plenty of time to reprimand Eric later, if it was necessary. She hoped it wouldn't be.

"I DON'T LIKE this color," Mrs. Gagglione said as she stared at the satin paper going up on the entryway walls. "I specifically said salmon."

"It is salmon," Zach said, showing her a color card.

"It's too pink. The salmon I looked at in the wallpaper warehouse was not that color pink. It was rosier."

Stifling a reflexive sigh, he rested his hand on his hip. "What do you want to do?"

Mrs. Gagglione waved her diamond-encrusted fingers at the walls. "Take it all off, of course." She moved her poodle to her other arm. "I guess I'll just have to go back to the warehouse."

"They'll charge you for both papers," Zach warned.

Mrs. Gagglione drew up to her full five-foot-one height. "No, they will not. They sold me the wrong paper. It is their loss, not mine! Come along, Millicent," she said to her squirming dog.

As Mrs. Gagglione stepped outside onto the front porch, Laura walked in. "Hi." She cast a glance from him to his customer. "Is this a bad time?"

"No," Zach said, his gaze lingering on her slim form. In a butter-colored skirt and sweater that made her brown eyes seem all the darker, she looked fresh and pretty. And she smelled great, too, like roses in the rain. "You've come at a great time." In fact, it would be a relief to talk to someone normal. Taking her hand in his, he led her to the bay windows in the formal dining room. "What's up?"

Briefly she told him about the conversation she had had with Eric the night before, ending uncertainly, "I don't know. Maybe we should cool it for a while." Her eyes filled with regret. "Maybe just let the kids see each other."

"Aren't you the one who told me problems don't go away by ignoring them?"

Looking torn, she swallowed hard. "Yes, but—"

"You can't let Eric dictate your life and make the rules. That's the parent's job, not the child's."

Laura bit her lip and looked at him uncertainly. "I can't just ignore Eric's feelings on this, Zach."

"If Eric approved of us seeing each other, the way Janey does, would you continue with the family outings?" Zach asked.

Laura flushed, her reaction an answer in itself. "But he doesn't," she protested.

"If he did."

She frowned and only answered, Zach suspected, because she knew instinctively he wasn't about to let her out of it. "All right, yes, if Eric approved I would...continue," she admitted grudgingly.

"But—?" he prompted when something else still seemed to be disturbing her.

"But I worry about what's going to happen if we continue to see each other as a group and it persists in being uncomfortable between you and Eric. If that occurs, you might want Eric and I both to stop seeing Janey...and now that she's finally starting to accept me, and I'm getting to know her, I don't want that to happen."

"Hmm." Restless, thinking, he walked over to the empty fireplace and rested one booted foot on the brick hearth. "There's only one way around that I know—to have you see Janey, like Eric does sometimes now, without Eric or I being there, too."

"You'd allow that now?" She seemed stunned. And very happy.

Thinking about it, Zach was a little surprised, too. His attitude had come a long way in the past several weeks. "I trust you not to try to abscond with her," he said softly, enjoying the sudden flush of pleasure in her face.

Zach moved closer, wanting, needing to be near her again. "Besides, it seems to be what Janey wants, and I want her to be happy."

"So do I," Laura said, surprising him with a soft, grateful touch of her hand on his. "Thanks, Zach. This means a lot to me."

He knew.

"You don't seem surprised that Zach's letting me see Janey alone," Laura commented to her father who was replacing the washers in the upstairs bathrooms.

"Your mother told me you were seeing a lot of him," her father said diplomatically, removing a faucet handle.

"Did she also tell you she thinks I've got plans to ensnare him so I can get Janey back?"

"It's not true, is it?" he asked, removing a packing nut.

"No!" Laura said, catching a glimpse of her indignant expression in a mirror above the sink.

"Then why let her upset you?"

Laura sighed. "Does she still want me to sue for custody?" Laura had been avoiding her mother like crazy since they had last talked, to stave off any further lectures on this subject.

Her father removed a worn misshapen washer and replaced it with a shiny new one. "She thinks you have a right to your own child. She still stubbornly refuses to think about the years and years the two of you have spent away from each other."

Laura studied her dad's impassive expression. As usual, it gave away nothing. "What about you, Dad? Have you changed your mind?"

He shook his head solemnly and looked her in the eye. "No. I admit I've thought about it, mostly because your mother can't think of anything else. I still think the child you raise is your own, regardless of his or her biological roots. You can't take Janey's past away from her, any more than you could take Melinda's from her. If she were still here with us, honey, I'd bet my last dollar you'd relive the Alamo before you'd let anyone take her away from you."

Laura nodded. "You're right. My home would be my fortress. I probably wouldn't want Zach near her if she were still alive."

"Which is understandable," her father agreed gently. "If you like Zach, you should continue seeing him."

''What about Eric?''

Her father gave her a reassuring pat on the arm. ''Eric'll come around, given time. He's a sensible boy. He's just hurting right now, is all. But he'll get past this. We all will.''

Her father paused, thinking, the reassembled faucet spindle in hand. ''It would be nice, though, wouldn't it? If you and Zach did eventually get together, like your mother keeps hoping, if you had a chance to raise Janey as your own daughter after all, if some good could come from this loss?''

Yes, it would be good, Laura thought. Almost too good to be true, too easy, too perfect. And for that reason, she didn't want to even think about it. Fate had a way of kicking you in the teeth when you least expected it. She couldn't afford to want too much. She'd already lost more than she could bear.

''DADDY, there's an Open House on Tuesday night at school. And I want Laura to come. Is that okay?''

Zach stared at his daughter, not sure what to say. Although he had just yesterday granted Laura permission to see Janey one-on-one, he hadn't even had a chance yet to tell his daughter of that decision. And now she was asking him for this?

''Are you planning to introduce her as your mother?'' he asked, careful to put no inflection of prejudgment in his voice.

Janey flushed. ''No,'' she said. ''If—if I did that,'' she stammered, ''people would ask too many questions. I just want her to come, you know, and see where I go to school and meet some of my teachers. Like a normal mom would.''

For not the first time in his life, Zach became acutely aware of how much his daughter had missed not having a mother. Still he found himself unexpectedly unwilling to grant her this. And it had nothing to do with the eyebrows people might or might not raise. It was because, prior to this moment, the turf of Janey's parent had been sacred ground, his alone.

It's only one night, and a rather stiff and formal affair at that, he instructed himself practically. It will be no sweat off my back to include Laura in it. "If it means that much to you, honey, I'll ask her."

"You don't have to do that," Janey said brightly. "I already did. I—I hope it's okay?" she said, when she saw the avalanche of hurt her unthinking remark caused.

"Sure, it's fine," he said hoarsely after a moment. "But let me call her to make sure," he continued, knowing all the while what he really wanted was to find out how this had all come about.

Laura picked up her phone on the third ring. After catching her up-to-date on his conversation with Janey, he said, "I think it's probably better if you go with me, rather than alone."

"Okay." Laura paused, then said almost apologetically, "Zach, I want you to know, I didn't initiate any of this—"

Remembering the eager look on Janey's face, he knew that was true. Still, he couldn't help but feel threatened.

He finally said, a bit more gruffly than he intended, "I gathered as much. But you didn't say no to her or even wait to discuss it with me first before you gave her an answer. And I admit that did bother me some."

On the other end, Laura drew in her breath rather suddenly. "Are you telling me she asked me before she asked you if it was okay?" She sounded shocked, Zach thought. So she wasn't working to separate them after all. And that was a relief.

"Yes," he answered Laura honestly. "She called you long before she talked to me."

"That's one of the perils of parenthood, I'm afraid. Kids want to make their own decisions and follow through, regardless of what their parents think."

Thinking of Harry Cole and the troubles he'd been having with Tabitha, Zach knew it was true. "You're right." Zach looked at the form Janey had given him detailing the Open House. "I'll pick you up at six-thirty."

"Sounds good," Laura said.

"And, Laura, I think I'll wait to tell Janey the two of you can see each other one-on-one."

Trepidation edged her voice. "You haven't changed your mind, have you?"

"No. But let's get through the Open House first," Zach said.

Chapter Eleven

"Where's Janey?" Laura asked as she met Zach at the front door Tuesday evening.

"Over at school. Members of the honor society were drafted to act as guides, to help parents find their way around. So we'll see her there."

Trying hard to keep her disappointment to herself, Laura announced steadily, "Harry Cole just called. He said to tell you a Mrs. Gagglione called. There's some sort of emergency over at her new-home site. She wants you to meet her there right away."

Zach swore and rolled his eyes. "That woman."

Laura offered gallantly, "Look, if you want to forget about taking me to Open House, I understand."

"No," Zach said, his expression adamant. "I don't skip anything this important to my daughter."

Something else they had in common, Laura thought. A heartfelt devotion to their children.

He frowned and glanced at his watch, adding, "I can stop by the construction site of Mrs. Gagglione's new home on the way, if it's all right with you, and still make Open House long before they close up at nine."

"Sounds great. Let's go." Laura grabbed her wrap and they were off.

The inside and outside of his Wagoneer were immaculate. Knowing how muddy it was around the construction site, Laura guessed he had washed and vacuumed it before picking her up. Knowing he'd taken such care made her smile.

"You sound like you don't want to deal with this Mrs. Gagglione," Laura said.

He sighed heavily. "I don't."

"You could always hand her off to one of your employees."

"No. They don't deserve that. I'll work with her. I just wish she had better timing, but I guess if she did, she wouldn't be Mrs. Gagglione."

Unfortunately his client was every bit as much a pain as Zach had implied. In a fur coat, with diamonds dripping from her ears, she was pacing back and forth in the foyer, a small white poodle cradled in her arms. She took one look at Zach and nearly burst into tears. "Have you seen the kitchen since they laid the tile?"

Zach shook his head.

"Well, come and see!" She led the way. Pointing, she said, "It doesn't match the granite countertops, not at all!"

She was right, Laura thought. It didn't match. But then, it wasn't supposed to color coordinate precisely. And it looked perfectly lovely against the white ceramic tile on the floor.

"Mrs. Gagglione, you picked out all the tiles and countertop materials yourself," Zach said.

"It was that interior designer you hired," Mrs. Gagglione wailed. "She talked me into these awful color combinations. When my husband sees it he is going to be furious with me." She turned to Laura, "It's our dream house, you see. And it's up to me to make it perfect!"

Zach said quietly, "What would you like to do, Mrs. Gagglione?"

"I don't know!" she sniffed helplessly.

"The countertops are lovely and all the rage," Laura soothed. "If I had a new kitchen, that's exactly what I'd put in it, and I'm a commercial cook."

"Really?"

"Really. But if you're concerned about color, you might want to change the tile a bit, put in something with just a touch of gray."

"Gray and white alone would be awfully plain, though," Zach cut in.

"I agree," Laura said. Able to see his client needed soothing more than anything else, she said, "Mrs. Gagglione? What do you think? Would you like a tile that has several colors in it, including gray? Or would you prefer to go with the plain white and add color in other ways, with drapes, for instance and rugs."

"I don't know," Mrs. Gagglione said miserably.

"Perhaps you should take a few days and think about it," Zach suggested gently.

Mrs. Gagglione sighed. "All right," she said finally, "I'll think it over. But, considering how this is turning out, you'd better get another designer to work with me."

"I will," Zach promised.

"Is she always this difficult?" Laura said after the client had left.

"Yes, unfortunately."

"How do you stand it."

"Isn't it obvious? I don't." His lips compressed grimly. "I mean I try to be patient, but it's hard. She's caused us so much extra work. Of course the cost overruns are all added to her bill. Still it's not easy telling the men to rip out tile they've just put in."

"Is she that insecure about everything?"

Zach nodded unhappily. "Afraid so."

Laura couldn't understand that. "Why? Is her husband hypercritical or something?"

"Just the opposite. I think it's her friends she's worried about. Mrs. Gagglione wasn't born to money, you see. They acquired it about five years ago, when some oil came in on their west Texas property."

"Oh."

"Since then, they've been very successful. Still she's not secure in her own worth. Hence, the hysteria over the house. She wants it to be perfect, to be proof that she is a special, competent human being. If it's a success, she'll be a success."

"I never thought of a house that way," Laura murmured.

Zach smiled. "That's because you have a lot more going for you. You don't have to rely on anyone or anything to elevate you to a position of importance."

"How'd you figure all this out?" Laura said, marveling at his insight. In the distance, the sun was slowly setting, basking them in an intimate, dusky glow.

Shrugging, Zach answered her question matter-of-factly, "My wife, Maria, was very much like Mrs. Gagglione. Maria didn't believe in herself, either. She was beautiful and smart and funny, but deep inside, she was insecure. I didn't know it when I married her but I found out later there were a lot of problems in her family. Neither of her parents had ever had much time for her, her mother because she was working almost constantly, and her father because he drank. She never really believed either of them loved her, and in the end she felt the same way about me."

Laura remembered how much it had hurt when her own marriage had started to go awry. "That must have hurt you."

He affirmed so sadly, adding, "I tried to convince her that I loved her very much, but there was no getting through to her."

Listening to him talk, realizing he'd struggled as she had to build a solid, happy life, her heart went out to him. "I'm sorry."

He shrugged, letting her know he had dealt with it long ago. "Life isn't perfect. I just wish, in retrospect, I could have helped her to believe in herself more."

Deciding a more cheerful topic was in order, Laura turned back to the kitchen. "The tile dilemma aside, Zach, this is going to be beautiful."

"You think so?"

"Oh, yes. What kind of refrigerator is Mrs. Gagglione going to get, do you know?"

"A stainless-steel Traulsen."

Laura groaned with undisguised envy. "I should have guessed. Only the best, hmm?"

He nodded. "Want to see the rest of the house?"

"Would you mind showing me?"

He looked at his watch. "Not at all. Open House runs until nine." And it was only seven.

They ended the tour on the third-floor balcony, overlooking the hills. "They're going to have a wonderful view of the city," Laura said.

"I kind of like the view now," Zach teased, looking at her.

Laura flushed with both pleasure and embarrassment. He wasn't so bad himself. He looked very handsome and very urbane. She was proud to be with him, relaxed and easy at his side. And those feelings of camaraderie surprised her. The heat still warming her cheeks unbearably, she moved away from him.

He stayed his ground with obvious effort. "You don't have to run away from me, you know," he said softly, his gaze still on her.

Afraid things were moving too fast, she ducked her head. "We better get going to Open House."

"I haven't forgotten." Zach stepped closer. Before she could protest, he had his arms around her, an intense, ardent look in his clear blue eyes. Knowing instinctively she'd be lost at the first touch of his lips upon hers, she started to resist but his mouth closed over hers with unapologetic hunger anyway. He took what she wasn't so sure she was ready to give, until her lips had parted and she had that familiar, unmistakable weightless sensation in her middle. Her head fell back, giving him freer access to her mouth and she moaned with disbelief, and joy, and wonder, unsure that this, the forbidden, was really happening, yet ecstatic that it was.

Slowly, inevitably, the tension left her body as his tongue continued to tenderly plunder her open mouth and she curled against him, pressing her thighs to his. With a groan of contentment, he slid his hands down her body to her waist and pulled her more firmly against him. Aware of his fierce desire for her, she felt an answering thrill where he held her cupped against him that soon turned to a white-hot throbbing. Her arms moved to wreathe his neck and she let her fingers tunnel through the silky thickness of his hair. His arms wrapped tightly around her, he continued to kiss her with spellbinding tenderness. How she had missed this closeness, she thought, this feeling of being absolutely, completely alive. Of being a woman. Of being wanted. Of having a life outside the boundaries of work and motherhood.

He may have been the aggressor, but she was more than compliant. As he kissed her, she felt the warmth and tenderness and the excitement that had always been missing from her life. And more: she felt cherished, just for being herself. So much so that she was shaking when they drew apart. This had been coming a long time, Laura realized looking up into his face, the fire within her still raging out of control. And now that it had, she wasn't sure she had the willpower to call a halt if he so much as kissed or touched her again.

To her credit and satisfaction, he didn't look any steadier than she felt. Or any more able to stop if they touched again.

But they were in a house still under construction, she reminded herself firmly. And what felt good tonight, might turn into a living hell tomorrow. She had been reckless once, in her youth, letting her passionate nature rush her into a marriage that had never been destined to last. She couldn't do that again, not with the happiness of both their families at stake.

"I better get you to the Open House," Zach said.

Knowing how close she had come to making love with him, right there and then, she didn't argue. Her heart was a little heavier as she made her way to the car.

"YOU MUST BE LAURA," Mrs. Bauer said the minute they walked in the door to Janey's Language Arts class.

Laura looked up, surprised. Recovering her equilibrium, which wasn't easy after Zach's passionate, unexpected embrace, she smiled and held out a hand. "How did you know who I was?"

Mrs. Bauer smiled. "Just a guess, really. You see, Janey wrote a poem. Maybe I should show it to you." Turning, she directed them to the back of the classroom.

Stunned, Laura moved closer to the feminine script and her heart in her throat, read Janey's poem.

It was entitled, "If I Had A Mom."

If I had a mom,
I'd want her to be,
    just like Laura.
Bright, cheerful, funny,
    Kind and sweet,
Always loving,

Always caring,
Laura.

Tears in her eyes, a happiness she hadn't felt in a long
while filling her soul, Laura stared at the handwritten poem.
Zach stared at it, too, but he looked more as if he'd been run
over by a truck than pleased by the expression of his
daughter's sentiments.

Mrs. Bauer beamed at them both, Laura especially. "It
was a lovely tribute," she said. "Janey must feel very close
to you."

"Closer than I knew," she admitted tremulously, while
beside her Zach said something equally inane.

As soon as they could, they left the classroom. How they
got through the rest of the night, Laura wasn't sure, only
that she and Zach met four more teachers in various classes
as well as Janey and several of Janey's friends, who were all
stationed strategically at various points around the sprawling four-story middle school. But over and over her mind
kept going back to the poem.

"Did you see it?" Janey asked en route home, having
opted for the back seat of the jeep, leaving Laura to sit in the
front with her dad.

"Yes, Janey, I did," Laura said. "It was very sweet."

Janey grinned, pleased with the heartfelt praise, and
leaned forward as much as her fastened seat belt would allow.

"Daddy?" Janey asked.

"Your ability to express yourself has really improved," he
said finally. "Listen, I'm going to drop you off first, so you
can go ahead and get ready for bed. I'll take Laura home
and be right back."

"That's a good idea," Janey said, a worried frown
crossing her face as she gathered her purse and several left-
over maps of the school.

"I'm sorry," Laura said softly, long moments later when they had reached her driveway. Alone again, she was free to tell him what she'd been feeling since the moment she'd spied Janey's poem. "I had no idea what was in store for us tonight."

"Obviously that's why she wanted you to be there tonight. So you could read the poem." And realize firsthand how much she has always wanted a mother of her very own, Zach thought. A mother she could go to for warmth and tenderness.

"It's not surprising she would have those feelings about me," Laura said, looking down at the house key she held in her hand.

"Isn't it?" he responded.

Laura shrugged expressively. "She wants a mother. All children do." It probably could have been anyone, any woman with a sense of tenderness and concern for her wellbeing, Laura thought. I shouldn't get carried away, she instructed herself sternly. But she wanted to get carried away. Knowing how Janey was beginning to open up to her, she wanted to fly.

"I guess you're right," Zach said tiredly, deciding he was overreacting, as he had so often these past few weeks, when it came to the subject of Janey and Laura. "After all, Janey's never known a mother. Maria died of a stroke when she was just a baby."

"All the more reason for her to latch on to me." Laura continued the conversation, thinking, there's no reason for you to be threatened by this, Zach. Janey loves you, too.

His shoulders lifted and fell, and he stared straight ahead. "You're right, of course," he said, but his words sounded dull and lifeless even to his own ears.

"And you're worried," Laura said, hating the anguish she saw in his eyes and wishing she knew some magic way to erase it.

Zach looked at her, for once not trying to hide behind an impassive front. "Wouldn't you be worried in my place?"

Laura wished she could say no, but she wasn't that noble and unselfish of heart, either. "Probably," she conceded with a small frown, hoping this latest action of Janey's wouldn't destroy the closeness she and Zach had begun to forge. Or the ardent desire she had felt in his kiss earlier. Because she had started to count on his friendship. And his support. And if it was too soon, or still unwise for them to make love now, maybe it wouldn't always be....

Again, they lapsed into silence. "You better get back to Janey," she said finally. She wished they could work this out now, but even as she thought it she knew it was foolish. It took a lot more than mutual love for a child to bond a man and woman together, to form a relationship that would last. And after her disastrous first marriage, she would no longer settle for anything less. There was simply too much at stake, for her and Zach especially.

"START, darn you!" Laura said Wednesday afternoon, pumping the gas pedal on her station wagon for the third time. The starter made a faint clicking sound but the engine didn't even begin to turn over.

The battery was dead and she had a three-tiered fiftieth wedding anniversary cake carefully loaded in the rear compartment. The party was due to start in another hour, and the cake was supposed to be there before any of the guests arrived.

Getting out of her car, she went back inside the house. She tried calling her parents, to no avail. The auto club couldn't send anyone for at least another two hours. The party giver's line was busy. And the local taxi service was fresh out of limousines—the only car with doors wide enough to allow her to house the gigantic cake.

She needed someone with a station wagon or a Jeep.

In desperation, she punched out Zach's number. "I wouldn't call unless I were desperate—" she began hesitantly.

He laughed softly. "Well, that's flattering—"

Flushing, she began to explain. Hearing, he said, "No problem. I'll come right over."

"You're sure you don't mind?" she asked cautiously.

"What are friends for?"

The moment she saw him she knew he had also had an incredibly busy day. His blue chambray shirt and jeans were dusted with streaks of white, blue, and mint green. Paint was smeared on his chin. His eyes widened at the huge cake. "I see what you mean about it being unwieldy."

"We're going to have to lift it up into the truck," Laura said frowning.

"No problem."

"It's heavy," she warned.

"I'll be careful."

With some difficulty, they managed to transfer the cake. Only when she was certain the cake was secure, did they shut the back door.

In tandem, she and Zach dashed toward the front of his Wagoneer. "Where to?" he asked genially.

She looked up the address she'd written on the invoice and they were off. "The client is going to be furious with me," Laura moaned as they waited impatiently at the third red traffic light. "I should have had this cake at the reception hall two hours ago. I would have, if everything under the sun hadn't gone wrong."

"Like what?"

"I ran out of bittersweet chocolate and hazelnuts and had to make an emergency trip to the store, then I got caught in traffic on the way back. The two bottom layers took an extra ten minutes to bake. I have no idea why. My stand mixer went on the blink, so I had to use my hand-held electric mixer to make all the frosting. I misplaced one of the parts to my electric food gun so I had to hunt up my pastry bag and put on all the swags and bows the old-fashioned way. Then, when I was putting on the names, as the client suggested, I forgot they spelled Karin with an *i* instead of an *e*, and misspelled her name, so I had to scrape off my error, redo the layer of frosting beneath it, make an extra batch of icing, and spell the name correctly.''

Just talking about it made her perspire anew. Zach laughed and shook his head in shared commiseration. ''When you have a rotten day, you go all out.''

Of course, the worst part of it all was she knew why she'd had so much trouble. The problem was she wasn't concentrating on her work. And the reason she wasn't doing that was Zach. Since he had kissed her, she hadn't been able to think about much else.

''Here we are,'' Zach said, pulling up in front of the reception hall. No sooner had he cut the engine than a woman came running out. ''We thought you'd never get here!''

''Sorry,'' Laura apologized. ''It's a long story.''

With Zach's help, she got the cake inside, out of the box, and safely situated on a table. Fortunately it was everything the celebrating couple had wanted in an anniversary cake.

Zach and Laura went back outside. ''I owe you for this one,'' she said, breathing a sigh of relief.

He smiled, liking the idea of that. ''Now what about your car?''

She fell into step beside him, glad he was there with her. She shrugged. ''I guess I call the auto club again.''

He slanted her a thoughtful glance. ''Want me to take a look at it?''

Laura thought of the mechanic's fee she could save, if he could locate the problem. ''Sure, if you don't mind.''

''No problem.''

"You may need a new battery," Zach said an hour and a half later. They had jump-started her car, charged it, then let it sit. When they tried to start it again, it was dead.

Laura sighed, thinking what that would entail: a trip to the shop, a wait, the price of a new battery plus a mechanic's fee.

"If you like, I could put it in for you," Zach said.

Laura looked over at him, amazed. Was there no end to this man's generosity? "I don't want to impose."

"It's no problem," Zach reassured her as Eric drove up and parked on the street.

"What's going on?" Eric asked, joining them. He looked from Zach to Laura.

"Your mother's car needs a new battery. Want to help me replace it for her?" Zach asked.

Eric looked at him, his wariness evident.

Ignoring her son's reticence, Zach continued pleasantly, "That way, you'll know how to replace the battery in your car, if and when it quits," Zach continued.

The opportunity to learn skills that would make him even more self-sufficient was too good to pass up. "Sure," Eric said. "I'll do it for Mom." And not, the unspoken declaration went, because Zach had asked him.

Ignoring Eric's subtle put-down, Laura said, "I'll need to get money for the battery."

Zach caught her wrist before she could depart. "That's not necessary. We'll settle up later."

She smiled. "You're sure this isn't too much trouble?"

"No, not at all. But you might call Janey and tell her I'll be late."

After the men left, Laura decided to do better than that. Rather than have Janey endure an evening alone because Zach was busy at her place, she decided to use Eric's car to go and get Janey and bring her back to her house.

"This car is so cool!" Janey said as the two of them rattled along in the old red Mustang. "I want one just like it when I learn to drive." Janey settled back into her seat with a contented sigh, looking so much like Eric at that moment that Laura thought her heart would break.

"So what's for dinner?" Janey asked, once inside the house. She settled in at the kitchen table with her homework, as Melinda used to do.

Her heart brimming with memories, Laura watched her open her algebra book. Janey was such a sunny child, so sweet and outgoing and giving. As Eric normally was. "What would you like for dinner?"

Janey slid the eraser end of her pencil behind her ear. "Do you know how to fix *fajitas*?"

Laura laughed and teased, "Are you kidding, girl? I'm a native Texan. Chicken or beef?"

"Either one."

Laura opened her freezer, glad it was well stocked. "How about both?"

Janey grinned exuberantly. "Radical."

Extracting two packages of *fajita* meat from the freezer, Laura put it in the microwave to thaw. Janey watched, entranced, as Laura quickly whipped up the marinade. Melinda had loved to watch her cook, too, Laura thought. She had missed having a daughter to talk to while she puttered around putting supper on.

"What's in the sauce?" Janey asked.

"Worcestershire sauce, garlic salt, pepper." Laura began slicing up onions to fry with the meat.

Watching, Janey giggled and shook her head in consternation. "I didn't think people who were dating liked to eat onions. Or garlic." At Laura's surprised look, Janey elaborated, "You know, 'cause if you kiss someone."

Laura flushed. Who did Janey think she was kissing? Had Zach somehow let on about Tuesday night? In an effort to recover, she retorted calmly, "That's true enough, but it's not a problem if the two people who are going to kiss eat the same thing."

"Oh, so it doesn't matter if you and my dad both eat onions and garlic?" Janey asked.

She's fishing, Laura thought triumphantly. And I almost fell for it. "If our respective dates also eat the same thing—" Laura began, returning Janey's too-innocent look.

"If who eats the same thing?" Zach asked, coming in the back door behind Eric.

The two of them were covered with black grime, from fingertips to elbows. "People who are dating," Janey replied. "Hi, Eric." She beamed as she looked at her older brother.

"Hiya kid." Grinning, Eric pretended to bop her on the head with one grease-smeared arm. Janey squealed and ducked.

"There's soap in the guest bath," Laura said.

"I'll show you," Eric said.

Laura noted that although Eric greeted Janey affectionately, he still wasn't all that warm to Zach. On the other hand, they had worked together on her car.

Seconds later, Eric returned. He pulled a cola from the refrigerator, and tossed one to Janey, who barely managed to catch it. "Eric Matthews, if those colas explode you will personally mop up the mess!" Laura warned.

"Relax." Eric grinned, winking at Janey. "I know an old trick. Just tap the top about five or six times, right over the cutout of the pull tab. See? And voilà!" He pulled it open. Nothing, not even a bubble fizzed over the top.

"Now you try it, Janey," Eric encouraged.

To Laura's amazement, hers opened without incident, too. Laura said. "Did you thank Zach for showing you how to change a battery?"

"He did," Zach said from the doorway.

Eric looked at Zach over his shoulder, his feelings of ambivalence simmering close to the surface again. "Come on, Janey," he said, inclining his head toward the door. "Let's go watch TV. There's a game on cable...."

"Can I get you something to drink?" Laura asked Zach. Zach nodded. "A beer if you have it."

"Coming up."

"Something smells good." He nodded toward the meat simmering in the skillets on top of the stove.

"Janey requested *fajitas*. I hope that's okay."

"One of my favorites."

"Great."

"Anything I can do?" He moved closer, yet retained enough distance to give her elbow room.

"Not really. I just have to set the table." He smelled like soap and man. It was a tantalizing combination and disconcerting to have him so close.

"What was all that about people who date having to eat the same things when I came in?" he asked.

Laura felt herself blush. "She wanted to know why I didn't mind eating garlic and onions. She was under the impression most adults who date don't do that."

"Ah," Zach said, his eyes sparkling in a way that let her know he, too, was remembering their first, and so far only, kiss. His impertinent grin said he was anticipating another.

Her heart thudding with telltale speed, Laura decided she had been on the hot seat long enough. It was time for him to have a turn. "Do you make a habit of not eating garlic and onions—for that reason?" she asked, careful to keep her expression innocent. "Is that where Janey got the idea?"

"I didn't," he admitted, owning up to the fact unabashedly, "until a few weeks ago. I guess since then I've been making more of an effort to have restaurants hold the onion and/or garlic. Mrs. Yaeger, too. I guess Janey noticed."

Suddenly Laura couldn't breathe. The sound of the kids, hooting over a game in the family room, sounded very far away. Attempting to diffuse the tension with levity, she said,

"If I didn't know better, I'd think you were trying to tell me something."

His eyes softened tenderly. "Maybe I am," he admitted quietly. She was backed up against the countertop with no place to go, a stack of plates in her hands.

He took them from her, and put them aside.

"Zach—" The word escaped her lips on a breathy sigh.

"I like the way you say my name," he countered, taking her into his arms. His mouth slanted over hers predatorily. Knowing a kiss was inevitable and that if she was honest with herself she wanted it as much as he, her head tilted back.

"And I like the way you look in that apron," he continued softly.

Anticipating, even welcoming his sweet caress, she linked both hands behind his neck and teased back softly, "I'm a mess."

"You're perfect," he murmured, his lips touching hers once, and then again and again. "And you know it."

And there the testing stopped. He kissed her again, even more passionately, until she was limp and acquiescent in his arms. Only the smell of nearly burning meat woke them up. Laura stared at him, wondering how she had ever gotten along without this man in her life, hoping she would never have to again.

She turned swiftly, avoiding another sensual pass of his mouth. "Dinner's ready," she said. "We need to tell the kids."

He gave her a long, sultry look that let her know he, too, felt they should tell the kids, and not just about dinner, but about the two of them, as well. "I'll get them."

Chapter Twelve

"This is so neat! Thank you for taking me shopping," Janey said as she and Laura walked in the entrance to the mall.

Laura smiled, already having fun. "You're welcome."

"How come Dad didn't come?" Janey asked.

Realizing she still had her car keys in her hand, Laura tucked them into the zipper pocket of her purse. "He thought you could use some girl talk, female bonding and all that." Plus, he was keeping his promise to let her develop a relationship with Janey on her own, so if anything did happen to make family outings impossible, she could continue to see her daughter with the least amount of awkwardness possible.

"Radical," Janey said, giving her highest stamp of approval to the idea of she and Laura doing things like shopping alone. Janey continued confidentially, "Dad doesn't really enjoy shopping anyway. He just wants to go in the store, buy what you need as fast as possible and get out. He doesn't like to look around or just hang out. Know what I mean?"

Laura nodded. "Eric hates shopping, too. Most men are that way, I think. Must be something in their genes."

"Or not." Janey laughed, explaining, "The shopping gene. They don't have it."

Laura laughed, too.

They passed a shop that carried only accessories. "Oh, would you look at those earrings?" Janey breathed, holding on to Laura's shoulder with one hand and pointing with the other. "Aren't they to-die-for? And they're clip-on, too!"

Laura noted Janey didn't have her ears pierced. For someone who adored earrings as she apparently was beginning to, that could pose a problem. The selection of clip-on was usually sparse when compared to the selection of pierced earrings. "They are pretty," Laura admitted.

"But they're seven dollars. I only have five," she said, disappointed.

"I could lend you two dollars. Actually, I'd be glad to buy them for you if you think your dad wouldn't mind me doing so."

Janey's expression was indignant. "Why should he mind? We're friends and friends give each other presents. But...maybe you're right." Janey frowned as if seeing a slight problem. "Maybe I should buy them with my own money."

"Then it's settled." Laura reached into her change purse and counted out two dollars. "This is a loan."

"Thanks, Laura!" Janey cried ebulliently. "Wait till the girls at school see these."

As they had predicted, the earrings looked terrific on Janey. Cute and young. Janey wore them the rest of the day and she still had them on when Laura drove her home.

Zach was working in the yard. His smile faded as Janey got out of the car. "Hi, Daddy!" she said buoyantly.

"Hi." His glance narrowed on her ears, then turned back to Laura. Seeing his obvious displeasure, she felt herself tense.

"Thanks for taking me, Laura," Janey said, moving forward to give Laura an impulsive hug. Affection for the child flowing through her in waves, Laura hugged her back. Withdrawing, Janey said shyly, "I had so much fun. It was neat to be able to do girl-stuff, just the two of us, like my friend Chrissy does with her mom. I wish we could be together all the time like that."

"So do I," Laura admitted, not ashamed of how much the time with her daughter had meant to her.

"I'm going in to call Chrissy," Janey said, dashing for the door. "I can't wait to tell her what I got!"

Janey disappeared, the door slamming behind her. Laura looked back at Zach. His face was a mask of displeasure. "Where'd she get the earrings?" he inquired crisply. His deliberate matter-of-fact tone didn't fool her. Zach was furious.

Trepidation making her legs tremble, Laura answered as serenely as she could, "Janey bought them with her own money plus a two-dollar loan from me."

He was incredulous. "You gave her money for those?"

"Yes."

"Why?"

"She admired them."

He leaned on his hoe and Laura could see he was struggling with his temper. "Did she tell you I've forbidden her to get her ears pierced?"

Laura's smile faltered, as did her equilibrium. "No, but those are clip-on earrings, Zach."

His jaw took on a stubborn edge. "I don't want her wearing those, either. I think she's too young. Janey knows that, Laura."

Embarrassed, she had to work to keep her gaze steady on his. "She didn't tell me that."

Zach sighed, realizing Laura had been hoodwinked. "Knowing how many times we've argued about that in the past, I don't doubt it."

Laura cast around for something to say. This was none of her business, she told herself firmly. Or was it? Janey was her child. And Zach was being unfair and dictatorial. Suddenly, she knew she had to come to Janey's defense. "Zach, they're just earrings. All the girls her age are wearing them."

The corners of his mouth curled downward. "I don't know how to say this without offending you, but those earrings make her look cheap."

Now he was being ridiculous. Laura stiffened her spine. "I disagree."

He shrugged. "Disagree all you want. Janey isn't your child. She's mine."

If he'd meant to hurt her, he had. She gritted her teeth.

Janey was back. She hurled herself into Laura's arms and gave her a heartfelt hug. "I almost forgot to say thank-you for the earrings."

"Janey," Zach interjected in a calm, cautious tone. "About the earrings."

At Zach's firm but weary tone, Janey's countenance turned stormy. "I can't get an infected earlobe from clip-ons, Dad."

"I still don't want you wearing them until you're older."

"Dad, I'm almost in high school—!"

"But you're not in high school," Zach countered.

Guiltily, Laura stepped in. She had made a mess of things here, albeit unknowingly. Never would she have undermined Zach's parental authority deliberately. "Your dad is the boss here, Janey. What he says goes. If he doesn't want you to wear earrings to school, you'll just have to wear them at home."

Janey looked at Laura as if she was a traitor. "I thought you'd be on my side in this," she said in a soft, hurt voice.

Laura felt she was caught between a rock and a hard place, with no way out. "I am."

"Sure you are," Janey mumbled. She turned and ran off.

Zach turned back to Laura, the moment the front door had slammed behind his daughter. "Satisfied?"

"Look," Laura began, "I know how this looks—"

"Like you're trying to start a war between my daughter and me?"

Laura imposed an iron control on her own rising temper and countered softly, reasonably, "I never tried to do that."

His blue eyes clouded with uneasiness, Zach shot back, "Maybe not deliberately, but you're doing a damn good job of it."

"Look," Laura insisted with returning impatience, "just because I happen to think you're unreasonable about this earring business does not mean I am trying to replace you in your daughter's affections!"

Zach swore beneath his breath and clenched his mouth tighter. "Be honest here, Laura, if not with me, with yourself. Admit it would suit your purposes just fine if you could usurp my role as parent and woo Janey away from me emotionally, become her favorite parent, and let me carry all the burdens of the disciplinarian. You get to take her out and have fun whereas I get to be the guy who stays home with her and makes sure she does her homework and doesn't act older than her age."

"I never would've permitted Janey to buy the earrings if I had known about your rule at the time," Laura said again.

"A lot of good that does me now."

She breathed an exasperated sigh. She knew he was jealous. She could hardly blame him. "I care about Janey, Zach. I'll be the first to admit that. I might even be starting to love her, but I have never tried to steal her away from you, and I never would. And if you think that even for an instant, you don't know me at all."

Zach studied her, his hurt visible. "Maybe not consciously," he said finally. "But Laura . . . you have to think about what you've just done."

"I have. And I have nothing to be sorry for. If anyone is acting like a jerk, Zach, it's you." Knowing it would be pointless to discuss this further until he calmed down, she turned on her heel and marched defiantly toward her station wagon.

As she suspected, he did nothing at all to stop her.

EARLY SATURDAY evening, Laura was on her knees, turning over the soil with a spade when a shadow fell over her. Shading her eyes with one hand, she glanced up just as Zach hunkered down beside her. His anger of hours before had faded and he was waving a small white flag, made out of a handkerchief and a small stick.

As their eyes met, he said softly, "Truce?"

Although a small part of her wanted to hurl herself into his arms then and there and just make all this unpleasantness go away, a larger part of her knew glossing over this bitter misunderstanding wouldn't help. They had to talk it out, as honestly as possible, even if it hurt them both. "Easier said than done," Laura said, digging even more sharply into the dirt.

He watched as she turned over another small row of soil.

"I'm sorry I said what I did. I know you didn't mean to come between me and Janey." At the genuine contrition in his voice, she looked up and met his eyes. They were laced with worry as he continued solemnly, "But you've got to realize that I'm Janey's dad. I have final say over what she does or does not do or wear or buy."

Her anger at his patronizing attitude flaring anew, Laura dug her spade even more sharply into the dirt. "And the fact I'm her mother counts for nothing. Is that it?"

She hadn't meant to say those words, hadn't even known she felt them, until now. As shocked as he was by the revelation of what was in her heart, she let her hand go limp. Her mouth dropped open. Zach was silent, too. Finally she dared a glance deep into his eyes and saw naked fear, the kind she had suffered when she'd first found out Melinda was going to die.

The breath left her lungs in one giant whoosh. Her jaw trembled, so did her hands. Tears welled in her eyes. "I'm sorry," she said softly, shaking her head and dropping her gaze. "I don't know where that came from." Somewhere, in the past few weeks, Laura had come to love Janey fiercely. She realized that now.

Looking stunned, Zach sat back in a patch of grass next to her garden, folding his legs in front of him Indian style. "Maybe we should talk about this," he said slowly.

Laura wasn't sure she agreed. They seemed to be on treacherous ground again. Opening a pack of lettuce seeds, she began sprinkling them one by one into the furrow she had created.

"Is that how you think of Janey?" Zach pressed softly. "Like she's your daughter?" he finished in a voice full of curiosity and wonder.

Although she wasn't looking at him, Laura could feel his eyes upon her, burning into her, wanting to understand. Feeling near tears, she shrugged with feigned indifference. "She's a lot like Eric—in looks, temperament, interests." And not at all like Melinda had been, she thought.

"That's not what I'm asking." When she continued to drop the seeds into the furrow, one by one, with abnormal concentration, he reached out and caught her wrist, holding it still until she was forced to meet his steady, unwavering gaze. "Do you feel she's your daughter?" he repeated in a husky, strained voice.

Laura gulped. She wanted to lie to him, but she knew she couldn't. One, she'd never get away with it. Two, her guilt would eat her alive if she did. She'd made so many mistakes already. Disavowing the depth of her maternal concern for Janey wasn't something she was willing to add to the list.

"Yes," Laura said, swallowing the knot of emotion in her throat, "I guess I do. I didn't at first," she added quickly, stung into softening her statement by the hurt look on his face. "But, as I've gotten to know her, I've felt a bond with her. I'm not sure I can explain it. I just know when I look at her that she's mine. In here." Laura placed a hand over her heart.

"And what was Melinda to you then?" he countered gruffly, an angry set to his jaw.

"She was mine, too, just the way Janey is yours."

Silence fell between them. Looking weary and emotionally embattled, he let go of her wrist.

"About the earrings," she said sitting back on her heels, "I am sorry about that. I never meant to help Janey have anything that was forbidden to her."

"I surmised that," Zach said. Idly he picked up a package of green bean seeds and turned it over to glance at the instructions on the back. With a flick of his wrist, he dropped them back on top of some other packets. His mouth thinned. "But that doesn't mean you should let it happen again."

Laura didn't want to interfere between Janey and Zach. But neither could she stand idly by and watch Zach repeat some of the mistakes her own mother had made when parenting her. "Zach..."

"What?"

For Janey's sake she knew she had to at least try to talk to him about this. He was setting a precedent here, whether he knew it or not. She took a deep breath and took off her gardening gloves. "There is such a thing as being too strict."

His face changed, his visage becoming most unwelcoming. "I thought you weren't going to interfere anymore. Laura—"

"I'm not. But what can be the harm in earrings? Those earrings are all the rage right now."

"Well, it's a rage she'll have to do without."

Anger flared in Laura. Zach was sounding exactly like her mother. "Zach, you're going to have a lot of battles with Janey over the next few years. Janey needs to assert her independence and decide what she likes, and not just do everything you want her to do, willy-nilly. That's how kids grow up and cut the apron strings.''

"It's also how they get into trouble," he prophesied grimly. "Today, it's earrings that are a little too flashy, then it's a skirt that's a tad too short. I know how these things work, too, Laura. Lots of men on my crew have teenagers who have or are getting out of hand. Harry Cole's daughter, Tabitha, was picked up for hitchhiking recently. Her only excuse was she wanted to fit in with the other kids. I'm not going to let that happen to Janey. And this is where it starts, with the little things."

Laura knew his concern was valid, one she shared. But he was going about trying to protect Janey in the wrong way. "You have to give her some breathing room," she persuaded practically.

"I will, but not about the way she looks," Zach said stubbornly.

Laura sighed. "I still think you're being unreasonable about this."

"Fine." His expression remained immobile. "I trust you'll keep your feelings to yourself and not let Janey know how you feel."

Laura knew that Janey was loved, nurtured. Zach was only doing what he felt was appropriate. Just as she did what she knew was right for Eric, even when others, like Zach or her father, thought she was being too lax.

Knowing she couldn't win, she gave in. "I promise I won't interfere."

Relief softened the line of his jaw. The beginnings of a smile curled his lips. "Then we agree to disagree and call a truce?"

Warmed by the new gentleness she saw in his eyes, Laura smiled, too. It seemed they were both as stubborn and opinionated as the day was long, and maybe that wasn't all bad. "All right. Truce."

"Are you going to plant this whole area?" Zach asked, changing the subject. He indicated a fifty-foot by ten-foot plot, partitioned off from the rest of the backyard by railroad ties.

"Yes," Laura said.

His brow furrowed. "And you're going to till all the soil by hand?" When Laura nodded, he asked, "Don't you have a Rototiller?"

"I wish. No, I don't."

"And I don't suppose you want to hire anyone to do it for you."

Shrugging, she admitted, "That seems like a lot of trouble and expense for a job I am perfectly capable of doing myself."

Zach frowned. "You really shouldn't have to work so hard," he murmured.

Wordlessly, she shook her head.

"What?" he prompted.

"I'm just not used to having anyone fuss over me, that's all. I've done it this way for years, Zach."

His brow furrowed. "Your husband never felt it was too much for you? He didn't help at least ready the soil?"

Laura flushed self-consciously. "He was in the Navy, remember? And even when he was here when it was time to plant, it never occurred to him to offer to help me care for the garden."

Zach frowned, looking chivalrous and disapproving again, as if he couldn't understand anyone being there and not helping. "That didn't bother you?" he asked softly.

At the time, Laura hadn't given it much thought. Or at least she had tried not to. Now that Zach brought it up, though, she realized she had harbored resentments about the life they had lived. Shrugging carelessly, she allowed, "We didn't share that much. I mean, how could we? He was always gone, at least half the year. At that time, they spent six months at sea, six months at home. When he was here…well, suffice it to say, the kids were all over him. They missed having a daddy. I didn't want to interfere in that." Suddenly needing the emotional release physical activity provided, she started digging again.

Beside her, Zach picked up a spade too, and began tilling the soil several feet away. "That's understandable," he said.

"Yes, but it wasn't any way to conduct a marriage." Laura sighed. She knew she had to be honest with him about this. She knew if he was ever going to understand her, she had to tell him what she'd not confided in anyone else. "The simple truth of the matter is, had Rob lived, we never would have stayed married. We would have been divorced by now." Zach wasn't the only one who'd had an imperfect marriage and maybe it was time he knew that.

Stunned, Zach momentarily stopped what he was doing and stared at her. "I'm sorry," he said.

Laura shrugged and kept digging. "We married too young, for all the wrong reasons. He wanted to have children, to have something and someone to come home to and I wanted to be on my own, grown-up. And for me, marrying Rob was the fastest way to get away from my mother and live my own life."

"So you married."

"Yes," she reported sadly. "Fancying myself a modern-day Juliet to his Romeo, I eloped with him. Only it wasn't as wildly romantic as I had thought it would be," she admitted, digging hard in the soil again. "When it really came down to it, we didn't have a lot in common and he spent a lot of time out with the guys when he was home."

"That doesn't sound like fun."

She shrugged again, realizing she'd just made Rob sound like an ogre. "It wasn't all bad. I mean the homecomings were very passionate and—" She stopped and blushed self-consciously, realizing what she had just blurted out in her effort to make him understand what her married life had been like.

He grinned. "Makes sense."

Blushing even more, Laura plowed on, explaining, "But his homecomings were always empty, too. We were like strangers. It was hard, getting to know each other again. I was going through a lot of changes while he was gone, growing, and then when the kids came along, it became even more strained between us. I ruled the house. Then he would come home and he would want the final word." She shook her head in regret, remembering how bitterly they had quarreled at times.

"A bit of a power struggle, hmm?"

Laura nodded sadly, admitting, "And then some."

"Is that why you would've divorced?"

Laura nodded. "The sad part is in retrospect I'm not sure I ever did really love him. Still I knew how traumatic it would be for the kids to go through a divorce, so I tried to work through the problems, only to find out the willingness to compromise and change was all on my side. He just didn't think it was necessary. And that's when his ship was sent to the Gulf of Sidra, off the coast of Libya. He was part of the U.S. Navy task force that was conducting exercises there. He was in a plane that was hit by an anti-aircraft missile and he was killed instantly."

"I'm sorry," Zach said softly, covering her gloved hand with his own.

She stared down at their entwined palms, his looking so solid and strong over her more delicate one. "I never told anyone what I just told you about the problems in my marriage," Laura admitted quietly, unable to help feeling ashamed about her failure. "I never even told my parents."

His hand tightened over hers. "Not to worry, kiddo. Your secret is safe with me."

Looking into his eyes, she knew she could trust him.

Suddenly she felt immensely relieved. As if she had been to confession and received absolution for her sins. Deciding a change of subject was in order, she said lightly, "I don't know about you but my throat is so dry it's killing me. How about a glass of lemonade, maybe a couple of cookies to go with it?'' She dusted off her gloved hands. ''I'd say with all the activity we've earned a caloric splurge.''

''Sounds good to me.''

Holding out a hand, he helped her to her feet. ''I'm glad you talked to me,'' he said softly.

''So am I.'' And she was glad they had stopped fighting about Janey. She didn't want to argue with him. It simply hurt too much.

THE NEXT DAY Zach went to work whistling. Harry Cole was already there, waiting in Zach's office. ''You're in early,'' he remarked, surprised.

''With good reason,'' Harry admitted in a fatigued voice. ''I know I haven't given you any advance notice, Zach, and I apologize for it, but I need a couple of days off.''

''Anything wrong?''

Harry nodded sadly. ''It's Tabitha again. She and her mother have been fighting all weekend. Mostly about this new bunch of friends Tabitha has. They've got Tabitha saying and doing all sorts of things.''

''Worse than the hitchhiking?''

Harry shrugged as if that were hard to decide. ''We found her climbing out her window Saturday night, trying to sneak out.''

''Tabitha?'' Zach did a double take. She was so young, the same age as Janey!

''Yes, anyway, I promised my wife I'd take the next couple days off. We're going to try to figure out what to do with Tabitha. We're thinking of putting her in a private school. There's one in Dallas we're going to drive over and look at. Oh—I know she's missed the last two practices and games, but I promise you she'll be there on Saturday for the last one. Her mother and I are both insisting. We're hoping if she's with a group of clean-cut kids again she'll realize how far off the track she's been."

"Well, if it will help convince her to come, we're playing a tough team. We could really use her," Zach admitted, as worried about Harry as he was about Tabitha.

"I'll tell her," Harry said agreeably. "In the meantime, maybe Tabitha will take her mother and I seriously and stop wearing all that trashy black and purple makeup on her eyes."

Remembering Janey's earrings and how he had successfully nipped that behavior in the bud, Zach asked, "You've told her it's forbidden?"

"Yes." Harry shook his head. "She wears it anyway. Says if her mother doesn't get off her back she'll dye her hair purple, too. Well, I better go. I'll be back Wednesday."

Zach nodded. "Take care of your family." That was the most important thing.

"Thanks, Zach," Harry said gratefully. As he slipped out the trailer door, a woman of regal bearing, in a starched yellow shirtdress and heels, walked in. "Mr. Anderson?" The woman, who looked vaguely familiar to Zach, held out her hand. "I'm Laura Matthews's mother, Grace. I hope you don't mind me dropping in like this?"

"Sit down." Zach said. He hadn't yet had time to make coffee. He searched around, looking for something to offer her, all the while hoping nothing was wrong with Laura or Eric. "Can I get you something to drink? A cola perhaps or a glass of juice?"

"No, nothing, thank you. I'm only here to ask you to dinner at my home. My husband and I would like to meet our granddaughter."

Feeling a little shaken, he regarded his guest cautiously. "Does Laura know you're here?"

Grace shook her head. "No. And I'm sure she'd be furious if she knew. You see, I've been trying to convince her to issue a similar invitation herself for weeks now."

"But she refused?"

"She thought it would be too hard on Janey." Grace fingered her pearls. "I would never want to do anything to harm her but I also think she has a right to get to know her natural grandparents."

Zach was silent. Laura had been right in initially warning Grace off about approaching him. A few weeks ago he would not have warmed to this idea at all, but now, it didn't seem like such a bad idea. Particularly since Janey's own grandparents were living far away, having retired in Florida and Arizona respectively.

"It seems like a fine idea, but my schedule is rather full at the moment. May I call you?" If he was going to do this, he wanted Laura and Eric there, too.

"Certainly." Looking victorious, Grace drew a small notepad and pen from her purse and neatly penned her telephone number. "I'll look forward to hearing from you, Mr. Anderson," Grace said as she rose.

Unhappily, Laura wasn't nearly as receptive when Zach dropped by and she heard what her mother had done. "I specifically told her not to call you!" she said furiously, her fists knotted at her side.

"Well, she didn't call me. She called on me," Zach joked, trying to ease the situation.

"You don't understand, Zach. She always does this to me! She feels she has to control my life!"

"It's just one dinner, Laura."

"It's the principle of the thing, Zach. I specifically told her not to do this and she did it anyway."

He knew how it felt to have someone go over your head. But he also knew a determined woman when he saw one and Grace was not about to give up. "Maybe you should just humor her, Laura. This once."

Laura continued looking at him as if he was the worst sort of traitor. "She thinks my opinions aren't valid. She thinks she is the only person who ever knows what is right."

"Then make her listen," Zach advised. "And don't stop until she does."

Laura looked up at him, stunned by his reaction. Obviously she had expected him to take her side regardless, but he couldn't do that. "I know how irritating parents can be sometimes, Laura," he said in gentle sympathy. "I've had problems off and on with my own, over the years. But they're not going to be here forever. Remembering that can make it easier to work things out. The bottom line is they love you."

Laura sighed. "Do you have to make so much sense?" she asked plaintively. Making a fist, she batted playfully at his chest.

Zach laughed and caught her hand in his, caressing it lightly. "Only when I'm right."

As Laura glanced up at him, her brown eyes grew velvet soft. Her lips parted slightly. Desire stirred inside him. He wanted to kiss her, but he had the feeling if he did that just now, he might not stop there.

His decision made, he took her by the shoulders, turned her around and pointed her in the direction of the phone. "Now call her. Set this dinner up and then forget about it." Contenting himself, for now, with only cursory contact, he pressed a kiss to the top of her head.

Laura groaned and murmured a reluctant, comical excuse.

"Do it. Because we have much better things to think about." He wrapped his arms around her waist and held her close, cloaking her with his body heat. She relaxed against him, feeling so soft and warm and right. It was all he could do to keep track of what he'd been about to say. "Starting with what we're going to do tonight. Maybe the four of us could go out to dinner."

Zach had sensed a definite softening in Eric's attitude toward him, since he'd showed him how to replace a car battery. And he wanted it to continue. Because only if Eric accepted him, as Janey had already accepted Laura, could he and Laura ever have a future together.

Chapter Thirteen

"I'm so glad you could come!" Janey said as Laura and Eric walked into the gym. "I really wanted you to see my last game."

"We wouldn't have missed it," Laura said, warmly returning Janey's welcoming hug.

"Yeah, and I brought our camera," Eric threw in. "So be sure you turn and smile in my direction as you're scoring all those points."

Janey scoffed at him. "You're crazy. I can't think about pictures when I'm playing a game."

Eric viewed her with mock skepticism. "I don't know why not," he said, his eyes glimmering. "All the girls I know spend every waking moment trying to look good." Seeing the growing outrage on Janey's face, he put up both hands in front of him, as if comically trying to ward off a blow. "Think of it as good practice for when you get older and are desperately trying to land a boyfriend."

"Very funny, big shot." Knowing it was expected of her, Janey landed a teasing blow to his shoulder.

Leaving the two to continue their good-natured bantering, Laura walked over to say hello to Zach. Several feet away, he had been watching the playful exchange between their two children with a look of quiet satisfaction on his face. She knew how he felt. It was good to see them getting along so well.

"Hi," she said shyly.

"Hi." He looked happy to see her, too.

Their increasing closeness left them both silent, searching self-consciously for something to say. "I hope Eric's being here won't distract Janey."

"I wouldn't worry about it," he advised with cheerful authority, looking very capable and handsome in his gold Lady Tigers shirt. "When the action starts, all her attention will be on the floor. The President could be in the stands and Janey would never know."

Laura smiled, feeling blissfully happy and alive. "I know exactly what you mean. Eric's the same way." It was all she could do to stand motionless and not stand on tiptoes to give him a pregame hug for good luck. "I hope you win."

"So do I." His eyes glimmered affectionately as they roved her face. "But either way," he promised, "we'll have fun."

Without warning, there was a commotion at the other end of the gym. Laura turned to see a girl with vivid purple hair and black eyeliner arguing with her father. She had on a gold shirt that identified her as being a member of Zach's team.

"Poor Harry," Zach murmured, concern radiating from his eyes. "He really has his hands full with Tabitha." He sent Laura an apologetic glance. "Since this is the first game she's been to in several weeks, I better go over and say hello."

While Zach walked over to join Harry and his wayward daughter, Janey walked up to Laura. "Can you believe what she's done to her hair?" Janey asked incredulously. "It used to be brown, like mine."

No doubt about it, Laura thought, Tabitha had ruined her hair. That color would probably take a year to grow out, and that was if she sacrificed a good deal of the shoulder-length strands.

Knowing this was the type of touchy situation that needed tactful handling, Laura advised, "I wouldn't say anything about the color to Tabitha, Janey. Just let her know you're glad she's here today and then concentrate on playing a good game."

"I will," Janey promised. "See you later, Laura." She ran off to join her father.

Laura climbed into the stands. With the exception of the purple-haired Tabitha, who remained slumped on a seat at the far end of the Lady Tigers bench, all the girls on Zach's team went through their warm-up drills. When their ten minutes had ended, they all gathered around Zach. Laura watched with a mixture of pride and affection, as Zach's team put their hands together and shouted "Go Tigers!" with a maximum amount of team spirit before running off onto the floor. It was clear, by the adoring way the girls looked at him, and the attentive way they listened to him talk, they all had a lot of respect for their coach. And it was a respect he deserved, she had decided by the end of the first quarter when the Tigers were ahead, 10 to 6.

As was the rule for league games, when the first quarter team came out, the second team went in. Tabitha was among those tapped to play. She left the bench reluctantly while her father glowered at her from the stands. She tromped over to Zach. It looked as though she was telling Zach she did not want to play.

Zach listened quietly while she talked, then put his hand on her shoulder and said something. There was a moment of silence between the two. Then amazingly, Tabitha went in.

The girls on the bench exchanged tense looks. Laura had an idea what they were feeling. As did Eric. "If this Tabitha screws up, the Tigers could lose their lead," he whispered.

"I know. Let's hope she gives it her all," Laura said.

Unfortunately she didn't. And by the time one minute had passed, two rival team players had gotten by her and scored to tie up the game. Zach signaled to his point guard, who called a time out. The girls returned to the huddle. Laura could see there was some fighting going on, as the other teammates, who were rightfully angered by Tabitha's attitude on the court, started in on her. Laura watched as Zach spoke to all of them, and then to Tabitha.

The game resumed. Tabitha did a little better, but because she was out of shape, she wasn't able to keep up with the others. The other team scored. Fortunately, despite Tabitha's sluggish performance, the Tigers were also able to score. By the half, the teams were tied again.

"Janey's doing great," Eric said as she scored her tenth point at the end of the third quarter.

"You've helped her a lot with her lay-ups," Laura responded.

"Yeah, well she's a great student," Eric said.

Yes, she was, Laura thought. And she had Eric's talent for handling the ball.

The quarter ended with the Tigers ahead by six points. The final quarter began. "I can't believe he's putting Tabitha back in again," Eric moaned.

"It's only fair," Laura whispered back discreetly. "All the other girls are playing two quarters each."

"Yeah, but, to lose now, because of her," Eric muttered.

Unfortunately her son's prophecy was right. The other team quickly took advantage. When the other team took the lead, because of Tabitha's mistake, one of the disgruntled fathers yelled, "Oh, wake up out there, will you?"

Tabitha burst into tears. Almost instantly, Zach was on his feet, calling time out. He jogged out onto the floor, toward Tabitha. Try as he might, he couldn't calm her. When the buzzer sounded, he had no choice but to call another player from the bench to replace her. Still sobbing, Tabitha stalked toward the exit. Her father ran to catch up with her. When he did, Tabitha whirled on him angrily, "I told you I didn't want to play!" she screamed hysterically. "I told you I was no good! But would you listen to me? No! You had to make me play! I hate you! Do you hear me? I hate you!"

She bolted from the gym, her distressed father following closely on her heels.

"Jeez," Eric said. "Was she ever upset!"

Laura silently concurred. Seeing how much pain they were in, her heart went out to both of them. Poor Zach; he'd been put in the middle of it.

Fortunately the game continued without further incident. Zach's team recovered the lead and amidst excited cheering from the parents in the stands, went on to victory. Afterward, the whole team went for pizza. Laura, Eric, and others tagged along. At six, Eric glanced at his watch. "I better go. I've got a date."

"Be home by midnight," Laura warned.

"I will. Bye Mom." He leaned over to kiss her on the cheek. "Zach." He held out his hand. For the first time in weeks, respect glimmered in Eric's eyes. "You were great, coaching the girls today," he said.

Zach beamed. He met Eric's gaze, man-to-man. "I'm glad you were there," he said simply. Eric nodded while a grateful Laura marveled over the peace that had been made.

No sooner had Eric left, than Janey came up to join them. "Chrissy's having a slumber party tonight for the whole team," she said without preamble, looking at Zach for permission. "Can I go?"

"Sure," Zach said. "Just do me a favour and try to get some sleep this time."

"Oh, Dad!" Janey shook her head as if he'd just said the silliest thing in the whole world. "Get real." Zach laughed and Janey continued, "Is it okay if I go home with Chrissy? Her parents said they'd drop by our house and let me run in and get my stuff."

Zach gave his approval. Seconds later, the restaurant had cleared out. "Some day you've had," Laura said, leaning back in her chair. Now that the rest of the guests were gone, the restaurant had a cozy feel to it.

Zach nodded. "Want to go home?"

Laura didn't even have to think about that. Her eyes still holding his, she shook her head. "Do you want me to?"

He shook his head. They both smiled.

His hand covered hers warmly. "So, what'll we do this evening?"

Laura shrugged, aware that both her heartbeat and spirits had picked up immeasurably in one short minute. She hadn't felt this happy or content in a long, long time. And it was all because of Zach. "I'll let you decide."

ZACH DECIDED on a movie. Afterward, still not ready to part company, they went back to his house for coffee. As it started to brew, he went to check his answering machine. "Any messages?" Laura asked, having an idea what was on his mind.

Zach shook his head and didn't try to hide his disappointment. "I was hoping I'd hear from Harry," he confided.

"Why don't you call and check on them?" she urged.

"You wouldn't mind?"

"Not at all." Laura smiled.

Unfortunately, when he came back several minutes later, he didn't seem cheered. Laura was seated at the kitchen table, cup of coffee in hand. "Well?" she prompted immediately, anxious to hear the news, good or bad.

Zach sighed heavily and reached for a mug. "Tabitha's still pretty upset. Harry said she's locked herself in her room."

"I'm sorry."

"I am, too. He's a nice guy." Zach sat down across from her and shook his head in bewilderment. "Tabitha used to be pretty sweet, too. I don't know what's come over her the past few months. Harry says she's been running with a wild crowd."

"Maybe he should ease up on her," Laura suggested.

"That's the problem," Zach disagreed. "I think he's been too easy thus far."

"You don't know that," Laura said quietly.

Zach nodded. "You're right. It's probably pointless to speculate. So let's not talk about them anymore. Let's talk about us."

Us. The word had a wonderful ring to it. Aware her heart was beating very fast as his eyes roamed her hair, her eyes, her mouth, she croaked, "What about us?"

He shrugged, a new and different light coming into his eyes. "Anything. Everything," he said, a possessive sound to his voice.

He was close enough for her to inhale the scent of his cologne, close enough she could see the sprinkling of hair above the open V of his shirt. He had changed into jeans in the locker room after the game, and those jeans, so soft and worn, clung to his thighs as though they were custom-made, revealing taut calves, powerful thighs. His stomach was as flat as a washboard and just as taut and strong-looking as the rest of him. And lower still, the denim was even tighter and more revealing. Shyly, her heart tripping madly in her chest, she forced her eyes away. She didn't need to see that, didn't need to think about it.

He clasped her hand and drew her slowly to her feet.

Although she was laudably inexperienced, having only ever been with one man, her husband, sex or the possibility of it had never scared her. But then, this didn't feel like simple desire. It felt like much more, like commitment, compromise, devotion. All the things she had tried to give before when she had failed.

"What about your coffee?" she asked, panicking ever so slightly as the erotic look in his eyes deepened and grew.

"My coffee can wait," Zach said softly, brushing the dark brown stands of hair from her face.

Whereas he evidently could not, for no sooner had he murmured the soft, decisive words than his mouth was on hers, evoking a sweet response. The dizzying anticipation faded as a languid, sensual weakness stole over her, pushing her doubts aside. It was as if she had waited a lifetime for this moment, to let their feelings for each other grow to fruition, to experience his gentle loving. "You feel good," he murmured, holding her close.

So did he.

His face very close to hers, his blue eyes both searching and intent, he said, "If you want me to take you home, I will." He paused and his voice dropped another emotional note, "But, if not—Laura—"

He didn't finish the sentence. He didn't have to. She knew to stay would be asking him to make love to her. And although there wasn't anything she wanted more in the entire world, her doubts about herself, her fears, were still plaguing her. She didn't want to lose him. And she was afraid. If she didn't measure up—Zach was a man who deserved, who commanded, so much....

Reading her indecision, knowing her personal history and perhaps guessing at the reason why, he gently pressed his mouth to hers, exploring the tender inner flesh with his tongue. His arms holding her possessively, he repeated the tender, evocative caress again and again, each time going a little deeper, a little slower. Never had anyone kissed her so passionately, with just the right amount of pressure and heat. The sharp urgency of desire melded with the wonder of finding themselves together, in this way, at long last. A part of her had known it would happen, almost from the first. She had a suspicion he had known, too.

Realizing the searing depth of her need and his, she pressed closer and gave a tiny moan. As they continued to kiss, sensations splintered through her until every inch of her body cried out with wanting him. But it was more than just simple desire driving her, she realized shakily, exquisite as their ardor was. Cradled in his arms she felt loved. She felt safe. She felt wanted. Important. As if for the first time in her life she was everything she was supposed to be. And more, everything he had ever wanted. And there was a part of her, however selfish, that just didn't want to let that go.

A shudder ran through his body at the completeness of her response. "Oh, Laura," he whispered, burying his lips in her throat. "God. I don't know...if...I can...stop."

That said, he kissed her again, demandingly. Trembling, snuggling closer and closer to the heat and power of his body, she erotically deepened the kiss, tasting him as he had tasted her until he could take no more and had to stop and draw in a ragged breath.

"Laura, my sweet lovely Laura," he whispered as their embrace softened tenderly and they kissed again, this time with gentle, fragile balance. Over and over they touched and caressed until she felt the insistent nudge of his arousal against her, burning and tempting. He skimmed his hands down her breasts. Her hands swept lower to his hips and thighs. And it was all there in an instant, the sensation she was losing control and wanting it that way.

In that second, time froze and the clarity and meaning of the moment struck her. What they were about to do would change their lives forever. And she wanted it that way, she wanted the passion and the sensation of being truly, completely alive for the first time since her daughter and husband had died. She knew she would remember forever the whisper of his clothes against hers, the warmth of his skin emanating through the cloth, the unique male fragrance of his skin and cologne, the gentleness of his touch, and the splendid sight of him, so tall and handsome, so drawn to her.

Finally she was experiencing the total love and adoration of a good man. She wanted to cherish it, draw it out, and make it last. So much of the good in her life had passed in an instant. But not this. This was one moment she was going to savor and hold on to for the rest of her life. "I want you," she whispered, "so much."

His hands captured hers, held them still. He didn't want to be accused later of unfairly seducing her. "You're sure?"

She nodded. "I've never been more sure of anything in my life," she avowed. And she meant it. Yet when he took her by the hand and led her upstairs, to his bedroom, she felt an unsettling and unexpected wave of anxiety. He slanted her an intrigued, compassionate glance. "This is a big step for you, isn't it?"

"Yes."

"And you're frightened," he said, taking her trembling hand in his and pressing a kiss to it.

"Not of you," she swore. But of my own inadequacy, she thought.

He lifted his head, his eyes searching hers. He didn't understand. "Then of what?"

She swallowed. "It's been so long. I'm not sure I—oh, Zach, I don't want you to be disappointed."

"Believe me," he said assuredly, lifting her chin and pressing a light, reverent kiss on her lips, "I won't be."

She lifted her head and saw all the tenderness she had ever wished for reflected in the depths of his blue eyes.

"If we're going to be absolutely honest, this isn't going to be so easy for me, either." He grinned self-consciously and in doing so, drew a smile from her, too. "In case you didn't know, I haven't exactly been hopping from bed to bed the past few years. If you think it's too soon. If you want to wait..."

Melinda's death had taught her to take each moment as it came, to savor the present as if there was no tomorrow. And that was exactly what she planned to do. But now he was the one who needed convincing. She took his mouth, showing him how much she cared about him, how much she had to give. Reassured he wasn't taking unfair advantage, he showed her all there was to discover. About herself, about him.

He kissed her cheeks, her forehead, her chin, then blazed an erotic path down her neck to the soft womanly curves of her breasts. The warmth of his hands followed the slow unbuttoning of her blouse, the unclasping of her bra. He knew how to touch her, how to mold and explore and caress. When his mouth opened hotly over hers again, she found herself clinging, holding nothing in reserve. And though kissing him, holding him, was wonderful, it wasn't nearly enough. Not anymore. She wanted to touch him as he was touching her. Her fingers managed the first button, and then the next, until she had uncovered his sleek-muscled chest with the tufts of light brown hair that arrowed down into the waistband of his jeans.

"I'm not in any hurry," he murmured languidly, looking very pleased as she slipped the cloth from his shoulders and his shirt dropped to the floor to join hers. "You?"

She shook her head and, gasping as his thumb rubbed over her nipple, caught her breath. As she swayed against him, an enervating, sensual weakness stole over her. "As far as I'm concerned, we could do this forever."

The rest of their clothes followed slowly, drifting piece by piece to the floor. When they were free of encumbrances, he buried his face in the fragrant depths of her hair and held her close. The sensation of being held skin to skin with him was electrifying, a hint of the fulfillment to come. Taking her hand, he led her to the wide comfortable bed with the crisp dark green sheets. He followed her down to the mattress and stretched out beside her. Lying side by side, they kissed and touched their fill. She couldn't remember ever feeling so whole. So free. So accepted for who and what she was. "You surprise me," he said as she moved over him.

She glowed with his throatily voiced praise. "I'm surprising myself," she murmured back. "And you know why?" She kissed the flat plain of his abdomen and tasted the salty tang of his skin.

He threaded an idle hand through the silk of her hair. "Tell me."

"Because there's never been—" and never will be, she amended silently "—a night like tonight."

"For me, either," he acknowledged softly. Catching her suddenly beneath the arms, he slid her up and over so she was flat on her back, trapped beneath the sensually pleasurable weight of his body and the mattress.

The time for waiting was past; they both knew it. His tumescent flesh throbbing, he slid between her thighs. She opened herself up to him and then he was inside her, ridding her of the deep, aching emptiness, filling her with pulsing male power, heat, and strength. For the first time in her life she knew what it was like to be loved and accepted completely. Happiness sifted through her as they began their slow, inevitably erotic dance. And then the last thin barrier of reserve was ripped away. She knew only pleasure as they moved together in delicate harmony, tears of release streaming down her face. She felt only the thundering of his heart against her breasts, felt only the love and care in the arms around her, and then all was lost in the consuming, enveloping heat.

LAURA LAY EXHAUSTED, her damp cheek pressed against his shoulder, his body still a part of hers, although he had rolled slightly, relieving her of the bulk of his weight. Delicately his hand dried the dampness on her face. "Why were you crying?"

She shrugged shyly. "For silly reasons." Feminine reasons. "Because it was so good. Because you made me feel so loved. Because I've never felt quite that way before. So abandoned and replete."

"Did I really do all that?" he asked in wonder. His hand cupped her chin, forcing her gaze up and his voice was very

soft and very tender. "I'm glad I made you happy, Laura."
His voice dropped a husky notch. "I wanted to make you
feel loved. Because you should be. You are one hell of a
woman, Laura Matthews."

The way he said it, the way he hugged her, made her
smile. She pressed a tender kiss to his shoulder. "And you're
the nicest, most loving man I've ever met." If only this moment could last forever, she thought, gripping him tighter.
If only they could hang on to these feelings of peace and
contentment. If only they didn't soon have to face the in-
truding reality of their everyday lives, with all the atten-
dant frustrations and complications that went with them.
But now that the passion had faded, reality had intruded
and she was thinking of how complicated their lives were
again. And how very much she didn't want to give this up.

"Why the frown?" He traced the furrows between her
brows, then lovingly drew his index finger softly along the
southernmost curve of her lip.

Laura sighed and cuddled closer, needing to feel his
warmth and strength for just a little while longer. The truth
wasn't going to be easy to say, but she knew he deserved to
hear it. "I don't trust unencumbered happiness," she admitted after a moment, thinking how little of it she'd had in
her life. "When something feels this good, I find myself
waiting for the next catastrophe to hit."

His eyes darkened compassionately. He reassured her
firmly, "You can trust this, Laura. What we've found with
each other is the kind of thing that lasts."

His confidence was catching. Laura smiled. He was right.
She was silly to be so wary of the future.

Unfortunately a glance at the clock beside his bed told her
it was after ten. Time was passing with alarming speed. She
frowned again, not happy about this, either. "I have to be
home by twelve, to make sure Eric makes his curfew."

Zach smiled and turned to her, so that she was once again
lying on her back, beneath him. "Well, then, Cinderella,"

he drawled, "I guess we better get started because you're not getting out of here until I show you how I feel, at least one more time...."

Laura was all for that.

Grinning, she smoothed her hands across his shoulders, and promised, "I've got a few things to show you, too."

"YOU AND LAURA have been spending a lot of time together haven't you?" Laura's father said several weeks later as he and Zach worked side by side to install a ceiling fan in Laura's kitchen.

Zach nodded. Since the night he and Laura had made love they'd managed to see each other or talk on the phone every day. "Does that bother you?" he asked as he tightened yet another bolt.

Her father shook his head. "I'm glad the two of you can be friends. Or is it more than that?"

Zach knew these were the kinds of questions her dad should be asking Laura. He also knew as private a person as Laura was, they were exactly the kind of questions she was likely not to answer. "It's more than that," Zach said.

"How much more? Enough to get married?"

Her dad didn't pull any punches. But then he had more or less suspected that about him the first time they'd met. Knowing his directness was prompted by caring, made it tenable. "Maybe," Zach allowed. Probably. They just weren't there yet. It was enough now that they were together, that Eric was beginning to accept him, and that Laura no longer interfered in his parenting of Janey.

"Can you hand me the third blade?"

"Sure." Reaching for it, Zach couldn't help but notice the picture of Melinda on the windowsill. It had been taken when she was still healthy. She was curled up in a chair, a book in her hands, her eyes sparkling merrily, a saucy grin on her face. She looked so happy there. As Laura must have been. What had it been like to lose her? Zach wondered.

What had she looked like when she was ill? he thought, and then as soon as the thought came, he pushed it away.

"You don't talk much about Melinda, do you?" her dad asked as Zach handed him the third blade and watched as he screwed it to the rotund brass base.

"Not a lot, no." Her father raised a brow, and Zach found himself adding, somewhat defensively, "There isn't much point, now that she's gone."

"Isn't there?" Laura's dad asked mildly. "Hand me that fourth blade, will you?"

Zach went to get it. Returning, he said, "No, there isn't."

Again her father raised a skeptical brow. "If you want to know Laura, you have to know about that time in her life."

Although normally open to discussion about most anything, Zach found himself resenting the older man's advice. Maybe because it was true and he knew it but didn't want to face it. "That's up to her, what she wants to tell me," he countered gruffly. *And when.*

"I suppose it is. Just bear in mind Laura's a sensitive woman. She knows what makes other people uncomfortable. She usually avoids it."

Her dad's words stayed with him the rest of the day, haunting him, long after he'd said goodbye to Laura and gone back home. By late evening, he knew what he had to do. He'd been putting it off too long.

He called Laura. "Are you busy?"

"No, just sitting here in the kitchen, winding down after a long day, admiring my new ceiling fan."

The pleasure in her low voice made him smile. It took so little to make her happy. "How's Eric?"

"He went to bed early. He was tired."

"So did Janey." Zach paused, knowing he was about to ask a lot of her, but knowing her father was right, it had to be done. "I know it's late, but would you mind coming over, just for a little while?"

Concern radiated in her voice. "What's up?"

Zach found he was clenching the phone cord. "I want to know about Melinda," he said calmly. "I think it's time we talked. Don't you?"

ZACH'S GUT was in knots by the time Laura arrived, a box of old photos in hand. "Are you sure you want to do this?" she asked. She knew how he hated talking about things that hurt. Whatever had prompted his decision, there was no denying it was a major step. One he had needed to make for a long time.

Needing to feel as close to her as possible, Zach laced an arm around Laura's shoulders and walked her into the family room. "I've been avoiding dealing with this a long time," he admitted candidly. He swallowed hard. "Maybe because I just wasn't up to it. But a talk I had with your father this afternoon made me realize I can't go on hiding from it forever." Zach shook his head, knowing how painful an occasional glimpse into Melinda's illness was, knowing he had to somehow find the courage to stop telling himself it didn't matter, and examine his buried feelings. He had to find a way to heal them. He knew, if anyone could help him, it was Laura.

Laura touched his arm, not only able to see his fear, but empathize with it, "Zach," she said softly, "if you want to wait on this, I'll understand."

He shook his head. "No. Sooner or later we have to talk about this, Laura, all of it. If we don't, it will always be between us." And he didn't want anything between them.

Her face clouded with uneasiness as she took his hand in hers and clasped it firmly. "All right. We'll talk," she said determinedly, a mixture of sadness and apprehension in her low voice. "But first we need some coffee because I think it's going to be a long night."

LAURA STAYED in the family room, sorting photos while Zach went to make their coffee. The truth was, she wasn't all that thirsty; she had just needed a moment to herself, to pull herself together.

She had never been able to talk about Melinda's death without breaking down. And being with someone who was sympathetic made it all the worse. Indifference, thoughtlessness, even cruelty she could handle, but kindness always undid her. And if there was one thing Zach was to his very soul, it was kind. And she knew right now, more than anything, he really needed her to be strong.

He returned carrying a tray with a thermal carafe, two mugs, and a plate of homemade chocolate-chip cookies. "Here we go."

Delaying the inevitable as long as possible, Laura picked up a cookie and bit into it. "Let me guess. Your housekeeper made these."

"For that, the lady wins a kiss." He leaned forward to touch his lips lightly to hers. She melted into the tenderness of his embrace. If only they didn't have to go through this, she thought. What if he felt she was to blame for Melinda's death? What if he thought there was something more she could have done, or should have known?

"Laura," he said gently, feeling suddenly like the worst kind of heel for putting her through this. "Are you okay?"

Looking at the strain lines around his eyes, she knew this wasn't any easier on him than it was on her. She took a deep, hitching breath. "Yes," she said, accepting the mug he handed her and curling her hands, with their telltale shakiness, around the fragrant, steaming warmth. "I am. I just don't know where to start, that's all."

"Start at the beginning," he said softly, feeling now that he wanted to hear everything about his natural child whom he had never known. "From the time you took her home from the hospital. What kind of baby was she?" Happy, he hoped.

Laura rooted through the pictures she had brought and found several of Melinda wrapped in baby bunting. "She was a quiet child, from the very first. Maybe it was because Eric was such a bundle of energy at that age, but she seemed content to just watch him running around or giggle at something he said or did. She rarely cried, and then only if she was hungry or wet. She slept through the night...."

As Laura talked, it became easier. Zach found himself relaxing as they covered Melinda's toddler years and went on up into elementary.

"She was ten when she first became ill," Laura said, a quiver in her voice. "We didn't know it was cancer right away, but I knew it was bad, Zach. All I had to do was look at the doctor's faces and know that this wasn't something that was easily fixed." Her throat began to tighten, but knowing how much Zach wanted and needed to hear this, she forced herself to go on. "Melinda, of course, was only concerned with getting through the tests. Some of them were very painful. I remember how she cried and cried, particularly after the bone marrow tests." She shook her head. "I felt so helpless. I wanted to make it easier for her, but I couldn't. All I could do was sit there and hold her hand, and tell her that it was going to be all right."

Zach thought about what that must have been like, knowing her child—his child—was going to die. He didn't know how she had ever gotten through it. And he felt incredible rage against fate, knowing that she had had to get through it. It wasn't fair, dammit, he thought, struggling to hold on to his tenuous control. If Melinda hadn't been stricken, she would be here now. And I would know her the same way Laura knows Janey, he thought. But she wasn't here. And they had to find comfort in whatever way they could.

He reached blindly for Laura. Able to sense how much she was hurting, too, he held her close and said, "I'm sure your being there meant a lot to her." His eyes burned as he struggled to hold back the tears.

Laura shook her head, the anger and exhaustion she'd felt then coming back to her with amazing clarity. Withdrawing slightly, she shook her head in helpless uncertainty. And that made Zach angry, too, that she could have doubts about her capacity to love, to help and to heal.

Tears streaming down her face, Laura said, "I don't know, Zach. Sometimes I think I was more of a hindrance." She wiped her eyes and a pain almost too deep to be borne radiated in her low voice, "You see, she knew she was going to die long before I did. But I wouldn't listen to her. I wouldn't even let her say it. But she tried to help me anyway. She tried to tell me it was going to be okay, that I didn't have to be scared for her because she wasn't afraid. I wouldn't believe it of course, any more than I really believed she had cancer." She gestured helplessly.

"It's like there was this part of me deep down that was so angry and so scared, a part of me that just refused to accept that it was all really happening to us. I kept thinking it was a bad dream and I would wake up and everything would be fine again. But I didn't wake up and Melinda kept getting sicker."

Zach sorted through the pictures in the box, each one tearing his heart out a little more. Melinda in her hospital bed and gown, looking frail and helpless, but doggedly playing a game of Junior Trivial Pursuit with a nurse. Melinda with her headphones on and an IV in her arm. Melinda with hair that was so thin in places you could see her scalp. And another where she had none, and was wearing a funky black-top hat to cover her head.

Seeing him looking at that photo, Laura said sadly, "She cried when she lost her hair, because she thought she looked so ugly."

"But she didn't," Zach said, really sharing Laura's pain for the very first time, because he knew now—he could see in these pictures—exactly what she and he had both lost.

"She had a beautiful soul," Laura said reverently. "She was so kind and giving. Always concerned about the other kids at the oncology clinic."

Zach picked up a photo of Melinda, the surge of protective feelings in him incredibly strong. "Did she wear the hat because of hair loss?" Zach asked, looking at the photo again. And loving the way she looked in the hat, bald scalp and all, so brave and saucy and willing to face the next challenge.

"Yes." Laura smiled through her tears. "Being an old stodgy, I felt we could do a little better than that. So I went out and got her all kinds of wigs—blond, red, brown, even brunette. She really didn't want one because she said it was stupid—everyone knew she had lost all her hair anyway, but I persisted and finally got her to try them all on and at one point it was just so silly...because none of them looked like her. I mean we laughed until our sides ached and tears rolled down our faces and then, we ended up in each other's arms, both of us sobbing as uncontrollably as we had laughed."

Laura's pain transmitted to him in heavy waves. Struggling to maintain his composure, Zach sorted through the pictures. "Which wig did she pick?" he asked in a low, unsteady voice.

Laura gave a bleak smile. "I let her pick out four, one in each color. She wore them all and made a joke of it, telling the nurses she was the only one of them who could have a different color hair every day of the week."

He stared at her in shock, not understanding the tastelessness of the joke.

"I know, it's pretty dark humor but it got her through the really tough days," she said earnestly. "Sometimes, if you can just find a way to laugh, even for a minute..." Her voice caught and she couldn't go on.

"Did it help?" he asked, hauling in a deep, shaky breath.

Laura nodded. "Some. And then there were times—" she teared up again, looking so vulnerable that his heart went out to her "—when nothing could help."

He gripped her hands tightly. "How did you ever get through it?" he whispered, a desolate look in his eyes.

Laura shrugged. The truth was she didn't know. "I took it day by day. One minute at a time." That was all she had asked of herself, and all she had continued asking of herself until Zach came into her life. Now, for the first time since she could remember, she was wanting a future again.

As if shutting out the pain he couldn't bear to feel, he closed his eyes, his grasp on her hands becoming almost painful. When he finally spoke again, his voice was so ragged and low it was barely audible. "Did she ever get well again?"

"Yes," Laura said, relaxing a bit as she thought about that happier time. A little of the boundless joy she had felt crept into her voice. "After about a year and a half of therapy she had one remission, a brief one for six months. And it was wonderful." Laura sorted through the pictures and found several photos.

Melinda had looked great, then, Zach thought. Her hair had grown back, she had gained weight, and had some healthy color to her face.

Laura sighed, admitting, "When this photo was taken at the beginning of the school year, we thought we had the whole world by the tail." Slowly Laura lost her smile. Zach's grip on her hand tightened. "But then it hit again, and when it hit the second time, it hit her very hard, physically and emotionally." A ragged, defeated sigh escaped her parted lips. Laura eased a breath past the terrible constriction in her chest and continued in a voice brimming with painful memories. "She lost the will to fight. Eric and I tried to lift her spirits, you'll never know how we tried. But at the end, she just couldn't go on."

Zach tried to imagine what that must have been like and found his heart filled with as much pain as Laura's low voice. He wanted to bring her peace and vanquish the hurt she still felt, but found instead that increasingly, he was the one in need of comforting. Zach suffered a swift irrational pang of guilt for not being there then, not knowing, not helping.

"She went into the hospital again with pneumonia and they did everything they could for her, but—" Laura stopped, her voice breaking, and pressed a hand over her eyes "—it just wasn't enough. Her body had no strength left to fight off the infection and she died two nights later."

"In the hospital?" Zach asked softly.

Laura nodded, looking both numb and emotionally exhausted as she recounted, "Yes. Eric and I were both with her. I'm thankful for that much. But, I wished we could have had her at home, you know?"

It was foolish for her to berate herself about that, Zach thought. Taking her hand, her said, firmly, "You had no choice but to keep her hospitalized, Laura. After all, there was always a chance, even a slim one, that the hospital might have saved her. At home, she would have had no chance."

She withdrew from his touch, in too much pain to accept his sympathy. "But they didn't save her," she said sadly.

He was silent.

He had no answer for that, no way to aid her. Cursing his own helplessness, he asked, "Was she in much pain?"

"No," Laura said. "At least I don't think so," she said softly, knowing she could ease his mind about this much. "She didn't appear to be. She was drifting in and out of unconsciousness. She just came to a couple of times and when she did—" Laura was unable to help it, she teared up again and began to tremble. Folding her arms tight against her chest, she said, "—I remember her being very concerned about the two of us. She didn't want Eric and I to be

sad because she wasn't. She was at peace with her dying."
Remembering, Laura shook her head. Even now, her
daughter's courage and wisdom amazed her. "But we just
kept trying to hold on to her, to urge her back to us." And
that had been selfish of her, she knew. Guilt flooded her
anew. "And then she was gone, Zach. And a part of me and
of Eric died, too."

"It must have been very hard," he commiserated gently,
holding her.

Incapable of speech, Laura nodded. Yes, she thought, it
had been very hard. And for a brief time, until she had
started concentrating on Eric's needs again, she had thought
her whole world had ended. She, too, had wanted to die. But
her love of her son had pulled her together and made her get
through that first day after the funeral and then the next and
the next. It was Eric who had saved her. And now there was
Zach, sweet, loving Zach....

At a loss for words, Zach stroked her hair and held her
fiercely. "It's funny, the things that go through your head
at a time like that," Laura said after a moment. "I kept
picturing her in heaven with her dad, with Rob. I kept
thinking that as long as she was with him it would be okay,
that I wouldn't have to worry about her."

Zach could picture her in heaven, too. Happy and free.
Well again. With Maria. "If I had only known," he whispered in a strained voice, her trembling confession making
him aware of all he had lost and could never recapture. Of
all he would give his life to experience. Just for a moment.
"I would have been there—I could have held her—I could
have helped ease her suffering. I could have done something!" he finished in impotent rage, angry at having been
deprived of knowing his child. It angered him, too, that
Melinda had never known *him*. For she would have loved
him. Just as he now loved her. He was sure of it.

"I wish you had known her," Laura said. Their anguished glances met. Her strength depleted, her voice caught

on a sob and she broke down. For several minutes, both of them simply held each other.

"I'm sorry, so sorry you went through that," he said at last, his sorrowful voice muffled against her hair. He felt devastated by the loss. As though a part of him would never get over it. Needing to hold on to something, someone, he embraced Laura tighter. Brokenly he whispered, "It hurts that I'll never know her."

Laura drew back to face him. "You would have loved her."

Zach nodded, his eyes locked with hers, accepting all he had refused to accept for so very long. "I know."

Chapter Fourteen

The alarm went off like a siren, blasting inside his head. Zach reached for it, and then lay there in silence, exhausted but awake. The talk with Laura last night had been cathartic. He never would have guessed how much. For the first time he felt he knew his natural daughter, and he understood the loss they all had suffered.

Unfortunately Janey wasn't in the best of moods. She snapped at him over breakfast and remained strangely sullen and uncommunicative on the way to school. "Everything okay with you this morning?" he asked, stopping her before she could get out of the Wagoneer.

"Why wouldn't it be?"

There was the faintest hint of derision in her tone. Zach shrugged and took a closer look. She looked as though she hadn't slept much and there were puffy circles around her eyes. As though she'd been crying. The last time she had looked that way, he remembered, she had been in a fight with her best friend Chrissy. She hadn't appreciated answering questions then. She wouldn't now. But if she was still this upset when she got home tonight, they would talk.

Deciding it would be wise to change the subject, he said, "Don't forget. We're supposed to go bowling again tonight with Eric and Laura, so try to get your homework done right after school if at all possible. That way, we can leave right after dinner and make an early night of it.''

Something flickered in Janey's eyes. She shrugged and grabbed her backpack full of books. ''Sure, Dad. See you later.''

''Bye.'' He watched her go, still puzzled over her strange behavior. If he didn't know better, he'd think she was a little miffed at him, but that was impossible. They hadn't argued.

Hormones, he decided. A typical teenage mood swing.

When he got home from work, hours later, Janey wasn't home. There was a note from her on the counter. He picked it up and read it quickly:

Dad,
    I went to the mall with Chrissy. Won't be home until late. Go bowling without me.

                             Janey

Zach frowned. She knew she wasn't supposed to go anywhere without asking permission and that went double when they already had plans. Clamping down on his annoyance—he could read her the riot act when he saw her—he reached for the phone and dialed Chrissy's number. To his surprise, Chrissy answered on the third ring.

''Chrissy?''

''Mr. Anderson.''

She didn't sound glad to hear from him, Zach noted, stunned. In fact, contrary to her usual vivacious greeting, her voice was full of dread. Anxiety edging his voice, he asked, ''Is Janey there?''

''She's not here, Mr. Anderson.''

''I thought the two of you were going to the mall. At least that's what the note she left me said.''

"I know," Chrissy evaded politely. "She wanted me to go with her, but I couldn't. Not tonight. My mom wouldn't let me...." Chrissy's voice trailed off reluctantly.

Zach had known Chrissy long enough to realize she was hiding something. His annoyance over his daughter's unexpected wayward behavior turned to worry. What was going on here? Knowing he had no other choice but to put his daughter's friend on the spot, he asked bluntly, "Chrissy, do you know where Janey is now?"

There was a telltale silence on the other end. Zach's sense that his daughter was in trouble increased dramatically.

"Chrissy, please. I'm worried about her." And if Zach was reading Chrissy's unusual unease right, she was worried about Janey, too.

"She might be at the mall."

Zach shook his head in confusion. "At the mall? How did she get there? If your mother didn't take her—" The two of them always went with Chrissy's mom. Another telling silence. Zach's panic began to mount.

Chrissy said, "Look, Mr. Anderson, you're a nice guy and all but please don't ask me any more questions because I don't rat on my friends."

So Janey was up to something shady and stupid. Zach warned firmly, "Chrissy, you either tell me all of what you know, or I come over and tell your parents. And then we'll all talk this out. But one way or another I am going to track my daughter down. If you care about her, if you're really her friend, you'll help me find her and make sure she's all right."

Chrissy sighed then asked hesitantly, "You promise you won't tell Janey how you found out she wasn't with me?"

Zach had no intention of destroying Janey's relationship with her best friend. He just wanted his daughter home, safe and sound. What in the blazes was going on with her? "I promise."

"Well, there are these guys that go to our school and they're kind of radical—"

"Speak English, please."

"Uh—wild. Anyway, they've been after me and Janey for a long time, trying to get us to sneak out with them. Like a date, you know?"

Zach felt sick inside as Chrissy continued to talk.

" . . . We always tell them no, but this morning when they asked if we wanted to go to the mall after school Janey said she'd go. I told her she was crazy and she got mad at me. We had a big fight."

"Did you make up later?"

"No. We still weren't speaking after school. I mean, I like to flirt with those guys, too. They're cute. But they're also bad news. You know, always getting into trouble with the teachers and everything. Janey's always had too much sense to run off with them. I don't know what got into her this morning. She was kind of angry, but she didn't tell me why. Did the two of you have a fight or something?"

"No, Chrissy, we didn't, and I don't know what's going on with her, either." He paused. "Do you have any idea how they got to the mall?"

"The city bus."

"And they planned to come home the same way?"

"As far as I know."

"Thanks, Chrissy."

Zach hung up and dialed Laura's number. There was no answer. Glancing at his watch, he realized she was probably still out delivering pies. He left a message on her recorder that because of a crisis at home, bowling was off. He promised to call her later, when he could.

Hanging up, he headed out to his Wagoneer.

Fortunately, Janey was just where she'd told her best friend she was going to be. She was standing in front of an ice-cream shop, surrounded by boys in faded jeans, black T-shirts, and denim jackets. All of them had earrings that looked like fishing flies dangling from one ear. Zach estimated the four boys must have each used a pint of mousse on their spiked hair, which was long on top and sheared very short on the back and sides. One had laced a possessive arm around his daughter's shoulder.

Zach started toward the group. Janey didn't see him until he was right on her. As she turned to look at him, the color left her face. The boy standing next to her realized who Zach was. No fool, he dropped his arm from her shoulders and stepped back.

Her shock over seeing him there fading fast, Janey stared at him with defiance. For a second Janey looked like a stranger. Oh, no, Zach thought. The tumultuous teenage years I've heard everyone else talk about—especially Harry Cole—have just hit me full blast. The more Janey looked at him, the more he was reminded of Tabitha.

"What are you doing here?" Janey asked rebelliously, very much aware she had an enthralled male audience on all sides of her.

"I could ask you the same question," Zach said levelly. Now that he knew she was all right, he wanted to deliver the sternest lecture she'd ever gotten in her life. But that would have to wait. Right now he had to get her out of here. Away from these boys. Who were, from the looks of it, providing support for her newfound truculent behavior.

"How did you know where to find me?" she asked.

"You left me a note, remember?" Remembering his promise to Chrissy, he looked around, "Where's Chrissy and her mom?"

Janey's lower lip slid out and she folded her arms defiantly across her chest. "They didn't come."

Janey continued to regard him contentiously. Zach sighed. This wasn't going to be easy. "Let's go."

Her jaw thrusting out even more, Janey clamped her arms even tighter against her chest and resisted his attempt to put a paternal arm around her. Hurt, confused, Zach let her go. They walked in silence to his Wagoneer.

They didn't speak on the drive home. Janey, because she was afraid—she knew she had been very disobedient and would have to pay for her infraction of the rules. Zach, because he was too careful to risk what was bound to be a heated argument or emotional scene when he was driving. He also wanted to look at her face when they talked. One way or another, he had to find out what was going on here, what was upsetting Janey so. None of this was like her at all.

Once inside the house, Janey headed for the stairs.

"Hold it right there, young lady. We're going to talk about this."

Her shoulders slumped. She sounded tired, defeated. "Do we have to?" Now that the moment of truth had come, she was practically begging for pity. But after what she'd put him through, Zach wasn't of a mind to let her off easily. Besides, if he did, she might think it would be worth it to try something like this again. And that, they simply couldn't have.

"Living room, Janey."

He followed her into the room and watched as she flounced down on the couch, her arms still folded defiantly in front of her. "You have some explaining to do. I suggest you start now. And I warn you, it had better be good."

She shrugged and gave him an unpleasant look. "What's there to explain? I didn't want to go bowling. So I did something else."

Zach stared at her. More confused than ever, he asked, "Since when don't you like spending time with Eric and Laura?"

"Since today," she replied, looking at him with eyes that were filled with hurt and anger. "I didn't feel like it, okay?"

"No, it's not okay," Zach shot back, just as furiously. "You had me worried sick." Realizing it wouldn't help anything if they ended this in a shouting match, Zach calmed himself with effort. "Janey, what is going on with you? What is—" Zach broke off abruptly when Janey turned her head and he saw the flash of silver in her ears. Stepping closer, he saw with shock that she'd had her ears pierced. Silver studs were in both ears.

Knowing he'd seen, she said defensively, "I did it with my own money."

"And without my permission." Was this what her rebellion was all about? he wondered, amazed. Because he had refused to let her wear those stupid earrings Laura had helped her buy?

"Only because you wouldn't give me permission!"

"Which was the same reason you went to the mall with those boys, because you knew I wouldn't let you do it?" They were heading into dangerous territory now. Fear that Janey would go off the deep end, the way Tabitha Cole had, made Zach even angrier.

Seeing his response, Janey got even more rebellious. "Why do you care, anyway?" she said, jumping up from the sofa. "It's not like I'm your real daughter anyway!"

Before Zach had a chance to call her back the doorbell rang. Resenting the interruption, he went to get it. His irritation faded when he realized who it was. "Laura," he said in quiet relief.

She looked as panic-stricken as he had felt upon arriving home and finding Janey missing. "Are you okay? Where's Janey?" She looked past him, to see Janey. She put her hand over her heart and sagged visibly. "Oh, thank goodness you're both all right. When I got home and heard that message on the recorder, I thought maybe there'd been an accident or—" Breaking off, she looked from Zach to Janey and back again. "What's wrong?"

"Janey went to the mall without permission."

"Zach is mad at me because I got my ears pierced!" Janey cut in rebelliously.

Zach? Where had that come from? She'd never called him by his given name before. It had always been Dad or Daddy. Never Zach.

"Oh." Laura said heavily, looking as if she'd just backed into a hornet's nest.

"Tell him, Laura," Janey insisted. "Tell him how unreasonable he's being."

Laura bit her lip, looked at him, concern radiating from her dark brown eyes and then back at his daughter. "Janey—" she began in a tentative, soothing voice.

"You're both mean, you know that?" Janey said, cutting Laura off. She raced up the stairs.

Her bedroom door slammed with a force that shook the house. Zach looked up the stairs after her. Tabitha, too, had demonstrated her temper with aggrandizing force. Whether Janey liked it or not, this was going to have to stop.

"Want to talk?" Laura asked quietly.

He didn't know if that would be a good idea or not. "It hasn't been a very good day."

"I can see that." She held out her hand anyway. Realizing he needed to talk to another adult, and more importantly someone who understood and supported him in this battle with his child, he took Laura's hand, and together they walked into the living room where moments before Janey had been vacillating between defiance and tears. Briefly he explained everything. Laura listened intently. When he had finished, she looked as worried as he felt. She cast a tentative look at the stairs. "Maybe I should talk to her."

"I don't know, Laura. She's awfully upset."

Laura was already on her feet, gently disengaging her hand from his. "At least let me try, Zach. Sometimes a girl her age needs a woman as a sounding board."

Was that all it was? Zach fervently hoped so, even as his every instinct told him it was much, much more.

Laura was upstairs for over an hour. When she came down, she looked grim, worried. "Well?" He was on his feet instantly.

"I still don't know what's going on with her, only that she wants to come home with me, Zach. Just for a couple of days. I said it was okay with me if it was okay with you."

"Without even asking me first?" he asked incredulously.

She blinked. "I'm sorry. I guess I wasn't thinking." Laura held out her hands in a helpless gesture. "She just seemed so upset. I think you're right, Zach, that there is something wrong, something terribly wrong."

"But you don't have even the slightest idea what it is, either, not after talking with her for an hour?"

At his question, Laura ducked her head. And in that instant he knew that Janey had said something to Laura. Reluctantly, Laura repeated, "She said she thinks you're 'unfair and mean' not to let her wear earrings."

He saw the tension in her slender frame, the worry that mirrored his own. "And you agree with her, don't you?" Zach demanded unhappily.

Laura nodded tactfully. "I think in this instance you are going a little overboard. We're just talking about earrings here, Zach. It's something all the girls her age do," Laura continued in the same pragmatic, accepting tone.

Aware this was the first disagreement he'd had with Laura since they'd become lovers, Zach's shoulders tensed. "Not my daughter."

"It's too late for that dictum, Zach. She's already done it and it can't be undone."

Looking at Laura's exasperation with him, he suddenly knew where Janey was getting her ideas. It was all he could do to keep his voice calm. "You encourage this in her, don't you?"

She looked at him in confusion. "What are you talking about?"

His resentment building he spelled it out for her, "The earrings."

"What is the harm in that?"

"I'll tell you what the harm in that is." Unable to stop, he heard himself thundering, "You've been undermining my authority with her from the first."

Laura's eyes flashed. "I have not."

"The hell you haven't."

"How have I been doing that?"

"By telling her I'm too strict!"

"I never said any such thing."

"Not in so many words, no, but the message was clear enough. 'What harm can there be in wearing the earrings around the house, Zach?'" he mimicked furiously in a falsetto voice.

Laura's jaw clenched. Riotous color spread across her cheekbones. "If you will remember," she said in a low, barely controlled but reasonable tone, "I also told her that as her father, your word was law."

"Yes, and indirectly that your word, as her mother, would be so much more lenient than mine."

Her fists knotted at her sides, Laura looked down at the floor, then slowly back up at him. "It probably would be since you are too strict sometimes."

They glared at each other. Realizing this was getting them nowhere, Zach stalked through to the family room, then slid open the patio doors and stepped out into the coolness of the night. It was a moment before he realized Laura had followed him and was behind him. "Please, Zach," she said softly, stepping nearer in the chill darkness of the night, "Let me take Janey home with me."

"Why?" *So you can brainwash her against me even more?*

"Because I understand what she's going through, even if she doesn't." He lifted a skeptical brow and she continued, even more urgently. "I understand that kind of rebellious behavior because I lived it. I also know there's a reason for it. Maybe it is the earrings, but maybe there's more to it. All I know for sure is that she is talking to me more easily than she is talking to you. If we're to solve this problem with Janey, she needs understanding. And that I have in abundance, Zach.''

"You're saying I don't?" he countered stiffly.

Her expression was gentle as she soothed, "Not at all. I'm saying you're confused and angry right now, and that the two of you both need time to cool off."

Zach almost gave in to her request before snapping back to his senses. If he let Janey go now, the damage would be irreparable. No one, absolutely no one, was going to separate him from his daughter at this late stage of the game.

"No," he said calmly. "I won't let you take Janey home with you."

It was Laura's turn to recoil in hurt and surprise. "Why not?"

"Because you're the reason Janey is so upset. You're the problem, Laura." He continued gently, knowing this had to be said even if it hurt her. "I know you care about her, but the truth of the matter is you've been a disruptive force. I won't let you take Janey home with you or drive the two of us apart."

"Is that what you think I'm doing?" The tears streamed down her face.

"I know it is." Maybe she hadn't meant to do this, but she had. It was up to him to find a way to stop it before the damage to his daughter was any more severe. And the first way to fix it would be to re-cement his relationship with Janey, not push her away, as Laura suggested.

But now Laura was angry and disapproving, too. As she faced him, he saw some of that wildness she had claimed to have in her youth. "You don't have any right to stop me, Zach. I am her mother."

"No, you're not. You'd only like to be."

Laura stared at him, unable to believe what he had just said. "Meaning what?" she demanded. "Either I do things your way, or everything else is off? My friendship with Janey, and my relationship with you?"

He hadn't wanted to be quite so blunt, but since she had put it that way, he knew she deserved a truthful answer. "Where my daughter is concerned, yes. There isn't any room for discussion on this, Laura. I am Janey's parent, not you. I will make the decisions that shape her life."

"Even if you're pushing her away from you?" Laura countered.

Her assault on him stung. "You're the only one pushing us apart," he said sadly. Because the truth was, until Laura had come along, he had not had one problem with Janey.

Laura reeled as if he had struck her physically. "I was a fool to think this could ever work out."

"Maybe you were," Zach said disconsolately. But he had been, too. Because he had really thought this would work. How could he have been so naive?

Regaining her strength, Laura said, "I won't let you separate me from my daughter now that I have found her."

"You have no choice," Zach warned, mimicking her tone to annoying perfection.

Laura's jaw jutted forward. "You're wrong about that," she said very quietly, letting him know in that second that it was all over. They were finished, forever. "Dead wrong, Zach." And then she turned and left.

Watching her go, knowing his daughter was still upstairs, and that both she and Laura now detested him, Zach had never felt lonelier or more bereft.

Chapter Fifteen

"What time should I be home, so we can go?" Eric asked as he grabbed his jacket and prepared to head out the door Saturday morning.

"What do you mean?" Laura looked at him, confused.

"Isn't tonight the night we're supposed to have dinner over at Grandma's, with Zach and Janey?"

Realizing this was so, it was all Laura could do not to moan. She'd completely forgotten about that. They'd arranged it several weeks prior. "Yes," Laura answered her son's question, all the while wondering how she was going to get herself out of this one. "Tonight was the night we agreed on."

"So, what time?" Eric demanded impatiently, a basketball cradled under his arm. In Central High sweats, he was anxious to get over to the gym and work out with the rest of his team. They only had a few games left as the play-offs approached, but they were going at them full tilt, hoping to at least win the district title.

"Be home by six," she decided, still not sure what she was going to do about dinner at her mom's.

"Okay. See ya."

"See ya." Laura echoed his enthusiastic adieu lamely then sat in silence after the door had slammed shut.

She hadn't told Eric about the fight she'd had with Zach, only that the bowling was off because Janey had gone somewhere without permission, and was in hot water with her dad. Having done a similar thing himself a time or two, Eric didn't question what Laura told him. Even though several days had now passed, memories of her fight with Zach were still raw and painful.

She had hoped that he had just been speaking in anger and hadn't really meant half of what he'd said, but as the third day passed with no word from him, she knew he hadn't relented in the least. He really thought she was a disruptive, damaging influence on his daughter. That alone had been bad enough, but his rigidly dictatorial behavior toward her had been even worse, reminding her of her overbearing mother and the Navy. Both had run her life for so long.

Well, Zach probably wouldn't want to go to dinner, either, she thought. If that was the case, then she would have to tell her mother. If Grace found out about this, she'd probably start harping at Laura to sue for custody of Janey. And right now, Laura just didn't think she could deal with that. Picking up the phone, she dialed Zach's number.

He answered on the fourth ring. "Anderson residence."

"Zach. It's Laura." Not giving him a chance to say anything, she rushed on, "About dinner at my mother's tonight—"

"She called just a little while ago to remind me," he said heavily. "I didn't know what to do. I gathered you hadn't told her we—our relationship—was off."

"No." Laura said, squeezing the words out of her aching throat. "I haven't."

"So, I told her we'd be there," Zach finished.

"Oh." She was so surprised she couldn't think of anything else to say.

"To be blunt, Janey really isn't up to it. Neither am I. But I figured it would be easiest to go. I hope you'll understand if we don't stay long."

His voice was so cool and formal it stung. He hadn't forgiven her, Laura thought, heartbroken, disappointed. Any more than she had forgiven him. But then what had she expected? She knew how different they were in outlook. The episode with Janey had just made them face it, that was all.

"I agree, leaving early would be best," Laura said.

"Fine, then I'll see you there," Zach said crisply, then hung up the phone.

Unhappily, the evening was every bit as tense as Laura had feared it would be. Zach and Janey arrived well after Laura and Eric. From the way the two distanced themselves physically from each other, Laura could tell they were still fighting. And although her heart went out to any child and parent locked in a dance of pain, she was also aggravated with Zach. If he would have loosened up a bit, and let her help out, the situation would already be back to normal. Instead, everybody was miserable.

"So, Zach," Laura's mother started in on him promptly, the moment Eric and Janey had moved off to nibble hors d'oeuvres and watch a movie in the den, "we understand you and Laura have been dating."

Laura gave her mother a sharp look, warning her off the subject. As always, her mother steadfastly ignored the visual clue.

"We've become acquainted," Zach said evasively.

Her mother persisted cheerily, "What does that mean?"

"It means the subject is off-limits," Laura cut in.

"Laura and I are just friends, although I think in the future, now that we've gotten to know each other, we'll be seeing less of each other."

"Why, for goodness' sake!" her mother retorted, with her customary lack of tact. "I thought the two of you had a romance going."

"That's true," Zach said curtly, rubbing his forehead as if the pain behind his eyes was intense and throbbing. "But people change." Avoiding Grace's searching glance, he looked at Laura, amending, "Or sometimes they don't."

"But what about Janey!" her mother sputtered. "She needs her mother!"

Zach stood abruptly. The subject of Janey's welfare was not something he was willing to discuss. "I think I need a breath of air. If you'll excuse me—"

Her father stood, too. "The patio is out back, son. Right through those doors over there."

Laura waited until Zach was gone, then turned on her mother. "How could you?" she demanded furiously. Grace had promised her this would be a fun, purely social evening with no demands put on anyone. She should have known better then to believe her.

"I didn't think I was asking anything forbidden," her mother countered defensively. "Of course if anyone around here ever bothered to fill me in on what's going on, it might be a different story!"

"Okay, so now you know," Laura hissed, hating the defensive way her mother always made her feel. "Zach and I have broken up. Is that enough of a news flash for you?"

Her mother's mouth tightened. "I'll get dinner on. And keep your voice down, Laura. Do you want the children to hear?"

No, she didn't. Fortunately, they were so engrossed in a movie on cable that they were oblivious to the activity in the other room.

"I'm sorry if there's a problem between you and Zach," her father said quietly as soon as her mother had disappeared into the kitchen. "But that doesn't give you any excuse to be rude to your mother."

Laura knew that, as nosy as her mother had been, she hadn't helped the situation any. Her curt, aggravated retorts had only made things worse. She took a deep, steadying breath, promising, "I'll try to cool it."

Her father nodded his approval. "Good. Your mother has worked very hard on this meal. For the children's sakes, I'd like it to be a success."

Thankfully the children carried the conversation at the dinner table. Eric and Janey continuously charmed them all as they cheerfully traded stories back and forth, all of them centering on the highs and lows of being a middle school student. "You'll like the senior high," Eric promised Janey. "There's a lot more freedom when you get to the ninth grade. You can hitch rides with your friends instead of riding the school bus."

Janey sent her dad a brief, aggrieved look. "I don't know if I'll be able to do that."

"Not when you're just a freshman," Zach agreed.

"Why not?" Eric turned to Zach, looking at him as if he had suddenly sprouted two heads. "She'll be in high school."

"Right and she'll be there for four years," Zach replied.

Eric looked at Zach and shook his head in mute remonstration. "That's . . . stupid," he said.

"No, it's common sense," Laura's mother cut in. "Young girls need to be protected. I often thought if I'd been stricter with your mother, Eric, she wouldn't have married so young."

If Grace had been stricter, she would have suffocated and died, Laura thought.

Zach shot Laura's mother a grateful glance for jumping to his aid.

Seeing the two of them in cahoots on any issue, made Laura all the more certain Zach was out of line. Plus, she couldn't bear the thought of Zach making Janey as forcibly repressed and miserable as she had been at that age, always fighting to be heard, always fighting to maintain something of her own identity despite the crushing demands and restrictions continually put on her.

"Dessert anyone?" Laura said, rising with her plate in hand.

"Good idea," her mother said, also rising. "I've got the most wonderful Mississippi Mud Pie in there just begging to be eaten..."

"I want you to talk to your son," Zach told Laura later, getting her alone.

Visibly uncomfortable, he seemed so at odds with the man she had fallen in love with. But maybe that, too, had been an illusion, Laura thought. Maybe she'd only been seeing what she wanted to see. Because of Janey. Because of everything. Her heart aching, she faced him apprehensively. "What about?" she asked.

Zach's answering look was filled with both remorse and gentle censure. "Janey doesn't need any more encouragement to rebel."

"Eric didn't mean anything by his remarks, but you're right, he shouldn't have commented." Laura sighed, then caved in reluctantly. "I'll speak to him."

"Thanks."

"But about Janey—" she began, watching him tense up again. "Zach, you can't keep—"

"Laura, I think it'd be better if we didn't discuss this again, and especially not here, in front of your folks. We both know where each of us stands. Nothing's changed."

They faced one another in abject misery. She saw he was blaming her and now Eric, too, for all his troubles with Janey, instead of looking to himself and his own behavior for the answers.

"I shouldn't have come here tonight," he said finally, his expression disconsolate.

No, she thought wearily, considering how everything had worked out, he shouldn't have.

"JANEY TOLD ME what Zach did to her at the mall, embarrassing her in front of all her friends," Eric said as the two of them drove home. He turned sideways to face her, his back lightly grazing the passenger door. "How come you didn't tell me that, Mom? You knew, didn't you?"

"Yes, I knew." Laura signaled for a left turn as she approached the next intersection.

"Well?"

Keeping her eyes on the road, Laura said civilly, "I didn't think it was any of your business." And she had feared if Eric found out about it, he, too, would be upset. He might even try to put himself in the middle of Zach's disciplining of his daughter, as he had at the dinner table tonight.

"Janey is my sister!" Eric said.

Laura sighed. "I know that, honey, but this was a fight between Janey and her dad."

"It's still my business," Eric said defiantly. "You want to know what I think? The guy's a jerk. Not letting her wear earrings—"

Laura wasn't sure why, but she found herself coming to Zach's defense. "Zach thinks they are inappropriate for someone Janey's age. He has a right to his opinion, just like you and I have a right to ours."

"Even when his opinion is dead wrong?" Eric asked. "All the girls wear them," Eric continued. "You know that."

"That doesn't make a bit of difference to Zach. He still doesn't approve of flashy earrings on thirteen-year-old girls."

"What a crock!" Eric shook his head. Settling back against his seat, he ruminated casually, "Janey says she and her dad are barely speaking."

Laura had suspected that might be the case. Seeing how upset her son was, she searched her mind for something positive to say. "They'll work it out in time."

"Not unless he changes his mind," Eric predicted grimly, glancing out the window as Laura turned onto their street.

Their moods quiet, depressed, she and Eric went into the house. Claiming fatigue, Eric went to bed and Laura followed soon afterward. It had been a horrible night, to be sure, a horrible couple of days. Surely it had to get better, didn't it?

IT WAS SHORTLY AFTER 2:00 a.m. when Zach heard the first of the sirens. Loud and blaring, they were close by. Alarmingly close! Swinging his body lithely out of bed, he padded to the window. As he drew the curtain aside, he could see flashing red lights of two police cars down the block, and another fire truck on the way.

Wondering if the noise had awakened Janey, he went down the hall to her bedroom. Her door was shut. He knocked lightly. No answer. He pushed open the door. In the shadowy confines of the room, he could see the outline of her figure in the bed. He was surprised the noise hadn't awakened her, but decided to let her sleep through it if possible. She'd been so tired lately, because of all their fighting. She needed her rest.

Down the block, the sirens increased in number. Zach knew there were several elderly people down the block. Maybe someone needed help. He could go see.

By the time he had dressed the sirens had stopped. He paused to check on his daughter. Janey's form was still immobile. Satisfied she wouldn't awaken, he went downstairs and quietly went outside.

By the time he arrived, quite a crowd had gathered at the corner. Many of the people were standing around in bathrobes and slippers. As he neared, he saw it had been a car wreck of some kind. One of the cars was a big Suburban and in that, the people appeared unhurt. The other was a red sports car. A Mustang.

"Crazy teenagers!" one of Zach's neighbors said. "There's no reason for a crash like this on a suburban street!"

One of the paramedics was ordering the crowd to move back. His heart pounding, filled with a feeling of dread, Zach pushed closer anyway.

LAURA STRODE through the automatic glass doors of the Emergency Room entrance, her heart in her throat, tears in her eyes. Her hands and legs were shaking so badly she could hardly walk. All she could think about was Eric. Her baby. It didn't matter what Eric was doing out driving around at two in the morning. They could sort all that out later. Right now, all she cared about, was that he be all right.

Hurrying over to the admitting desk, Laura told the nurse. "I'm Mrs. Matthews. You called. You said you have my son."

"Yes. He was in a car accident with Janey Anderson."

Laura's heart stilled. Her insides went cold and numb with shock. "Excuse me?"

"Janey Anderson. That was the name of the young girl who was with him at the time of the wreck. Her father's already in the treatment room with her."

"Is she going to be all right?" Laura asked.

"The doctor is still with her," the nurse said in a crisp, professional tone.

"My son—" she croaked.

"Is back there, too. Would you like to be with him?"

Laura nodded, her vision blurred with tears. "Please." The nurse signaled to an aide who'd just walked up. "Show Mrs. Matthews to her son Eric."

"He's in a back bed, over here," the aide said as she led Laura past several curtained beds.

In the next to last curtained area, Laura saw Zach. He was standing next to Janey's bed, tightly holding one of her hands. Hearing her quick intake of breath, the stilled footsteps, he looked accusingly at Laura, then back down at Janey, whose arms were a mass of bandages. A long white bandage ran the length of her forehead. Blood was matted and drying in her hair and there was a large bruise on her cheek.

Laura wanted to say something, but there were no words that could begin to convey what she was feeling. She hurried after the aide and into the curtained area where her son lay.

He looked so small and vulnerable. For the first time, she realized with startling clarity just how young sixteen was. She thought of him as an adult now, so much of the time, but in his heart and mind he was still a child in many ways.

Like Janey, he looked as though he had been through sheer hell. His eyes were closed. His hair was matted with blood. His face was bruised. Two strategically placed butterfly bandages closed the worst of the wounds.

His eyes opened as she moved next to him and took his hand. "Mom." He croaked the word and tears poured from his eyes. "I'm so sorry."

She bent close and squeezed his hand reassuringly, all the love she had for him in her heart flowing into her soft, low voice. "It's all right, honey," she reassured softly, meaning it. "I'm not angry."

"But—"

"We'll talk about how it happened later. I just want you to rest."

"Janey—" Eric whispered, distressed.

Laura squeezed his hands harder. "She's close by. Her dad is with her."

Eric relaxed slightly and shut his eyes briefly. "Is she okay?" he asked in a trembling voice.

Laura had never seen her son look so afraid. "I think so. I'll have to talk to the doctors but she looked stable." Eric sighed in relief.

"Mrs. Matthews? We're going to move him upstairs now. We want to keep him overnight, just to be sure there are no internal injuries."

"Mom?" Eric asked, when she moved back to let the orderlies close enough to work.

"I'll stay with you, honey," she promised, leaning over the gurney.

It was almost five before Eric fell into a deep, exhausted sleep. Her mind full of questions, Laura started for the coffee machine. Farther down the hall, she saw Zach must have had the same thought for he was coming out of a patient room and heading in the same direction.

They met at the coffee machine. He had never looked more alone. Her heart went out to him. She still didn't know what had happened, but she knew he hadn't deserved to suffer though this. None of them had. "Janey asleep?" she asked softly.

"Yes." Zach nodded solemnly. "She's asleep. What about Eric?"

"He's asleep, too." Silence fell between them. Laura took a sip of her coffee and found it bitter. They stared at each other awkwardly. "I'm sorry," Laura said finally, wishing fervently that they had never fought. She would understand if he were furious with her for this. The last couple of hours had given her time to think, to realize that Eric was at fault, both for driving and having Janey out at that time of night. She shrugged helplessly. "I don't know what was going on."

"It's pretty obvious," Zach said, his voice hoarse with a mixture of hurt and disbelief. He sighed heavily, looking as if he had the weight of the world on his shoulders. "She had a suitcase in the back of Eric's car. She'd made up her bed to look as if someone was sleeping there."

Shock held Laura motionless. "Eric was helping her run away?" she gasped, stunned.

Zach nodded and his lips thinned. "The accident happened a little over a block from my house, at the intersection. The driver of the other car said Eric was driving with his lights off. They hit head-on."

"Oh, my God," Laura gasped. They could have both been killed. At the stark realization, all the strength left her. Somehow she managed to right her precariously tilting cup and then groped behind her for a chair and fell weakly into it.

"The Suburban wasn't damaged too badly but Eric's Mustang is totaled. Neither Janey nor Eric were wearing seat belts."

Knowledge of that made Laura furious. "He knows better."

"So does Janey," Zach said.

"Was anyone else hurt?" Laura asked, still feeling too shaky to stand.

Zach's expression remained wearily remote, as if he wanted to keep all his hurt locked deep inside. "No."

He blames me for this. I know it. Distressed, Laura buried her face in her hands, aware she was trembling visibly yet able to do nothing about it. The past week rivaled the worst times of her life. Melinda's final days, the days immediately after Rob's death. She didn't know how much more she could take.

Beside her, Zach was silent, too. He knew this accident was his fault. He should've seen it coming. But he hadn't because he'd been so wrapped up in his feelings for Laura, in trying to figure out if there wasn't some way to surmount all the obstacles in front of them. He wanted to find a way to make their relationship work, instead of giving i up for the lost cause it really was. And because of his self absorbed attitude, his daughter had almost died. Well, h had his priorities in order now. His love for Janey cam first, even if it meant giving up the best time he'd ever ha with a woman. He couldn't afford to lose Janey the way Laura had lost Melinda.

Laura heard him move to the window. When she looked up again, he was standing, staring out at the first pearly gray light of dawn on the horizon, a look of grim self-indictment on his face.

Wearily, Laura stood. She wanted to say something. She just didn't know what. Nothing could make things better at this point. Zach didn't speak to her again and she left silently.

"MOM, PLEASE. Do we have to talk about this now?" Eric grumbled as he attacked the breakfast the nurse had brought. He looked even worse than she felt. "My head is killing me."

"I don't wonder," she retorted sarcastically. Now that she knew he was all right, her anger and disappointment in him had reached mammoth proportions. Unable to wait any longer, she demanded, "What were you thinking last night?"

Eric's lip shot out truculently. "She's unhappy there. She wanted to get away. I said I'd help her." Eric put a fork into his scrambled egg, then looking nauseous, pushed the whole plate away.

"With no thought to the trouble you were causing?"

"Causing who?" Eric demanded, just as contentiously. "Zach?" When she flinched, he went on, "I care about Janey, okay? She is my sister. Zach—well—Zach is just going to have to worry about himself. I've got to worry about Janey."

"I see. And were you worried about Janey when you were driving without seat belts and headlights?"

He blinked, severely taken aback by her censuring tone. Recovering, he crossed his arms over his chest, then restlessly disengaged them. "We were trying not to be seen. How was I to know some big car would round the corner?"

"Don't blame this all on the other driver. If you'd had your headlights on, this most likely would not have happened!"

"I said I was sorry."

"Well, in this case sorry isn't enough."

Eric looked at her, distressed. "What do you mean?" he asked apprehensively.

"I mean you're grounded," Laura shot back. And the moment the words were out of her mouth, she knew it was the right thing to do. Having always been a parent who prided herself on not harshly confining her children in any way, she knew the time had come for her to take a stand and let Eric know his behavior had been unconscionable.

"You're kidding." He looked her up and down, with suspiciousness.

"No," Laura enunciated clearly, "I'm not."

Eric's jaw set. Long minutes passed in which neither of them spoke a word. "When am I getting out of here?" he demanded finally.

"By noon, the doctor said last night."

Eric's jaw turned even more rigid. Laura knew it wouldn't be easy taking him home. But then getting a phone call from the hospital in the middle of the night hadn't been easy, either.

She couldn't go through this again, wouldn't go through this again. And somehow, someway, Eric would just have to understand that. And, in the meantime, there were some things Zach would have to understand, too.

"ZACH, can I talk to you?" Laura said, from the doorway of Janey's hospital room. He looked up from his daughter's bedside. Like herself, Zach was still wearing the clothe he had hurriedly pulled on the night before.

Janey had been lying prone against the pillows, but at th sight of Laura she sat up gingerly. "I want to talk to yo first, Laura. Please?" She looked at her dad, sensing rightl that he was about to object. "Alone? It'll just take a minute."

Zach sighed and dragged a hand through his hair. "All right. I was about to go down to the business office anyway." He looked at Laura, his eyes direct, but his feelings, whatever they were, successfully hidden from her. "I'll meet you in the lounge down the hall in ten minutes."

"Thank you," Laura said and nodded graciously at him as he passed her, even though she knew he was only accommodating his daughter because he had nearly lost her.

"Don't be mad at Eric," Janey said. "It wasn't his fault. I asked him to come and get me."

Eric hadn't told her that. Laura let that fact sink in. So, this hadn't been all Eric's idea after all. "Maybe so," Laura countered gently but firmly, "but he knows better than to drive without lights at night. That was incredibly dangerous and foolhardy. The two of you are lucky you're still alive."

Janey hung her head. "Dad says he's going to be taking me home in a little while." She gulped. "Laura, I don't want to go. I want to go to your house. That's where I belong now. Before we didn't know who my real parents were, but now we do and I just think that's where I ought to be."

Laura regarded Janey carefully. There was no doubt in her mind at all the child thought she knew what she was doing. But Laura wasn't convinced. When all this had started Zach and Janey had been so close. Janey had been suspicious of and mistrustful of Laura, friendly only to Eric. She hadn't wanted to be taken away from Zach. Now, suddenly, she did. The fight about the earrings aside, it didn't make sense. More had to be going on here. She sat down on the edge of Janey's bed and took her hand in hers. "Your dad loves you, Janey." More than life.

"But he's not my real dad," Janey sniffed. "Please talk to him."

Sitting on the bed next to Janey, holding her close, the way she had once held Melinda when anything was wrong, Laura felt a surge of maternal affection. And although she had promised ten minutes, it was more like half an hour before Janey was composed enough for Laura to leave her.

Zach was standing at a window. One look at his tense expression told Laura he had seen her holding Janey. Briefly she wondered what else he had seen and heard. "Janey wants me to take her home."

He kept his back to her and responded evenly, "I told you before, that is not an option."

Janey didn't need stubbornness from him, she needed understanding. And so did Laura. "Do you want her to run away again?" Laura queried insistently.

That caught his attention. He whirled on her, doing his best to hide his hurt. "Did she tell you she was going to do that?"

Laura shook her head slowly. "No, but she's done it twice in the past week. Once to the mall, and once with Eric. I'd say that makes her intentions fairly clear."

Zach paced back and forth, his frustration with the situation evident.

Zach had known guiding his daughter to adulthood would be complex, full of ups and downs, but he had never expected it to be this emotionally draining or devastating. Not so very long ago he had been his daughter's hero, confidant, and conscience, all wrapped up into one. He'd been privy to her worst fears and her loftiest dreams. He'd felt so close to her then. He knew in his heart Janey still loved him deeply and always would, but knew they were no longer so close. And that hurt, almost more than he could stand. Still, he hoped her deliberate distance would pass. And be replaced by something deeper yet.

He didn't see how he could let Janey go. If he did, before they worked things out, he feared they might continue thi parent-child stalemate indefinitely. "She's upset," Zach said. She's young and impulsive, not thinking things through, but living moment to moment, like Laura.

"Maybe that's true, Zach. Lately her judgment has been off. But that doesn't change the facts. She's still my daughter," Laura said in a soft, persuasive voice. "And she wants to be with me. And because I love her, I can't deny her that, even though I know it means I'm hurting you."

Fear ran through Zach. He felt as though he was living his worst nightmare. He turned, his blue eyes narrowing dangerously as he looked at Laura. "What are you trying to tell me, Laura?" he asked, hanging on to his composure with a thread. "That you want her back?"

Tears filled her eyes and she looked at him with guilt and indecision. "I never meant to go back on my word—" she began gently.

Considering what was at stake, Zach didn't want her kindness. "But you are now anyway, right?"

"She's unhappy, Zach. Right or wrong, she needs a woman in her life now. She needs me."

He shook his head in abject misery. Janey was young enough to want to go where the grass was greener, but he hadn't expected this from Laura. "This—from the lady whose other, real child just landed mine in the hospital?"

Laura stood firm. "If you love her, Zach, you'll let her go."

He shook his head and moved farther away from her. He thrust his fists into the pockets of his jeans. The loss of Laura and Janey was enough to bring him to his knees permanently. "You don't know what you're asking," he said very low, fighting the tears that threatened.

"Yes," Laura said slowly, "I do."

"You wouldn't turn your back on Eric."

"Yes, I would. If it was the only way to reach him."

"This isn't."

"I think it is. Zach, she almost died last night, trying to get to me. I agree it was stupid and senseless but that's the way kids are at that age. They think with their hearts, not their minds." Her eyes filled with tears. "I can't stand idly by and watch this happen again."

He weighed her plea before responding. "You won't have to," he pronounced calmly. "This time I plan to keep a better eye on her."

Laura took a deep, bracing breath. "What are you going to do? Stand watch over her night and day? Run your home like a prison?"

Zach shrugged, the images Laura was concocting not appealing to him at all. "If I have to," he admitted reluctantly, "until she starts talking to me again, telling me what's going on with her." He would do anything to break the cycle of hurt and alienation that had been started.

Seething with frustration, Laura fell silent.

If she thought Zach's plan would work, she'd be all for it. "At least give me time with her, then," she urged passionately, knowing in her heart she could make a difference, that with time she could reach her.

"I can't," he said in a voice laced with deep regret. "Not when your involvement with her is what started this." Stepping closer he said softly and seriously, "For the time being, I don't want you to see her at all, Laura. Not until her life is back on an even keel again and maybe not even then. It's too confusing for Janey."

"Please reconsider," she whispered, feeling as though her heart was breaking.

"No."

"Zach, please. Don't force me to—"

"To what?" he asked, waiting.

Laura searched vainly for the words that would prompt him to do what she wished. "To take you to you to court." She hadn't meant to say the words, but once they were verbalized, she knew it was the only path.

He stared at her as if seeing a stranger. "You promised me you would never do that," he accused hoarsely in disbelief. He stepped closer. "I have your pledge in writing."

Laura knew that. And if Zach had been reasonable, it never would have been necessary. But looking at his closed expression, she knew that was never going to happen. And as such, he left her no choice. "All contracts can be revoked, Zach," she said firmly, hoping he would buckle under when he saw how serious she was. "Sometimes, like now, circumstances change."

Although her demeanor was calm and matter-of-fact, he was furious, seething. "Don't threaten me, Laura," he warned.

Stubbornly she held his penetrating gaze and refused to give in. "Then don't keep me away from our child." Seeing he was still unreachable, she braved his scorching look, knowing he was no longer going to forgive her for this. But somehow, she had to get to the root of Janey's troubles, so she could mend his relationship with her. "It's been an upsetting week," Laura said finally, furious Zach still wouldn't relent. "I'll give you until next Wednesday to reconsider."

"And if I don't reconsider and let you see Janey?" he queried harshly, his face a mask of pain that almost broke her heart.

Only if and when the two were close again, would they ever be happy. And the only way to get that to happen was to get Janey to open up. Even if that meant sacrificing Zach's trust and the possibility of them ever reconciling. She looked at Zach and pressed ahead bravely, because she loved him and Janey, because she had no choice. "Then I'll file suit."

Chapter Sixteen

"Why didn't you tell us what happened?" Laura's mother said, the moment they walked in the door Tuesday evening. "We had to hear about Eric's wreck at the grocery store!"

In the middle of cooking dinner and unable to indefinitely leave the pork chops she had simmering on the stove, Laura led the way back to her kitchen. "I didn't want to worry you until I knew how bad the situation was," she explained.

"You could have called us when you knew he was going to be all right," her mother chided, aggrieved.

"Yes, I guess I could have," Laura said. But frankly, her mind had been so full of Janey and Zach that she hadn't thought of her parents. "I'm sorry," she said.

"It's all right. We understand," her father said, patting her on the shoulder. He stepped back and gave her the kind of thorough once-over a general gave those he was inspecting. "But we are concerned about you and Eric. I hope you understand that."

"I do."

"I also hope you've taken corrective action with your son."

Laura smiled faintly at her father's military way of putting things. Although more sensitive to others' feelings than her mother, he, too, felt the world ran on discipline, and floundered hopelessly without it. "He's grounded. And the matter of whether or not he will get another car is yet to be decided."

Her father nodded approvingly.

"What about Janey?" her mother asked. "How is she doing?"

Laura pretended to busy herself tearing lettuce for salad. "I haven't heard but she was recovering when I left the hospital."

"What did Zach have to say about all this?" her father wanted to know.

He blames me for all of it, Laura thought, depressed. But unable and unwilling to go into that with her parents, she said only, "He was very upset with both of them."

"Was the rumor true?" her mother persisted. "Was Janey trying to run away?"

Wishing she could avoid this question entirely, Laura said, "Yes."

"And?" Grace persisted.

"And obviously she didn't get very far."

"Is that all you're going to say?" her mother prodded, hands on her hips.

"Yes, as a matter of fact, it is." Laura picked up a cucumber and began slicing it in neat quarter-inch rounds.

"Well, it's not all I have to say. I think it's high time you consider doing what I've advised all along—suing for custody," her mother said.

Laura knew her mother's heart was in the right place. She just wanted Laura to have everything that was coming to her. But Janey wasn't a commodity to be bandied about between Zach and herself. Deciding however, the only way to get her mother off her back was to level with her, Laura said, "I thought about it. I even talked to Zach about Janey coming to live with me, just for a little while."

"And?" her mother asked with bated breath, one hand clutching the pearls she wore around her neck.

"And I decided I couldn't do that to her," Laura said in a voice laced with sorrow. "She's already been through so much. I can't put her through a custody battle. I can't let her be dragged into court."

"Even if it's the best thing for her in the long run?" her father asked gently.

Laura sighed. She had thought about this long and hard and had come to the only conclusion she could. "Zach loves her and she loves Zach. They will work things out, given time and opportunity."

"And if they don't?" her mother asked, her eyes narrowed disapprovingly as she broke the heavy silence in the kitchen.

"They will," Laura said firmly, tightening her hands into fists at her sides. She had to believe that or she'd go crazy.

"You're doing it again," her mother exclaimed, upset.

Laura turned to face her mother, aware her face was growing red as she asked, "Doing what?"

Her mother stared at her, tight-lipped, then shook her head in silent disparagement. "Taking the easy way out, that's what. What you have always done from the time you ran away and married that sailor—"

Laura's temper flared at the cruel and inaccurate recitation. "Rob was a Navy officer, Mother."

Ignoring Laura's icy correction, her mother continued accusingly, "I don't know why. Heaven knows I tried to bring you up right, but you never could manage long-range plans."

Nor could I ever manage you, Laura thought. But maybe it was time she started. Gathering her courage, she faced her mother resolutely.

"If you won't sue for custody then we will," her mother declared.

Before her astonished father could reply to that, Laura cut in, "No, you won't, Mother. You'll do nothing of the kind." Her mother's mouth dropped open in mute surprise at the way Laura was suddenly fighting back. Knowing she was doing what she should have done all along, Laura continued, "This is my problem. I'll handle it."

"If only that were true!" her mother asserted, ready and willing to take control of Laura's life once again.

Laura wiped her hands on a dish towel in front of her. She knew she was about to lose her composure, but for the first time in years she didn't care. Some things had to be said. "Mother, I swear to you, if you interfere in this, if you say one word, if you so much as think about picking up that phone to talk to Zach, I'll cut you out of my life. For good."

Her mother's cheeks grew spotty with color, too. "You have no right to talk to me that way!" Grace swore.

Knowing she had a right to happiness, too, Laura said, "I have every right. I am a grown woman, fully capable of making my own decisions, and living with the consequences. Yet you treat me as if I am incapable of thinking for myself and worse, in constant need of rescuing. This is just not true, Mother. I can stand on my own and I have been doing so for a very long time. You just haven't noticed."

Laura's father grinned at his only child. "Bravo," he said to Laura in an approving undertone, and then to his wife, "Come on. We've done enough damage here. It's time to go home."

"Wait a minute." Grace dug in her heels. "You're going to let her talk to me like that?" In the past, Laura knew, her father had always insisted Laura treat her mother with respect, regardless of what her mother had said or done. But not this time.

Her father shrugged. "Like Laura said, she is a grown woman, perfectly capable of making her own decisions."

Her mother gasped. Outraged, she clamped her lips shut, picked up her coat and purse, and marched from the kitchen.

Her dad paused for one bit of advice. "Follow your heart, hon. It won't steer you wrong." And with that, he, too, was gone.

JANEY CAME DOWN to supper wearing the outrageous earrings Laura had helped her buy at the mall. Because she still wasn't talking to her father, she sat down in silence and began picking at her food.

She didn't look good. Her color was pasty. Her face and right arm still bearing the scars of her battle with the Mustang's windshield. The only time she had spoken to Zach since he had vetoed her going to Laura's and brought her home from the hospital was to ask him to help her wash the blood out of her hair. She wasn't allowed to get the stitches on her forehead wet. He knew if she had been able to keep her forehead dry and wash and rinse her hair alone she would've done so.

In the forty-eight hours since then, she had been totally silent. She went to school, but didn't say a word coming or going. If she had been giving him the silent treatment in overt rebellion, it would have been one thing. But she was just sad. For some reason, Janey had become inexplicably depressed. And he didn't know why. He didn't have so much as one damn clue. He had tried everything, from acting normal, to giving her space, to just being with her. Nothing worked.

"Do you want me to help you wash your hair again tonight?" Zach asked, passing the basket of rolls her way.

Janey nodded, the frivolous earrings bobbing on both earlobes, reminding him of Laura.

She had said she would sue him for custody of Janey if he didn't make arrangements to let her see her daughter by Wednesday. That meant he had twenty-four hours, maybe less.

He wasn't sure what hurt worse, that Laura was going back on her word to him, or that she didn't seem to believe he really loved his daughter. Her doubts were all too reminiscent of what he had suffered with Maria. Always having to prove his love, his goodness, his commitment.

He had promised himself he would never get involved with anyone who couldn't believe in his capacity for love or the worth of his devotion. And yet apparently he had. What kind of fool did that make him? he wondered. What kind of fool did that make Laura?

ZACH WAS STILL in a glum mood when he went to work the following morning. But he wasn't the worst looking guy there. Harry Cole was.

"You okay?" he asked as, blueprints in hand, the other man stepped into his trailer.

"No, as a matter of fact, I'm not," Harry admitted glumly. His eyes filled with tears. "We had to hospitalize Tabitha last night."

For a moment, Zach was too stunned to move. "Damn, Harry. I'm sorry. So sorry." Because Harry looked as if he was about to collapse, Zach pushed him into a chair.

His face devoid of all color, Harry related what had happened in a shocked monotone. "She tried to swallow a bottle of sleeping tablets. She did it in front of one of her friends. The friend called us. We got there. The psychiatrist said because she did it in front of a witness she obviously wasn't trying to kill herself. If was just a cry for help."

"Have you talked to her since?" Zach asked, horrified.

Harry nodded. "Yeah, my wife and I both saw her this morning, briefly." He sighed heavily and related in a hurt, bewildered voice, "She said we haven't been listening to her, Zach, that we haven't heard anything she's had to say. That she's been unhappy for a long time."

Galvanized into action, Zach said, "Whatever the costs are, whatever the insurance doesn't pay, I'll help you."

"Thanks," Harry said, looking relieved about that much.

Zach wished he could have reversed what had happened, or known enough to offer help earlier. Barring that, he suggested, "Why don't you take the day off?"

Harry nodded indicating he would. "I'd like to be with my wife. This has been really hard on her. They don't want us seeing Tabitha for a few days. They think it'd be better if we let the doctors get her settled in."

Zach nodded, listening.

"Then we're supposed to start family therapy." Harry shook his head and swore. "I wish I hadn't let it come to this...."

I wish I hadn't let it come to this.... The words echoed over and over in Zach's ears all day long. It hadn't been that long ago that Tabitha and Harry had been blessed with a happy family relationship. Could what happened to them happen to him and Janey? *I want to go live with Laura, Dad....* Zach pushed the words from his mind. The situations weren't the same. They weren't the same at all. But they could be, given more time and difficulty, and he knew it in his gut.

"HAVE YOU HEARD from Janey?" Eric asked Saturday morning when he sat down to eat the pancakes Laura had set out for them. After breakfast, as arranged with the conditions of his grounding, he was going to clean up the backyard and spend the rest of the afternoon writing to various colleges, asking for information about admission requirements. Never having grounded Eric before, Laura mainly wanted to keep him busy and productive. And she seemed to be doing that with ease.

What surprised her was Eric's attitude. Rather than chafing constantly at the restrictions on him, he had accepted them with equilibrium. Not that he always enjoyed the yard work and cleaning chores she had assigned, but he seemed to know it was only fair.

Reminded of her son's question by his expectant glance, Laura answered. "No, I haven't heard from Janey." Nor had she talked to Zach. That wasn't particularly surprising, either, considering the ultimatum she had flung down the previous Sunday. That had been foolish on her part and ill conceived. Remembering it, she was embarrassed by the shrewish way she had behaved. She still felt she was right, in wanting to see her child, but she also knew Zach and Janey had a lot to work out by themselves too. And as hard as it was for her to admit, she was getting in the way of that. Janey saw Laura as a magic cure-all. Laura had come to love Janey, but she knew her feelings still must pale in comparison to Zach's. Janey needed Zach right now, even if she didn't yet know it.

In the background, the doorbell rang. Laura motioned her son to stay where he was. "I'll get it. You stay and eat."

She was half expecting her mother, even though they hadn't spoken since their fight. She was stunned to see Zach. Janey was beside him, and she had a suitcase in hand. Her heart lodged in her throat, Laura opened the storm door and let them in.

"Hi," Zach said.

Janey's eyes brimmed with tears. "I've come to stay," she choked out, her voice little more than a hoarse whisper. "If you'll have me."

If she would have her? Her heart brimming over with love and compassion, Laura reacted instinctively and held out her arms. Janey tumbled into them. As Laura held the sobbing teenager, she met Zach's eyes. Like Janey, he was in unspeakable pain. "I thought it over," Zach said thickly. His eyes held hers as if begging for forgiveness. "I decided Janey and you were both right. Maybe she should spend time with you."

Zach must feel as though he is losing Janey forever, Laura thought. With effort, she held back her tears. "I'll take good care of her," she finally managed. "We'll have lots of talks. And do girl-stuff, too."

"Can we go shopping again and maybe cook together?" Janey asked. Despite her bright tone, she looked as miserable as Zach. And yet oddly relieved too.

Laura nodded. "Sure." She helped Janey out of her jacket. "Why don't you go into the kitchen and say hello to Eric? He's been thinking about you a lot. I'll be there in a minute."

"Okay." Janey turned to give Zach a fleeting look, full of misery and hurt, and then went on her way.

"Thanks for the girl-stuff," Zach said with difficulty. "She sure can't get that from me." Even though he wished with all his heart he could give it to her.

But she had gotten that from him, Laura thought guiltily, before I came on the scene. Janey'd had plenty of good times with her dad, plus a sense of closeness that had been almost impenetrable. And now—now they were barely speaking. But hopefully, that wouldn't last, Laura thought determinedly.

Knowing the next part had to be spoken, she said, "Zach about the lawsuit. I—I never would have really done that. I just said it because I thought it might make you see reason. When it didn't, I knew I couldn't tear the two families apart or take this to court and make it a public battle. I love Janey—" And you, she wanted to say, but couldn't, not when he no longer felt the same.

"I love her, too," Zach said with difficulty. "That's why I'm here, because I knew she needed to be with you."

Laura reached out and touched his arm. "I'll take good care of her," she promised finally. At least he understood now that she'd been acting out of love for their child, not because she wanted to hurt him.

"I'd like to say goodbye to her, if I could."

"You can stay a while, can't you? Have some breakfast or a cup of coffee?"

"Maybe some coffee," he agreed reluctantly after a moment. But that's all I'll be able to stand without breaking down. "And then I really have to go."

Swallowing her disappointment, Laura said, "Okay. Coffee it is then."

She led the way into the kitchen. Janey and Eric looked up as she came in.

"Have you had breakfast?" Laura asked her daughter. Janey shook her head, looking shyly at Laura, but avoiding Zach altogether. And though Zach didn't react in the slightest, Laura could sense his hurt. "Well, how about some pancakes?" Laura asked cheerfully, trying to end the tension. "And then when you and Eric both finish," she suggested to Janey, "the two of you can go out and work on the backyard together."

Stilted minutes later, the kids were out back, wrestling with rakes. As Laura watched them go at their mutual chore, her heart filled with the picture they presented. So much love, she thought. If only she and Zach could have shared this, as man and wife.

"You're sure it's all right—Janey staying?" Zach asked, looking as though he wanted to bolt.

Laura studied him, aware that, in his eyes, he had lost his daughter. And Laura was the woman who had stolen her away from him. Collecting herself, she assured him in the levelest voice she could manage, "Yes. I'd love to have Janey with me, however long she needs to be here."

He nodded, his expression relieved and sad. He glanced over at her, his mouth compressed apprehensively. "I won't lie to you. She's in bad shape. She said more to Eric this morning than she has to me all week." He swallowed hard and the confession tore at her heart. "I want her to be happy, Laura. For whatever reason, right now she just isn't when she's with me."

Laura wanted to reach out and cover his hand with her own, but not sure how the gesture would be received, she held herself in check. She said, "I told you before I thought something more was bothering her. Seeing her this morning, the way she burst into tears when she came in, I still think that's true. Maybe she'll open up and tell us what's on her mind."

"I hope so," Zach said. He sighed, not looking convinced.

Silence fell between them. She studied his strained face and the circles around his blue eyes. She wondered if anything else was adding to his pain. "Has my mother called you lately?" Laura asked, hoping not.

To her immense relief, Zach shook his head.

At least they were making progress in one area, she thought. Now if she could only make some headway in others.

"DON'T YOU THINK it's time you told me why you are so angry with your dad?" Laura asked Janey the following evening as the two of them worked together, folding a load of laundry.

"What makes you think I'm angry with him?" Janey evaded, smoothing a washcloth into a neat square.

"Oh, I don't know," Laura said idly as she picked up another towel and shook it out. "Maybe the fact you're here with me."

Janey's back stiffened. "He's too strict," she complained.

Laura's maternal instincts told her this was just a smoke screen, but she decided to play along. "Hmm, back to the earrings again."

Janey's chin took on a stubborn tilt. "He gets mad every time I wear them, even around the house."

Maybe because they remind him of me, Laura thought. How could we have thought the two of us, as different as we are, could have a lasting relationship? No, as much as she loved Zach, they just weren't right for each other. Not wh he felt she was too flighty and shortsighted, and when he could never seem to look at anything but the big picture. They would never be happy.

Laura looked at Janey. She was wearing her earrings now. "How long have the earrings been an issue between the two of you?" she asked lightly. "How long have you wanted them?"

"Since I was eight."

"Oh, dear. That long?" Laura asked.

Janey shrugged. "We fought about it off and on every year. It always ended with him saying no. He didn't want to hear any more about it, period."

"But you never ran away before," Laura guessed.

"No." Her expression dejected, Janey looked down at her lap.

"Why did you run away this time?" Laura asked.

Janey was silent a long time. When she looked up again, her eyes were awash with tears. Her bottom lip trembled. "Because h-he was s-sorry he had me."

Laura stared at Janey in bewilderment. "Honey, what are you talking about? Did your dad say something to you, during a fight?" Something Janey had totally misunderstood? She knew Zach. He loved his daughter more than life.

"Not to me." Janey shook her head, looking even more disheartened.

"Then I don't understand."

"To you."

"To me?" Laura splayed a hand over her heart.

"The night you came over with all those pictures of Melinda. I—I overheard the two of you talking. I heard Daddy crying and saying how sorry he was she had died. How sorry he was he'd never known her." She clasped her hands together tightly and said in the softest whisper, "And I knew then that he was sorry he'd gotten me at the hospital instead of her. Because if he hadn't, he would have had her as his daughter." She finished on a tearful hiccup. Embarrassed, the tears stilled streaming down her face, she pressed a hand to her mouth.

As Laura took in what she'd said, she felt an incredible mixture of emotions. Relief that this was all it was. Compassion for what Janey had needlessly suffered. And aggravation for not having suspected this.

Her brow furrowed as she struggled to put it all together. "The day you went to the mall without permission. Was that the day after your dad and I talked about Melinda?"

Janey nodded mutely, looking more miserable than ever. "Oh, honey." Laura held out her arms and Janey went into them gladly. They rocked together, mother and daughter, for several minutes. Tears slipped down Laura's face. "If we had only known what you'd been thinking and feeling...." Laura said, distressed. She drew back so Janey could look into her eyes and see for herself that Laura spoke the truth. "Don't you know how much we all love you?"

"But—" Janey sputtered in disbelief.

"Your father was just sad about Melinda," Laura reassured her softly but firmly. "That's all. I was sad, too. I helped us to talk about it." Studying Janey's distressed expression, a light bulb went on in Laura's head. Maybe there was a way to help her. "Maybe it would help you to talk about her, too," Laura suggested. Maybe if Janey dealt with this directly, the way Zach had, it would be as cathartic.

"Do you want to do that?" Laura asked softly, wanting the final decision to be Janey's.

Slowly, Janey nodded and wiped at her tears. "Would you mind? I know how upset you get talking about her."

"I don't mind. In fact, talking about things that hurt with someone we love makes it easier."

"Okay," Janey sniffed. "Let's do it."

"Atta girl," Laura said, rising and taking Janey's hand in hers. She led her toward the living room and the box of photos she kept there.

"Laura," Janey said, her tears fading as they sat down to look at the pictures. "After we look at the pictures, would you mind very much if we called my dad?"

Laura smiled through her tears, knowing at last their hopes had been answered. "I think Zach would like that very much."

"SO ALL THIS wild and crazy behavior was because you thought I didn't love you?" Zach repeated in a shaky voice as he regarded his daughter in astonishment.

Janey nodded. During the past four hours, she hadn't stopped crying for more than a few minutes at a time. Janey's eyes would be swollen tomorrow, Laura thought, but her heart would be freer than it had been in weeks.

"Janey, I will always love you. Always," Zach promised firmly, taking her into his arms. He drew back to look at her. "I have been so miserable the past few weeks, not knowing what to do or say to you, seeing that you were hurt, not knowing how to help. For the longest time, I blamed Laura. I see now that I was wrong." He looked over at her. "And for that, I'm genuinely sorry," he said softly.

Laura accepted his apology with the same goodwill it had been tendered, soothing, "It's been an upsetting time."

Janey looked at Laura. "Would you mind if I went home with my dad?"

Laura swallowed around the burning lump in her throat, glad she had been able to reunite father and daughter, while at the same time acutely feeling her own loss. "Honey, that's where you belong," she said softly.

"I'll go pack my things." Still wiping her eyes, Janey scampered up the stairs.

Left alone, Laura and Zach stared at each other. So much had happened. But they had worked through the worst of it, she knew. "I don't know how to thank you," he said thickly, looking a bit overcome himself.

Laura shrugged off his kind words. She didn't want his gratitude. She wanted his love. And if she couldn't have that, the rest was just too painful to contemplate. "Just be happy," she advised, keeping a tight rein on her own spiraling emotions. She gulped hard. "Be good to her. And Zach—"

He waited, not moving in the slightest, totally in the dark about what she was going to say.

"—think about those earrings," Laura advised softly, feeling as if her heart was breaking all over again as she prepared to say goodbye to this man one more time. "Maybe you can buy Janey some sedate ones she can wear to school all the time since her ears are already pierced."

Zach nodded, his eyes never leaving hers as he said slowly softly, "I'll keep it in mind."

Janey was back, having packed in an amazingly short time. "I'm ready to go!" she announced. Zach gave Laura another reluctant look, then thanked her again and followed his daughter out the door. Laura watched them go, glad it had all worked out for father and daughter, wishing it could have worked out for the two of them, too. But that was foolish of her, and not very realistic, and she knew it. Knew it only too well.

"OUR HOME is way behind schedule," Mr. Gagglione complained the moment he stepped into Zach's downtown office. "And I'm tired of all the excuses! I want an explanation!"

Zach looked at the irate businessman, then over at his wife. Mrs. Gagglione had her poodle along with her, as usual, but beneath the layers of rouge and makeup on her face, she was deathly pale. Worse, she seemed to be silently pleading with Zach not to let her husband know the delays were the result of her constantly and irrationally changing her mind.

He swore inwardly. Now what was he supposed to do? Be a gentleman and bail Mrs. G. out? And let the reputation of his business be ruined? Or be a gentleman and take the blame. Perhaps, he could just be diplomatic.

He turned to Mr. Gagglione. "You're right, sir," he said smoothly. "We are way behind on the work. Mrs. Gagglione and I are both aware of that, but it's not for lack of time put in. We've been working very hard to create the home of your dreams."

Mr. Gagglione growled impatiently. "I just want a place I can entertain in. What's so hard about that? Meanwhile, my current place is going to blazes because she is always over here."

"I see where that might be a problem," Zach agreed. The truth was, he could do with less of Mrs. Gagglione.

Ignoring Zach's response, Mr. Gagglione continued his tirade, "The servants need direction! They can't get a thing done! In fact, I think they sit around watching TV all day. Two days ago I walked in with guests. Dinner was a half an hour late, not even the canapés were made!"

"I got caught in traffic on the way home," Mrs. Gagglione interjected weakly.

Listening to the couple argue as if he weren't even in the room, it soon became apparent to Zach what the problem was. The Gagliones were both perfectionists. That's why they couldn't get anything done. Mrs. Gagglione couldn't make a decision because she feared it would be the wrong one. Mr. Gagglione was staying out of it completely, or trying to, so he wouldn't be to blame for the final product.

Maria had been a perfectionist, too. Expecting a dreamy type of romance instead of marriage, thinking he didn't love her when her vision of what should be failed to jibe with the reality of what was.

Laura, on the other hand, was not a perfectionist. She strove for excellence, loved it, but also knew there'd be plenty of problems along the way. She strove to meet them with equanimity. He'd been so afraid of failure, with Janey and with Laura that he'd been too rigid, too unwilling to compromise. Like Laura's first husband, he had acted as if there was only one way to do things—his. No wonder Laura had given up on him.

A decision made, Zach turned back to the still quarreling Gaggliones. It took some time and effort on his part, but he finally persuaded Mr. Gagglione that he needed to have more input on the house, to relieve Mrs. Gagglione of shouldering the burden alone. And that settled, he turned his attention to his own life.

"So, THAT'S ALL it was," Eric mused the morning after Janey had returned to Zach's. He downed a glass of orange juice. "Weird, isn't it, how people can jump to the wrong conclusions?"

"Yes," Laura said. It was weird. And sad. Because if it hadn't been for all that jumping to conclusions, if Janey had just told them initially what she had overheard, maybe she and Zach would still be together.

"Gotta go. I'll see you tonight," Eric said. He slammed out the door, just as the school bus roared down the block and came to a brake-squealing halt two houses south of theirs.

Laura went to her calendar and looked at the orders she had today. Mondays were always busy, and today was no exception. She had over a dozen pies to bake, plus four layer cakes. Well, she thought, I still have my business. And Eric's doing well. My mother is at least out of my hair for the moment. I ought to feel good. But she didn't. Couldn't. Life without Zach just wasn't the same.

But it was over, all over. When would she get that through her thick head? And it was then that she heard the sound of footsteps on the back steps and saw Zach. Hoping nothing was wrong with Janey, she waved him into her kitchen.

The back door shut softly behind him and they faced each other awkwardly, the morning sunlight streaming down between them. "You probably want to kick me from here to Arizona," he remarked in a highly reasonable tone.

"I probably should," she agreed slowly, apprehension coursing through her veins.

He stepped closer, the apology in his eyes heartfelt. "But I wish you wouldn't," he confessed softly. Still studying her quietly, he continued, "I was up all night, thinking. About Janey, Melinda. You. Me. We've got one helluva complicated situation on our hands. It seems like it can blow up at any time, and who knows, it probably will again. When we least expect it."

Laura nodded, unable to stop looking at him, unable to stop wanting to be held in his arms.

"But I love you. And dammit, I know you love me."

Her heart was pounding and it seemed she had forgotten how to move. She didn't want to misinterpret this. "What are you saying?" she asked thickly.

"Well," he drawled and looked at her uncertainly. "You know those earrings you've been encouraging me to buy my daughter? I think it's high time I did that." His blue eyes burned into hers. "So, want to go with me to the jewelry store?"

Laura's heart fell, she'd been hoping for so much more. But at least this was a start. If they couldn't pick up where they had left off, they might be able to work up to that point again. "It'll have to be after five."

"That's fine." Zach smiled, adding a mysterious stipulation of his own, "as long as you have time to help me pick out something else, too."

Laura's heart began beating very fast. "What?"

"An engagement ring and a pair of wedding bands, the kind that pledges you'll love me forever and I'll love you." His voice thickened and he went on, drawing her into his arms, weaving a hand through her hair as he spoke. "The kind that will bind us together through thick or thin, past or present, and well into the future.'' He tipped her head back, so she was looking deep into his eyes. ''Do you think you can do that?'' he whispered emotionally. ''Do you want to?''

''Well—'' Laura said, as his eyes searched hers.

He tightened his grip on her possessively. ''I promise I'll be less hardheaded in the future.''

She smiled, buoyed by a joy so intense she felt she was on cloud nine. She liked a man who could compromise. And she liked all the love she saw in his eyes. ''That sounds reasonable.'' Knowing it was her turn, she confessed softly, honestly, ''But you aren't the only one who needs to change, Zach. I've realized something, too. I can't go on living moment to moment. It was important when Melinda was dying. We needed to hold on to every precious second and it was too scary then to contemplate the future. But that time in my life has passed. I've got to take a longer view. And—'' this confession came harder ''—I've got to stop calling you a tyrant whenever your opinion is different than mine. Adults can have different views and still get along. Or at least they should be able to when they love each other as much as we do.''

Moving closer still, Laura hugged him tightly. And then looked up at him through her tears of happiness, her gaze sure and steady. Zach took her face in his hands and bent to kiss her. ''You're all I ever wanted,'' he whispered.

''And you're all I want,'' Laura echoed fiercely. In his arms, she felt at last, as if she knew what love was all about. It was about holding on and it was about letting go. Most of all, it was about Zach and her and the love they had found in each other. Everything was going to be all right. She just knew it.

MILLION DOLLAR JACKPOT
SWEEPSTAKES RULES & REGULATIONS
NO PURCHASE NECESSARY TO ENTER OR RECEIVE A PRIZE

1. Alternate means of entry: Print your name and address on a 3" ×5" piece of plain paper and send to the appropriate address below.

In the U.S.	In Canada
MILLION DOLLAR JACKPOT	MILLION DOLLAR JACKPOT
P.O. Box 1867	P.O. Box 609
3010 Walden Avenue	Fort Erie, Ontario
Buffalo, NY 14269-1867	L2A 5X3

2. To enter the Sweepstakes and join the Reader Service, check off the "YES" box on your Sweepstakes Entry Form and return. If you do not wish to join the Reader Service but wish to enter the Sweepstakes only, check off the "NO" box on your Sweepstakes Entry Form. To qualify for the Extra Bonus prize, scratch off the silver on your Lucky Keys. If the registration numbers match, you are eligible for the Extra Bonus Prize offering. Incomplete entries are ineligible. Torstar Corp. and its affiliates are not responsible for mutilated or unreadable entries or inadvertent printing errors. Mechanically reproduced entries are null and void.

3. Whether you take advantage of this offer or not, on or about April 30, 1992, at the offices of D.L. Blair, Inc., Blair, NE, your sweepstakes numbers will be compared against the list of winning numbers generated at random by the computer. However, prizes will only be awarded to individuals who have entered the Sweepstakes. In the event that all prizes are not claimed, a random drawing will be held from all qualified entries received from March 30, 1990 to March 31, 1992, to award all unclaimed prizes. All cash prizes (Grand to Sixth) will be mailed to winners and are payable by check in U.S. funds. Seventh Prize will be shipped to winners via third-class mail. These prizes are in addition to any free, surprise or mystery gifts that might be offered. Versions of this Sweepstakes with different prizes of approximate equal value may appear at retail outlets or in other mailings by Torstar Corp. and its affiliates.

4. PRIZES: (1) *Grand Prize $1,000,000.00 Annuity; (1) First Prize $25,000.00; (1) Second Prize $10,000.00; (5) Third Prize $5,000.00; (10) Fourth Prize $1,000.00; (100) Fifth Prize $250.00; (2,500) Sixth Prize $10.00; (6,000) **Seventh Prize $12.95 ARV.

   *This presentation offers a Grand Prize of a $1,000,000.00 annuity. Winner will receive $33,333.33 a year for 30 years without interest totalling $1,000,000.00.

   **Seventh Prize: A fully illustrated hardcover book, published by Torstar Corp. Approximate Retail Value of the book is $12.95.

   Entrants may cancel the Reader Service at any time without cost or obligation (see details in Center Insert Card).

5. Extra Bonus! This presentation offers an Extra Bonus Prize valued at $33,000.00 to be awarded in a random drawing from all qualified entries received by March 31, 1992. No purchase necessary to enter or receive a prize. To qualify, see instructions in Center Insert Card. Winner will have the choice of any of the merchandise offered or a $33,000.00 check payable in U.S. funds. All other published rules and regulations apply.

6. This Sweepstakes is being conducted under the supervision of D.L. Blair, Inc. By entering the Sweepstakes, each entrant accepts and agrees to be bound by these rules and the decisions of the judges, which shall be final and binding. Odds of winning the random drawing are dependent upon the number of entries received. Taxes, if any, are the sole responsibility of the winners. Prizes are nontransferable. All entries must be received at the address on the detachable Business Reply Card and must be postmarked no later than 12:00 MIDNIGHT on March 31, 1992. The drawing for all unclaimed Sweepstakes prizes and for the Extra Bonus Prize will take place on May 30, 1992, at 12:00 NOON at the offices of D.L. Blair, Inc., Blair, NE.

7. This offer is open to residents of the U.S., United Kingdom, France and Canada, 18 years or older, except employees and immediate family members of Torstar Corp., its affiliates, subsidiaries and all other agencies, entities and persons connected with the use, marketing or conduct of this Sweepstakes. All Federal, State, Provincial, Municipal and local laws apply. Void wherever prohibited or restricted by law. Any litigation within the Province of Quebec respecting the conduct and awarding of a prize in this publicity contest must be submitted to the Régie des Loteries et Courses du Québec.

8. Winners will be notified by mail and may be required to execute an affidavit of eligibility and release, which must be returned within 14 days after notification or an alternate winner may be selected. Canadian winners will be required to correctly answer an arithmetical, skill-testing question administered by mail, which must be returned within a limited time. Winners consent to the use of their name, photograph and/or likeness for advertising and publicity in conjunction with this and similar promotions without additional compensation.

9. For a list of our major prize winners, send a stamped, self-addressed envelope to: MILLION DOLLAR WINNERS LIST, P.O. Box 4510, Blair, NE 68009. Winners Lists will be supplied after the May 30, 1992 drawing date.

Offer limited to one per household.

HARLEQUIN®
OFFICIAL SWEEPSTAKES
RULES

NO PURCHASE NECESSARY

1. To enter, complete an Official Entry Form or 3" × 5" index card by hand-printing, in plain block letters, your complete name, address, phone number and age, and mailing it to: Harlequin Fashion A Whole New You Sweepstakes, P.O. Box 621, Fort Erie, Ontario L2A 5X3.

   No responsibility is assumed for lost, late or misdirected mail. Entries must be sent separately with first class postage affixed, and be received no later than December 31, 1991 for eligibility.

2. Winners will be selected by D.L. Blair, Inc., an independent judging organization whose decisions are final, in random drawings to be held on January 30, 1992 in Blair, NE at 10:00 a.m. from among all eligible entries received.

3. The prizes to be awarded and their approximate retail values are as follows: Grand Prize — A brand-new Mercury Sable LS plus a trip for two (2) to Paris, including round-trip air transportation, six (6) nights hotel accommodation, a $1,400 meal/spending money stipend and $2,000 cash toward a new fashion wardrobe (approximate value: $28,000) or $15,000 cash; two (2) Second Prizes — A trip to Paris, including round-trip air transportation, six (6) nights hotel accommodation, a $1,400 meal/spending money stipend and $2,000 cash toward a new fashion wardrobe (approximate value: $11,000) or $5,000 cash; three (3) Third Prizes — $2,000 cash toward a new fashion wardrobe. All prizes are valued in U.S. currency. Travel award air transportation is from the commercial airport nearest winner's home. Travel is subject to space and accommodation availability, and must be completed by June 30, 1993. Sweepstakes offer is open to residents of the U.S. and Canada who are 21 years of age or older as of December 31, 1991, except residents of Puerto Rico, employees and immediate family members of Torstar Corp., its affiliates, subsidiaries, and all agencies, entities and persons connected with the use, marketing, or conduct of this sweepstakes. All federal, state, provincial, municipal and local laws apply. Offer void wherever prohibited by law. Taxes and/or duties, applicable registration and licensing fees, are the sole responsibility of the winners. Any litigation within the province of Quebec respecting the conduct and awarding of a prize may be submitted to the Régie des loteries et courses du Québec. All prizes will be awarded; winners will be notified by mail. No substitution of prizes is permitted.

4. Potential winners must sign and return any required Affidavit of Eligibility/Release of Liability within 30 days of notification. In the event of noncompliance within this time period, the prize may be awarded to an alternate winner. Any prize or prize notification returned as undeliverable may result in the awarding of that prize to an alternate winner. By acceptance of their prize, winners consent to use of their names, photographs or their likenesses for purposes of advertising, trade and promotion on behalf of Torstar Corp. without further compensation. Canadian winners must correctly answer a time-limited arithmetical question in order to be awarded a prize.

5. For a list of winners (available after 3/31/92), send a separate, stamped, self-addressed envelope to: Harlequin Fashion A Whole New You Sweepstakes, P.O. Box 4694, Blair, NE 68009.

PREMIUM OFFER TERMS

To receive your gift, complete the Offer Certificate according to directions. Be certain to enclose the required number of "Fashion A Whole New You" proofs of product purchase (which are found on the last page of every specially marked "Fashion A Whole New You" Harlequin or Silhouette romance novel). Requests must be received no later than December 31, 1991. Limit: four (4) gifts per name, family, group, organization or address. Items depicted are for illustrative purposes only and may not be exactly as shown. Please allow 6 to 8 weeks for receipt of order. Offer good while quantities of gifts last. In the event an ordered gift is no longer available, you will receive a free, previously unpublished Harlequin or Silhouette book for every proof of purchase you have submitted with your request, plus a refund of the postage and handling charge you have included. Offer good in the U.S. and Canada only.

HCFC-SWPR

HARLEQUIN® OFFICIAL SWEEPSTAKES ENTRY FORM

4-FCARS-2

Complete and return this Entry Form immediately – the more entries you submit, the better your chances of winning!

- Entries must be received by **December 31, 1991.**
- A Random draw will take place on **January 30, 1992.**
- No purchase necessary.

Yes, I want to win a FASHION A WHOLE NEW YOU Classic and Romantic prize from Harlequin:

Name _____ Telephone _____ Age _____

Address _____

City _____ Province _____ Postal Code _____

Return Entries to: **Harlequin FASHION A WHOLE NEW YOU,**
P.O. Box 621, Fort Erie, Ontario L2A 5X3   © 1991 Harlequin Enterprises Limited

PREMIUM OFFER

To receive your free gift, send us the required number of proofs-of-purchase from any specially marked FASHION A WHOLE NEW YOU Harlequin or Silhouette Book with the Offer Certificate properly completed, plus a check or money order (do not send cash) to cover postage and handling payable to Harlequin FASHION A WHOLE NEW YOU Offer. We will send you the specified gift.

OFFER CERTIFICATE

Item	A. ROMANTIC COLLECTOR'S DOLL	B. CLASSIC PICTURE FRAME
	(Suggested Retail Price $60.00)	(Suggested Retail Price $25.00)
# of proofs-of-purchase	18	12
Postage and Handling	$4.00	$3.45
Check one	☐	☐

Name _____

Address _____

City _____ Province _____ Postal Code _____

Mail this certificate, designated number of proofs-of-purchase and check or money order for postage and handling to: **Harlequin FASHION A WHOLE NEW YOU Gift Offer, P.O. Box 622, Fort Erie, Ontario L2A 5X3.** Requests must be received by December 31, 1991.

ONE PROOF-OF-PURCHASE

4-FWCAR-2

To collect your fabulous free gift you must include the necessary number of proofs-of-purchase with a properly completed Offer Certificate.

© 1991 Harlequin Enterprises Limited

See previous page for details.